I0689843

# CREATOR

## A Superhero Epic

### 2nd Edition

# JAIME MERA

# Dedication

I dedicate this book to my lifelong friends who inspired me to write this superhero series. Science fiction is best experienced with a creative imagination and open mind. I hope this story inspires us towards all of those possibilities in life.

**A Superhero Epic Series**

Creator (2004, 2014)

He is Known as Ego (2006, 2014)

Guild Without a Name (2014)

The Galaxy is Ours (2014)


**Non-Fiction Books**

Jesus and the Paint on the Wall, What Do People Live For? (2012)

# Preface

✠ - ✠

No technology, scientific intellects, or metaphysical elites could undisputedly answer the questions raised in newspaper headlines: "Where Do Superhumans Come From and Why Are They Here?" The truth was simple—*too* simple to accept. Superhumans had been on Earth since the beginning. Mutations of human DNA resulting from radiation, chemicals, electromagnetic forces, genetic engineering, and other catalysts were just pieces of a more complex puzzle. In the days of old, superhumans had been known as druids, wizards, magicians, soothsayers, demons, angels, and even dragons. Now the world saw a new breed of magic-users and called them superhumans.

They emerged in the 20th century to fight for justice and the pursuit of happiness. But some superhumans had traveled a different path. They desired more power, more wealth, more control. Some even thought of themselves as super beings—as *gods*. War between superhumans and humans, and between factions of superhumans, seemed certain. It was a time of reckoning and a time of change in which the world faced civil war and possible extinction.

In the wake of the Cold War, select humans and special superhumans proposed a merger with the CIA to combat crime and promote justice. Superhuman hero groups emerged to fight superhuman villains whose aim it was to invade and conquer whatever territories of the world they could reach. The death of Nuetronium, the most admired superhero of the time, gave villainous factions a chance of getting away with the most heinous of crimes. But, Nuetronium's death caused superhumans and humans to work closer together and create the most powerful network of crime-fighters ever imagined. In the mist of the rising fame of superhumans and law-enforcement agencies emerged new governments and countries with national might that surpassed the United States and Soviet Union. South America and Australia became superpowers in the time of the Information Age, soon to be the Space Age. The Special Intelligence Agency (SIA) evolved out of the government elites which ran all investigations dealing with superhumans and anything which the Presidential committee requested. In the growing pains of stardom, a superhero group of superhumans called the Eternal Champions would be born with the support of the SIA. The Eternal Champions come together by chance; if destiny is not in your vocabulary. The members are by far the most well balanced and effective team in history, but they would have to prove themselves to the public, law enforcement, and themselves. The era is a stepping stone for the group in their fight against evil, but also the beginning seed of a galactic war with Earth as a prime target.

# List of Characters

**Richard Octavian / Creator**—Leader of the Eternal Champions

**Larcis G. Draven / Night**—Member of the Eternal Champions

**John Goodman / Mindseye**—Member of the Eternal Champions

**Erica**—Member of the Eternal Champions (Super Artificial Intelligence computer)

**Elizabeth Armstrong / Isis (Katherine Fletcher)**—Member of the Eternal Champions

**Susan M. Sawczer / Pandora (Lynda Manchester)**—Member of the Eternal Champions

**Sedric**—Leader of the Galactic Guardians (born on the planet Tir Goth)

**Medroc (Patrick Lawrence)**—A Galactic Guardian (born in Seattle, WA)

**Princess Navia**—Princess of Dothoria, the largest realm in the Argonian Empire

**Queen Omia**—Sole ruler and queen of the Argonian Empire

**Elexsuia**—Second in command of Princess Navia's flag ship

**Randolph Maximilian**—Director of the Special Investigation Agency (SIA)

**Steven Zack**—Agent in charge of Blue Sector Fort Lauderdale SIA field station

**Robert Thorn**—Field agent for SIA, Superhuman Recovery Division

**Rick Tyler**—Oakland, field agent for SIA

**Sargon**—Telekinetic super villain, ruler of Complex San Francisco

**Brandon Lester**—Chief Marshal of Complex San Francisco

**Jack T. Lochnir**—Pilot of flight UA-0292

**Samuel Stevens**—Co-pilot of flight UA-292

**Coy Patterson**—Navigator of flight UA-0292

**Cindy Colone**—Flight attendant

**John Wilkens**—Flight attendant

**Nadine A. Tess**—Flight attendant

**Senator John G. Fence**—Texas State Senator

**Blake Gardner**—Director of Space Operations, NASA

**Lt. General Thomas P. Cartier**—Newly appointed DDCI (Deputy Director of Central Intelligence)

**Major General Eugene Fox**—USAF Space Program director

**Jeffery Samuel**—CNN correspondent, on flight UA-0292

**Wendy H. Palmer**—Presidential adviser and investigator

**Captain Nancy McDanials**—Military Intelligence adviser

**Jacoya Su-rak**—Owner of Hon-su-rak Electronics, (major space technology builder)

**Linsan Hitoshi**—Secretary and adviser to Jacoya Su-rak

**Patricia Ortiz**—South American Space Program representative

**Rebecca Martinez**—South American Trade and Commerce representative

**Jeremiah Allen**—Senior Secret Service agent

**Robert L. Hains**—Secret Service agent

**William C. Ottis**—Secret Service agent

**Tanya Makan**—Wife of Landon Makan

**Brittany Makan**—Daughter of Landon Makan

**Jean Lorenz**—Director of the Counterespionage Agency (CEA)

**Theodore Patterson**—CEA agent, and second in command of CEA

**Jared Erickson**—Special operative for CEA

**Natasha Erickson**—Sister of Jared and special operative for CEA

**Carlos P. Hernandez**—Captain of the South American cruiser, Doris

**Luis Meza**—Lieutenant Commander of the South American cruiser, Doris

**Lieutenant Roberto Alejandro**—Beta Team Leader (South American special operations team)

**Master Sergeant Rivera**—Beta Team Assistant Team Leader

**Quatris**—Leader of Energy, Fire and Light (EFL, superhero group in NY)

**Hellfire**—Member of EFL (second in command)

# Contents

# Chapter One

✠ - ✠

# Save the Queen

K yos, a port for thousands of planetary travelers, spun out of control as it plummeted toward Polare, the fourth moon of the planet Nakei. The four-mile-long cylindrical spaceport expended its remaining emergency boosters trying to re-establish its orbit around the icy satellite. Polare's gravitational hold seemed too strong. The silver-plating protecting Kyos' outer structure dulled as Polare hid the dwarf star's light rays of a new day on the space port. Large landing-bay doors opened at each end of the port to reveal empty internal docking platforms and railways.

The last seven of forty-two spaceships of various sizes and shapes exited the port in hopes of escape as the Argonian Space Destroyer Huron closed in on Kyos. The main propulsion system of the spaceport once again failed to activate, its engineering section having suffered a critical hit by a thermo plasma beam shot from a Drakon mercenary cruiser. Kyos would break apart and fall through Polare's krypton-based atmosphere before hitting solid ice.

The Huron came within 500 meters of Kyos, matching its speed and trajectory. It had destroyed the Drakon cruiser but had appeared on the scene too late to thwart the plot to assassinate Omia, queen of the Argonian Empire. The queen's guards watched in frustration, as the Huron remained at a distance, unable to physically attach itself to the spaceport docking arms or enter the landing bay.

One of the queen's elite guards, a Galactic Guardian named Sedric, exited the Argonian destroyer's personnel chamber and flew into space. His body glowed yellowish-white as he came within fifty meters of Kyos' secondary transport landing bay. Sedric disappeared into nothingness, and then reappeared inside the bay. Sedric's exposed skin revealed extremely well defined muscles. His seventy-four inch tall body and excellent physique personified the perfect human specimen even though he was not human. One of the Imperial Guards, with four of his comrades surrounding him, held the queen's limp body in his arms.

"Sir," said one of the guards to Sedric, "the queen is dying!"

Although Sedric's body continued to glow, his heart sank upon hearing those words. He was almost unable to believe that the queen was physically here in the spaceport. He had known before leaving the destroyer that he was on a rescue mission. But now it seemed that he was too late.

The landing bay shook violently as a fusion reactor at the other end of Kyos exploded. Three of the Imperial Guards, who were unable to keep their footing, fell on the platform floor. Sedric floated above the floor and flew in between the guards, touching the queen's arm. The queen's skin, normally almost silver, was now dull, and a dark blood spot appeared on the left side of her dress. Her beautiful face was pale and long blond hair was turning gray. The wound was deep, but it was not the cause of her deteriorating situation.

Sedric extended his free hand toward the guard nearest him.

"Take my hand," said Sedric. "The rest of you join hands and make a chain around the queen."

Sedric spread a yellowish spherical force field around the group and lifted all of them from the floor of the landing bay. As they moved toward the barrier that sustained the atmosphere within the spaceport, the energy barrier collapsed. The emptiness of space sucked the air out of the bay along with Sedric and his group. Pieces of machinery, scrap metal, tools, and other equipment burst from the port and flew out with them toward the Huron. Sedric, although he was worried that he would not be able to keep the force field on the group for very long, betrayed no signs of fear. He knew that the Imperial Guards needed his reassurance.

The destroyer quickly moved away in self-preservation as the last six reactors on Kyos exploded, shattering the spaceport so that debris flew in all directions. Twisted and scorched pieces of the structure, some of them five meters long, streaked past

Sedric's force field, spinning and striking one another in mid-space.

"Sir," screamed one of the guards, "we're not going to make it!"

Sedric looked back toward Kyos. Three great metal scraps were hurtling their way. He was uncertain whether he could destroy them without dropping his force field. Alone he would have had little trouble getting to the Huron. But he wasn't alone and protecting the group drained a lot of power.

"Hold each other tighter!" Sedric yelled as he focused his energy on the force field and himself. Using all of his willpower, he projected a bolt of energy that formed just outside the force field, launched itself toward the center object, and disintegrated it into a vaporous cloud. The other two objects splintered and veered from the group.

Thousands of bits of debris continued twirling toward them. Sedric had used a great deal of power already and doubted that he could go on protecting himself, the guards, and the queen all the way to the destroyer. He had been in worse situations before, but this time there were no other guardians to aid him. This time it was up to him and him alone to determine a course of action and see it through.

Sedric decided to warp himself and his group through space toward the Huron and hope that they could outrun the debris or avoid being hit if they were overtaken. In a split second, they were traveling 3,000 miles per hour toward the retreating destroyer. Small pieces of debris, in the two-ton to three-ton range, struck Sedric's force field, but inflicted little damage. Still,

Sedric was taxed from using many of his special powers at the same time, after having already used his powers in the adjacent space sector less than thirty minutes ago. Although he was closing the distance between himself and the Huron, debris was steadily trailing behind him. The destroyer slowed to near 1,000 miles per hour.

Sedric hoped that the destroyer wasn't slowing so that he and his group could board it. If he slowed, the debris was likely to rupture his force field and kill the guards and queen, who couldn't survive in a space environment with their injuries. He maintained his speed and tried to fly over and around the Huron, placing the destroyer between the group and the debris. He strained with all his might only to slow down as his energy started to quickly fade. The Huron was within a few thousand meters, but the debris was now almost on top of them.

At that moment, a blast of plasma energy streaked pass the group as the Huron fired its main guns at the debris and Kyos. Large sections of wreckage evaporated, and what remained of Kyos was cut in half as if a miniature nuclear bomb had hit its main structure. Debris scattered in all directions, a few pieces still heading toward Sedric's group. Sedric had to come to almost a complete stop as he conserved his energy to maintain the force field. The guards looked at Sedric, wondering why he had stopped.

Sedric looked at the queen. He wished only to be forgiven for failing to save her. The Huron could not fire its guns again with the debris so close to the group. Besides, it was at the wrong angle to get a clear shot. The guards held each other tighter, hoping for another miracle.

Sedric looked up to see a piece of debris that seemed to increase in size as it approached them. But out of the corner of his eye he saw a beam of light shoot past their front and destroy it instantly.

"What was that?" one of guards said as they looked out into space.

A blue and white spaceship resembling a tall, fat SR-71 Blackbird fuselage with small round trimmed wings came up to within twenty meters beside them. The craft was no more than seventy meters long and had no planetary markings on it, but its speed was incredible, and its shiny metallic skin seemed so transparent that stars could be seen beyond it.

"It's my ship!" Sedric said with relief.

Three of the Imperial Guards were in awe seeing the one-of-a-kind stealth scout ship. It was in this ship that the legendary Galactic Guardians were said to have started their appointment as the queen's personal elite guards enforcing the queen's rule over the empire. Sedric was the second Guardian picked, creator of the stealth ship, and Captain by default. It was this ship that the Guardians used to travel the galaxy and maintain the peace.

The Huron moved around next to the group and scout ship. Sedric's ship shot multiple energy beams at all debris still speeding their way. Sedric regained his strength as the destroyer opened its landing-bay doors on the port side. He flew into the bay next to a standby emergency medical team.

Sedric removed the force field and the yellowish aura around him resided back inside his body. The guards spread out and allowed the ship's surgeon to treat the queen as she was placed on a floating white bed no more than six inches thick. Sedric called the Captain of the Imperial Guards. He noticed black burns on the guards' suits and knew that they had recently been in a firefight. The suits were strong enough to protect them and the queen, but something must have gone wrong. The Captain of the Guards stood at attention before Sedric as everyone else left the bay and moved toward the medical center.

"Tell me what happened in Kyos."

"Sir, we were on a diplomatic mission to meet the chancellor of Nakei. The queen's mission was supposed to be a secret even to us until we were informed prior to entering Kyos. I protested because this was completely out of security procedures, but the queen wouldn't hear of it. Four of my guards and I escorted the queen into Kyos, waiting for the chancellor's envoy. We didn't know we had walked into a trap until a sniper shot the queen with some kind of phase rifle. We surrounded her, but it was too late. There was an explosion on the bridge while we killed the assassin. Twenty men in the main transport chamber were strategically located around us and attacked us with plasma rifles. We fought our way back to our ship, but before we entered the main loading dock our ship was blown up. It was all planned out, and we would have died if you hadn't arrived."

"Did the queen tell you why she was meeting with the chancellor?"

"No, sir, she didn't seem too concerned about meeting him, seemed to me like it was a routine covert meeting."

"Do you know who these assassins were?"

The one assassin we could get a hold of before he died was a Drakon spy. We made it back through the port up to the landing bay where you found us. It was a miracle you showed up, sir."

Sedric thought carefully about what the captain had reported.

"Yes, well...that's all for now. Go and take care of your men and get the ship's guards to relieve you and your men for a few hours."

"Yes, sir!" The Imperial Guard said and bowed.

Sedric bowed his head and turned toward the open landing-bay doors. The Imperial Guard quickly walked away as Sedric viewed his scout ship a short distance from the destroyer. A smile came over him as he saw his best friend exit the ship and fly towards him.

Medroc wore his guardian uniform, black with sliver gloves, boots, and belt. Medroc's thick black hair was brushed back. His handsome face resembled that of many male supermodels on Earth. He flew through the bay's energy force barrier in front of Sedric.

"It's good to see you, Medroc." Sedric reached out and shook hands down close to the elbow.

"We were in the area and responded to the distress call from Kyos, and then I heard you needed some help and had to come and save the day."

"Really, what took you so long?" Sedric asked, knowing it was a one-in-a-quadrillion chance Medroc was there by accident.

Medroc grinned and felt good seeing his friend for the first time in more than six months.

"Princess Navia will be here shortly. She's about ten minutes away."

"What?" Sedric asked. "How? Why?"

"We are her invisible escort. But the little bird that came to me didn't tell me the queen was here until we spotted you trying to dodge those bullets."

Sedric was used to hearing Medroc use English metaphors, but his slang caught him off guard this time.

"What little bird?" Sedric asked all confused.

"I'll explain it to you later." Medroc laughed.

"Right. Come; let's go see how the queen is fairing."

They ran to medical center only to find the queen being moved back out to the loading dock. Sedric stopped the captain of the Imperial Guards and demanded an explanation.

"Sir, Princess Navia demands that the queen be present when she boards this ship."

Sedric knew that something was going on with the state of the empire and royal house, but what?

"What else did the princess demand?"

"She demanded yours and Guardian Medroc's presence, Sir."

Sedric allowed the crowd to continue moving the queen to the loading dock and pulled the chief surgeon aside to get the queen's diagnosis.

The royal shuttle wasted no time entering and landing in the dock. There were more than forty people waiting for the princess to emerge from the shuttle as a ramp extended from its side. The metal door slid open to reveal the Princess of Dothoria, the largest realm in the Argonian Empire.

Princess Navia stepped onto the ramp wearing a green gown draped to her feet and extending several feet behind her like a wedding dress. The dress seemed to shift from emerald green to a shiny silvery green and was trimmed in light blue from chest to waistline. An emerald rested on a chain about her neck. Her silky silver hair flowed down to mid back, and her tan complexion brought out her cheekbones and rose-colored lips. Her beautiful green crystal like eyes normally brought happiness and comfort at a glance, but timing was everything, and they now showed only distress. Her aunt, Queen Omia, was dying. The only way to save her, Navia knew, was to become a temporary living host.

Sedric and Medroc stood next to the queen as Princess Navia quickly, but majestically, walked toward them. Although

Queen Omia was present, everyone in the dock knelt before the princess. She reigned as long as Queen Omia was incapacitated.

"Your Eminence, the surgeons cannot stop the queen's body from deteriorating," Sedric reported in perfect English. "They say she has less than one hour to live."

All stood as Sedric informed the princess of Queen Omia's fate. A glimmer of hope came back to Princess Navia's eyes as she placed her hands on the queen's head.

"Then it is not too late," the princess said in a soothing voice. "There is no time to lose. I will absorb her essence now."

Sedric and Medroc stepped away from the princess and queen. Princess Navia's entourage of personal guards and advisers began walking down the fifteen-meter ramp, but stopped halfway. Everyone stood silently waiting to see if the princess could save the queen's life force.

The dock was silent except for the faint humming of the floating magnetic bed where the queen lay. Princess Navia's hands started to glow with a pure white light as she bowed at the waist and placed her forehead on the queen's forehead. It was a tense moment for everyone except the princess' soothsayer.

Sedric looked at Princess Navia's advisers and stopped his gaze on Navia's soothsayer. Now he understood how it was that he, Medroc, and the princess were all here at the same time. It couldn't have been coincidence. The royal family did not normally venture into deep space as a group. Kyos was in the far corner of the empire's realm, and he had been given instructions to take the *Huron*, the Argonian destroyer, to this sector in search of pirates. He was specially selected for missions by the Queen herself and had not seen his scout ship for the past six months. Princess Navia was also probably in the area, but for a different reason judging by the formal dress she wore. What he couldn't understand was why the queen had come to Kyos without his knowledge. The soothsayers were masters of predicting the future and had a good reputation with the royal family, but he knew they advised only on what needed to be heard by their distinguished audience.

Princess Navia broke the mental bond after several minutes.

"It is done," she said.

The queen's entire body turned a bright reddish color as her cosmic energy dispersed with the collision of energy particles moving through the space of the universe. Soon only her clothes remained on the bed. Princess Navia carefully took the queen's necklace and coiled it in her hand.

The five nurses and three doctors were unsure, hesitant to move the empty bed. But Sedric stepped up and grabbed the bed with one hand and flung it aside for them to take away.

Princess Navia stepped forward, giving the group on the ramp enough room to come down and join her. The others stepped away, maintaining their distance from the princess as she moved out into the middle of her people.

Sedric and Medroc, quickly assuming their duty of protecting the queen, stayed close to the princess. Princess Navia turned to face the group coming off the shuttle ramp. She stood gazing into space as if in deep thought. She didn't wait for everyone to get off the ramp but slowly approached Filia, her personal soothsayer.

Everyone in front of her bowed.

"Think carefully before you speak," Princess Navia said in a threatening tone of voice. "I will tolerate no deception. You will tell me everything of my task ahead in front of everyone here as witnesses."

Filia had kept the queen's fate hidden from her until the last minute, which made the princess very angry. The soothsayers had been playing with the royal family's destiny, and she hated knowing that they were the ones really in control of the future. She had no choice but to use them to restore the queen to the throne.

Filia spoke boldly. "Your Highness, the queen's life force must be fused with the Chosen. You must travel to a planet called Earth in the thirty-fourth quadrant of the empire. Once the queen is in the Chosen, she will stabilize the empire and rule for thousands of years to come."

Princess Navia was learned in ancient history and remembered the prophecy about the Chosen, the queen who would bring lasting peace through a reign that would last almost an eternity. Princess Navia doubted the prophecy, but Filia's demeanor was serious and strong.

Medroc's eyes fixed on Filia as she spoke about Earth. He was from Earth, as were three other Guardians who had returned there after completing their five-year quest. He had not been to Earth in more than six years and wished he could visit his home state of Washington, but he knew that his duty was to protect the empire.

Sedric also looked at Filia, having recruited Medroc, known as the earthling Patrick Lawrence, and the other Guardians many years before. He recalled the blue planet and how many superhumans lived there. The queen's cosmic powers were close to being omnipotent and would require a special body that could manipulate the energy. The Earth was a perfect choice since it held rare and unique humans who might be able to do just that.

Princess Navia turned to Sedric and spoke.

"You and Lord Medroc will hunt down and find these murderers. You will find the traitors who dared to take the throne away from our queen. I do not care if royal blood is spilled. I want all of them found and executed."

"Princess," replied Sedric, "please let Lord Medroc go with you to Earth. He is a human from Earth and knows it better than anyone here."

"No, I need you and Lord Medroc to take the fleet and find the traitors. I know the royal family is involved, and you will need Lord Medroc to keep the empire from civil war. I will go to Earth, and Queen Omia will reign again."

Sedric and Medroc bowed at the waist.

"It will be done as you command, my princess," said Sedric with certainty.

The princess and her crew departed the landing bay immediately making their way towards Earth, while Sedric and

Medroc made preparations for finding and destroying the traitors with a vengeance the galaxy was yet to witness.

# Chapter Two

⊠ - ⊠

# Creator

F ew students roamed the campus during the weekend break. Most stayed indoors or left campus to see family and friends or go to the beach or any number of things Floridians do in near-perfect weather. Unlike most days, Richard Octavian was one of those students who stayed in his room simply trying to relax. He was not a normal student, as was evident from his older appearance and disciplined demeanor. He had spent long hours during the week working on his dissertation on quantum data processing for artificial-intelligence computers, so instead of going out with fellow students, he sat on his sofa with his feet propped up on a small table enjoying one of his favorite movies, *Aliens*.

His black hair was finely cut away from his ears and tapered in the back. If he'd worn glasses, he might have been mistaken for a computer nerd. But his well-defined muscles, masculine voice, and handsome face said otherwise. Other students respected him for being outgoing, assertive, and always there when someone needed help with schoolwork or personal matters. He was, by and large, a smart but otherwise normal student. But his true origins were clouded with destruction and mystery. His pure black eyeballs, pointed ears and six foot two inch tall stature hinted that he was a descendant of what some people would consider as dark elves in a fantasy game or movie.

Richard Octavian was, in fact, a superhuman and was approaching his ninety-second birthday. For as long as he could remember, he had possessed the power to shape shift and mentally focus an energy field using telekinesis. He could use telekinesis to propel himself through the air and create a force field around his hands able to project telekinetic bolts through the air. Fortunately his parents had kept him at home until he was able to control his powers at the age of ten.

Richard had learned at an early age that he was different from other people. And through the watchful upbringing of his parents he had learned to see the folly of letting normal people know about his powers. It was later, during the post-World War I years after his parents' deaths that he decided to disappear from the face of the Earth and resurface where people would need him most. He spent many years in third-world countries where he helped the poor, sick, hungry, and homeless. In the midst of misery and the death of his fiancée, he joined British Special Forces during World War II and then the Central Investigation Agency during the Vietnam War. He hoped to fight for a larger cause in finishing a war that others had started.

He liked being in the shadows and using his powers whenever he could. The CIA gave him the opportunity to work alone or with select people who knew all there was to know about unconventional warfare and special operations. Richard saw and learned many things in Vietnam and became extremely proficient in assassination and demolitions. The horrors of war and political deception, however, took their toll on his conscience and desire to fight for the downtrodden. He regretted getting involved with the CIA and hated being used by the government. He got out of the agency and tried to make a living with several business ventures, but none of them panned out. His last remaining relative, Derrick Octavian, invited him to live with him in Florida and start a new life. Richard gladly accepted. Derrick was his nephew by birth, but they forged documents to make it look as if Richard was Derrick's only remaining son. Richard used his connections to ensure that his history was hidden from the world during his new life as a University of Miami student.

It was almost dinnertime when a knock at Richard's dorm room door disrupted his movie watching.

"Who is it?" Richard yelled from his beat-up sofa while watching Sigourney Weaver torch the alien pods at the colonial base.

"I have a Domino's delivery for a Thiman Clones," a male voice answered.

*Pizza?* Richard thought. *Man, I could go for a pizza right now.*

"Wait a minute," said Richard, although he had not ordered a pizza.

*Too bad for you, Thim, or whoever you are. This pizza is mine!*

Richard answered the door wearing a worn-out Black Sabbath T-shirt and black shorts. His pure black eyes changed to light blue, and his pointed ears shaped shifted to normal human ears. He opened the door and saw a man in his thirties wearing sunglasses and holding a pizza box.

"You've come to the right place, buddy," Richard said.

"Yes, I know," the man replied as he raised a weird-looking pistol, with a glass like cylinder type hollow barrel, from underneath the box and pulled the trigger. A beam of light and heat pulsed through the air and hit Richard square on the chest. Richard fell back eight meters against his bookshelf next to his dorm-room window. The man ran down the hallway as Richard looked down at the hole burned through his shirt.

"What the hell!" Richard shouted as he jumped up and rushed after the man who had just burned his favorite shirt.

Larcis G. Draven, a sophomore who lived down the hall, had heard the deliveryman. His door was open for ventilation during his bimonthly clean-up-the-room day. The sound of a video-game blaster and Richard falling against a bookcase caused him to look toward his opened door. He saw the deliveryman, carrying a weird-looking gun, sprint by. Richard followed a few seconds later. As Larcis stepped into the hallway, he smelled the residue of a fire but saw no smoke. He quickly pursued the two men downstairs toward the front entrance.

The mystery deliveryman flung open the glass double doors of the dormitory entrance and jumped into the back seat of a black sedan. Richard, at the man's heels, hurled himself onto the driver's door as the car sped away. Larcis caught up to the car, matching its speed right behind Richard. Richard grabbed the edge of the door with both hands while being slightly dragged along the pavement.

Lightning and thunder shot from Larcis's hand and struck the left rear tire. Fragments of burned rubber sprayed everywhere, and molten metal streaked across the black pavement. The sedan went out of control as the man in the back seat fired his laser pistol in Richard's general direction, hitting the driver, the driver's seat, Richard, and the roof of the car.

Richard released his hold on the door, swung his arm over the driver, and hit the deliveryman on the head, sending him into a coma. The car struck a three-foot sidewall and stopped.

"Who the hell sent you?" Richard screamed at the driver while grabbing him by the throat. The driver, bleeding from a gaping hole in his head, said nothing.

"Hey, Richard, I think he's dead," Larcis said in response to Richard's question.

Common sense replaced Richard's anger. He realized that he would not find out from these two men who had sent them to kill him. Richard let go of the dead man's throat and glanced at the pizza deliveryman. He was unconscious and bleeding from his nose, mouth, and ears.

"Yeah," said Richard. "I guess they both are."

Students came out of the woodwork to find out what was going on. Richard stood erect as the Black Sabbath T-shirt turned into a black Led Zeppelin T-shirt—without a hole in the middle. He turned toward Larcis.

"So what's your story?"

"I'm Larcis. I'm new here."

Until now, Larcis had thought he was the only superhuman on campus. He was two inches taller than Richard, but was thinner in physic, and not as muscular as Richard. His short blond hair, blue eyes, and well structured facial bones made a very good impression on the girls as a clever and handsome young man.

Richard paid more attention to what Larcis was wearing than anything else. Larcis had a dark brown polyester long sleeve shirt with the sleeves rounded up and dark blue slacks. He wore black leather shoes and a black Timex watch. Either he was a geek, was about to go out, always dressed that way for picking up girls or simply dressed well due to his upbringing. Richard thought. In any case, he felt a little relieved that Larcis was a superhuman and would not be ratting him out for being a superhuman himself.

"How do you know who I am?" Richard asked as if interrogating Larcis.

"Everyone knows you, Richard," said Larcis. "Even the teachers refer to you as a computer genius and say that you are Mr. Octavian's only son."

The two men turned their attention to the gathering crowd. Sirens faintly sounded over the normally peaceful campus.

"So, how are we going to explain this?" Larcis asked.

"Lucky for us, there were no witnesses, I think." Richard said as he looked around and stood behind Larcis as his shorts turned into a pair of blue jeans.

"The weekend helps out too," Larcis added not paying too much attention to what Richard just did with the pants. "But I have never told a lie, and I will not start now, even if it means getting expelled or thrown into jail."

Richard looked intently at Larcis. "Are you for real? If anyone finds out what just happened, we'll be put in a laboratory and experimented on like rats. By the way," Richard added sarcastically, "why did you have to melt half of the car?"

Larcis looked at the melted tire hub.

"Yeah, well, I never really used my lightning powers on a car."

Larcis and Richard stopped talking as several students came within hearing distance.

"What the…"

The awed students looked at the dead men and destroyed car and fearfully backed away from Richard and Larcis.

"Okay, just avoid telling the *whole* truth. Use the Fifth Amendment if you have to. In fact," Richard commanded, "promise me you will go along with what I tell the police and nothing more."

Larcis thought about it for a few seconds.

"I'm not sure."

"Promise me or I swear I will kill you myself!" Richard whispered. "As long as we tell the story right and stick with it, everything will be okay. I will explain what happened, and hopefully, we won't get thrown out of school."

"Yeah, sure. You seem to be very calm all of the sudden," Larcis doubtfully remarked.

The two men quickly talked about what to say as they went back to their rooms and got ready for the police to pick them up.

Miami-Dade police officers arrived at the scene and took Richard and Larcis into custody. The dead men and the car were taken away within an hour, while Richard and Larcis sat in separate holding rooms at the police station.

"So," said Detective Andrews, "you say the two men drove up to the door and started to fight each other while in the car? You and your friend ran up to stop the fight when they bolted out and crashed into the concrete wall by the building?"

"That's correct, detective," Richard calmly answered.

"So what is this about you killing the guy in the back seat, and what about the rear tire?" barked Andrews's partner, Detective Harris.

"If I did kill the guy in the back seat, detective, how could I have done it?" Richard challenged him, knowing that his telekinetic punch through the car's body left no evidence of his blood, sweat, hair, or skin on the man.

"It seems that your so-called friend said you did," Detective Andrews stated.

"I doubt he did because neither of us did anything wrong, and I know my friend wouldn't make up a story or lie," Richard said without a twitch.

Harris and Andrews scrutinized Richard, trying to find a flaw in his body language or expressions.

The door opened and a man wearing a dark gray two-piece suit entered the room.

"Detective Andrews, Detective Harris," the man said, "may I have a word with my client?"

"And who are you?" Detective Harris asked.

"I am Richard Octavian's lawyer, Robert Thorn. So if you please, leave the room now so that I can talk to my client."

Harris and Andrews glanced at each other in frustration and confusion as they left the room. Robert intertwined his fingers behind his lower back as he stood in front of the table. Richard looked at him, a little confused himself.

"I didn't call a lawyer," Richard said, "especially since I don't have a lawyer to call."

You're right," Robert replied, "you didn't call me. However, your benefactor, by whom I'm employed, knows you and wants this incident kept from over inflating. So in order for me to get you out of here, you will need to work with me as honestly as you can. Now, tell me what you told the police and whatever else you wish to tell me and only me."

Richard told Robert everything he had told the police, adding no details or reasons for his having been near the entrance of the building or what had happened to the car or the passengers.

"I see. Your friend Larcis has been pleading the Fifth and has not talked. He's waiting for a lawyer, so I will go to his rescue."

Robert assured Richard that the incident was closed and that he would take care of it.

"I am required to tell you that Dean Whitmen will want to see you and Larcis when you get back to campus," Robert added.

"Of course. As long as I can graduate, I'll settle for one of his lectures. But now that I think of it, who is my benefactor?"

"Dean Whitmen, of course. You should be out of here in about ten minutes," Robert said as he exited the room.

Robert closed the door behind him and searched for the two detectives. They were agitatedly waiting in the captain's office. Robert stormed into the office and pulled out a badge.

"Gentlemen, as you're aware by now, I have taken over your case."

Robert glanced at Captain Landers.

"You will release Mr. Octavian and Mr. Draven immediately on grounds of insufficient evidence. In addition, you will destroy all documentation of their involvement in this matter."

"Where the hell do you get off destroying evidence in a homicide?" Detective Andrews interrupted, while rising from his chair.

"This is where I get off, detective!" Robert flashed his Special Investigation Agency (SIA) badge a second time. "It might not mean much to you, but as per direct authority from the President of the United States and Supreme Court ruling 878, I can tell you or anyone else in this department to eat crap and like it!"

Special Agent Thorn frowned at Detective Andrews.

Captain Landers sprang between the two men.

"Cool down, you two."

Landers placed his hand on Andrews's shoulder, pushing him back into his chair.

"Okay, Agent Thorn," said Landers, "we'll do it."

Andrews and Harris sulked in their chairs.

"However, you will tell me what is going on before I let anyone go. And don't give me this jurisdiction stuff of yours. I'll make extra red tape, which I know and you know we don't want."

Robert looked at the veteran police captain and took a deep breath.

"Alright," Robert replied. "I guess I can do that much for you." He placed his briefcase on the table. "As you know, SIA investigates terrorist groups, hate groups, anti-social groups bent on not only the overthrow of the U.S. government, but our way of life. The two dead men at the scene were members of an anti-social group called the Pillars of Society. This group is bent on killing students, teachers, religious leaders, and potential political or technological leaders who would assist our country in revolutionary ideas and technology. The ideas and technology would be used by our government to exploit society, especially the young minds of our nation—so they think. They have telepaths who comb universities, churches, and other assemblies, reading minds and finding those gifted and nonconformist potentials that would stand in their way. The two men were there to assassinate someone, and those two students who you have in custody simply got in the way. They defended themselves, but they're scared to tell the truth because they might get kicked out of school. I don't know if Richard Octavian was the target, but I *do* know he is one of the leading experts in computer science and has not even graduated. So was he the target? It doesn't matter. If they get kicked out of school, the Pillars of Society have won a small victory and delayed Richard's potential contribution to society."

Robert relaxed, keeping an honest, cool face.

"We have been tracking the group's whereabouts, and I am telling you that they are the ones who are responsible for any wrongdoing. In the meantime, SIA will investigate the incident in case Mr. Octavian and Mr. Draven are guilty of anything. But it will be handled through SIA and not by this department."

Robert placed his hand on his briefcase.

"Is that enough for you, Captain Landers?"

Captain Landers had twenty-six years under his belt as a Marine Corps sniper, police officer, federal marshal and police chief. He once attempted to enter SIA but failed the training and induction phase of the hardest school he had ever experienced. The SIA field agents were among the best in law-enforcement agencies and military branches. He understood and admired the agent before him and knew that the story was just that. Robert would not tell him the whole truth—if any of his stories were true at all—because SIA would not let him. The field agents were held accountable to SIA by the use of chronicles, file recordings, and telepaths. The bad agents were weeded out and dealt with severely. If Robert was holding back or misleading them for any reason, it was a good one.

SIA had been created in the wake of the death of Nuetronium, the legendary all-American superhero, as an all-powerful law-enforcement agency with the authority of executive decision to protect national interest and Americans against superhuman criminals, terrorists, and agents of espionage directed against the United States and allied countries. Any and all investigations or directives SIA chose to enforce had to be followed by all U.S. military, police, or alphabet organizations (CIA, NSA, FBI, DEA) or severe consequences would follow, including the death penalty, which had occurred only once in SIA history. SIA was the ultimate law-enforcement agency, with direct channels to the president and the Supreme Court.

"That's enough for now," Landers said. "But I want a report of your findings on my desk no later than a week from today."

"It will be on your desk," Robert said with a nod. "If that is all, gentlemen, I have one last demand. No one will hint to those two students that SIA is involved in any way, only that I am an attorney working on behalf of the university." Robert looked each of the three men in the eyes. "Understood?"

Harris and Andrews anguished the idea but went along with their captain's acceptance of Robert's demands. Harris was a veteran cop and knew the outer workings of SIA, but he considered SIA to be corrupt and misguided. Andrews was a rookie detective, but he also saw SIA as an egotistical secret police agency that liked to be above the law. Robert left the office as quickly as he entered.

"Sir, you don't believe that crap story of his, do you?" Harris asked Landers.

"No, but it doesn't matter. He represents our boss," Landers said.

"Our boss? I don't care if there *is* an executive order, this is *our* case!" Harris retorted.

"Captain, what the hell are we doing here if we can't do our jobs?" Andrews added.

Landers glanced sternly at each of his officers.

"Look, I know how you feel. But the executive order is the problem, and if you violate that order, you will be just like one of those guys you put behind bars. Go and take the rest of the day off, and I'll see both of you tomorrow morning."

Landers sat back in his chair and tapped his fingers on his armrest, waiting for a reply.

Harris stood. "I guess I'll be able to pick my kids up from school after all."

Andrews looked at Harris and then the office's glass wall. He saw Robert preparing to enter Richard's questioning room.

"Too bad he's not off today," Andrews said with a slight grin. "Then I could kick his ass and shove that badge of his back where it came from."

Landers smiled as he heard the words come out of Andrews's mouth.

"I don't think that's a very good idea, Mat. I've seen you fight, and believe me; I know you can fight. But he would kick your butt."

Andrews doubtfully looked at the captain and said, "He's nothing but an over glorified pencil-pusher. He's probably never fired a weapon in his life, just like those FBI desk-jockeys."

Landers smiled again. "Let me tell both of you something about SIA. SIA doesn't have flunkies. They train ten times harder than we do. Their training carries into their everyday life. Every agent knows at least three different martial-arts styles. They don't just do Katas; they *fight* with each other, full contact; with knives, sticks, swords, common household utensils, you name it. They know two to four languages; fluently. They are all sniper trained and experts in guerrilla warfare and small-unit tactics in all types of terrain. They all have a master's degree or higher in criminology, computer science, counterintelligence, or even astrophysics. Believe me; I know what I'm talking about. So the next time you want to jump into an SIA agent's face, make damn sure you can win."

Landers concluded his pep talk as he watched Robert and Richard exit the holding room. Concern filled his mind as the three men prepared to leave his building. SIA had something special for those two students. Landers could only hope that SIA was doing the right thing by protecting them.

Robert took Larcis and Richard to the property clerk on the third floor. Larcis and Richard were given back the personal possessions that had been confiscated from them at the time of the incident—two wristwatches, spare change, one wallet, one set of car keys, and a pair of Ray-Ban sunglasses. Richard scrutinized Robert as he completed the release documents. Richard had served in the CIA, as a special black operations agent in Vietnam, and Robert seemed to remind him of those old times. He had disguised himself with his shape-shifting abilities for six years with the CIA only to disappear from the face of the Earth after the war. Richard was confident that his cover was foolproof. The mortuary files had been altered to keep his past lives and aliases buried six feet under and him free to live a normal life.

After completing the release documents, Robert gave the two men his business card. They were to stay in Dade County until his legal team took care of the situation. Robert escorted them down to the entrance of the police station, where he offered them a ride back to campus.

A handsome gray-haired gentleman stood just inside the entrance. Waving his hand, he called out.

"Richard! Is everything alright?"

Richard's face brightened as he approached the man.

"Yes, dad, everything's fine," Richard greeted him. "Dad, this is Larcis, a student friend of mine, and this is Robert Thorn, an attorney for the university."

"How do you do, Mr. Octavian," Larcis said, extending his hand. "It's a pleasure to meet you."

Derrick Octavian shook Larcis's hand as he spoke.

"Thank you, Larcis. I trust that you've been looking after my boy."

"Yes, sir," Larcis replied proudly.

Robert likewise extended his hand to Derrick.

"It is a pleasure, Mr. Octavian. However, I must apologize, but I'm in a bit of a rush and it seems that your son now has a way to get home."

Robert looked at Derrick and Richard, attempting to excuse himself with a last note. "If there is anything you need from me concerning your case, call me. It was nice meeting you, Mr. Octavian."

"Of course," Derrick said. "And thank you for helping my son and his friend."

"It isn't over yet, so please don't thank me," Robert countered.

"Yes," said Derrick, "but if it was bad enough, they would not be leaving the station right now, so I'm assuming that you had some degree of influence in the matter. In which case, thank you anyway."

Robert smiled, bid goodbye again to his clients and Mr. Octavian, and left the station in his fashionably expedient lawyer speed march.

Derrick escorted Richard and Larcis outside.

"So what happened to you two?" Derrick said while disarming the alarm and doors to his dark green Jeep Grand Cherokee.

Richard looked at Larcis while motioning him to get in the back seat.

"You did good, but we've just started."

Larcis sighed, nodded affirmation, and got into the Jeep.

Richard sat in the front while Derrick started the car.

"Dad," Richard said, "do you remember when I told you I wished I could find a close friend who would understand my problems?" Derrick smiled slightly and looked at Larcis in the rearview mirror. "Someone tried to kill me with a laser gun. Larcis here helped in stopping the men by vaporizing part of their getaway car. I killed one man and the other died from laser wounds shot from his own partner's weapon. I know the police don't believe our story and neither does Robert Thorn. But, for some reason, Robert Thorn is the key to this mess. They don't have hard evidence, but they had enough to keep us overnight. Robert pulled some strings, and I just have this feeling about him that I can't put my finger on."

"Yeah I don't trust him." Larcis added.

"Do you want me to see if I can find out some information on this Robert fellow?" Derrick asked.

"No, Dad. Not just yet. If he isn't an attorney like he says, he probably has covered his tracks and expects us to spy on him right about now. In the meantime, Larcis and I have a lot to talk about, especially what we are going to do about our future."

Richard looked back at Larcis, who sat in a state of confusion or awe while father and son conversed. Larcis's parents and friends spoke of Derrick Octavian, who had been police commissioner a few decades before, as a legend in law enforcement. He was expected to emulate the legend. Larcis understood that his life would change drastically with this newfound friendship. He loved adventures and as a boy had dreamed of becoming a police officer or spy. Many superhumans had stepped forward in the name of justice, and he knew he was somehow going to get a piece of the action. He was young and was sure Richard had the experience to be the leader of a superhero group he had brainstormed since childhood. The Emerald Legion and EFL (Energy, Fire and Light), two of the major superhero groups on the planet, spurred him on to find fellow superhumans to fight crime and evil. And now his dreams were becoming a reality.

The three men went to Derrick's Coral Gables house. It was roomy and seemed deserted since the deaths of Derrick's wife and four children. The house was safeguarded by a security system that Derrick had developed himself. Richard knew that it was safe to speak freely with Larcis and Derrick in the house. His CIA experience had left him with paranoia concerning intelligence surveillance operations. The Miami Police, as far as he knew, did not have the authority to conduct high-tech surveillance on him, especially without due cause or criminal activity. Government agencies and the people who had sent the men to kill him might have such technology and resources, however.

Richard was also uneasy about Robert's sudden appearance at the police station. Richard's superhuman identity had been discovered, and this could be done only by using high-tech bio-scanners, telepaths, or electronic listening devices. Richard had not used his powers or spoken of them since entering the university. So obviously a bio-scanner or telepath had been used to find him. Whatever the case, he was now forced to trust Larcis Draven.

The men took snacks—foot-long turkey and beef subs, pizza leftovers, hot wings, and iced tea—from the kitchen to Derrick's den. The small room was dimly lit with a directional lamp hanging down five feet from the floor. The cleverly scattered pictures and trinkets spanning sixty years made the room seem tranquil. Richard and Larcis sat across from each other on plush leather sofas. A small circular table covered with a dark blue tablecloth separated the two men. Derrick sat in his recliner in his favorite corner of the room.

Richard gave Larcis the third degree. He questioned him about his childhood, his family and friends and enemies, his habits and hobbies, his religious and philosophical views as well as his views on women. He asked about Larcis's dreams, goals, and prejudices, his educational background and work experience. Richard also questioned Larcis about his superhuman abilities before asking for a day-by-day, hour-by-hour accounting of his activities over the previous two weeks.

The informal interrogation lasted four hours. Larcis enjoyed opening himself up to Richard and answered every question down to the minutest detail. He could not—*would* not—lie, which meant that his secret as a superhuman had been kept from everyone, even his family, until now. At times Richard worried that Larcis might be too candid for his own or anyone else's good.

*Oh, boy,* Richard thought. *Are reporters going to have a field day with you!*

"So now that I know a lot about you. Do you have any questions for me?" Richard asked. He was merely going through formalities, knowing that Larcis had a million and one questions.

Larcis glanced at Derrick, who was still sitting comfortably in the corner of the den, and then turned back toward Richard.

"You probably think I have a million questions," Larcis stated with an expectation of a reply on his face but continued to talk as if a reply was not required. "And I do. But ninety-nine percent of those will be answered by spending time with you as a friend. So for right now, I have only a few questions."

Richard was surprised and impressed with Larcis's keen logic and maturity. He smiled his uncanny smile.

"Go ahead," Richard said. "Shoot."

"What do you think about superhero groups like EFL, the Emerald Legion, and the Defenders?"

Richard thought for a few seconds. "I think its good there are groups of superhumans fighting crime and upholding justice; and there should be more groups like that who will carry on with their work before they fade away like ninety-nine percent of the groups that get started."

"I was wondering why you never joined one of those groups," said Larcis.

"I'd get in somebody's way...or somebody would get in mine." Richard bit into a hot wing smothered in sauce. "As you've noticed, I don't like to take orders and my temper can get out of hand."

"So why don't you start your own group? As leader, no one will get in your way, and you will have many opportunities to vent your temper on the bad guys?"

Richard continued to eat and answered without missing a beat. "To be leader of a group, there must be a group to lead. The group has to have a common purpose; the members also must have secret identities and a secret rallying point or headquarters. In order to have a headquarters, you have to have money, technical support, and law-enforcement or governmental backing to some degree. Since we don't have any of these, starting a group is not on my to do list."

"Hmmm," Larcis said. He leaned back in thought. "It seems that you forgot another thing that there has to be."

"Oh, what's that?" Richard asked, looking amused.

"There has to be a dream to start it all and make it come true. You know, Richard, I think it was destiny that brought us together. I mean, what are the chances of us meeting the way we did? I just happen to be there when you used your powers and all. We get picked up by the police and our identities as superhumans are protected by some lawyer who comes out of nowhere." Larcis' sarcastic face was a portrait of disbelief and annoyance.

Richard thought about that for a second. True, it was extremely uncanny that they had met in such a random way. The odds had been over a trillion to one. And yet Richard was hesitant to get involved in a superhero group. The commitment of resources and time was so great. And then there were the financial, technical, and logistical considerations. Also, Richard did not want to deal with the attention such a group would attract. Still, it did seem that he and Larcis had been brought together somehow and for a purpose.

Richard nodded and mumbled, "Hmmm. Tell me something. If we did start a group, how do you think we would do it?"

"All we need now is for us to have a third superhuman to officially have a group," Larcis answered without seriously considered the consequences of his statement.

"Do you think it's wise to have secret identities and a secret base of operations?" Richard asked while looking at Derrick.

"Of course it is." Larcis replied. "We can't have people know where we live and who we really are. Our families and friends would be in danger from fanatics and psychos wanting revenge or wanting to satisfy their egos. But if we can get hooked up to the right people, we can be like the Emerald Legion. They've been a group for more than eighteen years, and no one knows who they are or where they live."

Richard grinned. "I've lived in the shadows and know things like that don't happen very offend," he said. "I don't trust anyone right now outside of us three. So for us to keep from being compromised as a semi-superhero group, we must find those bastards who sent those two fools after me. We can't do anything until we find out how they knew I was a superhuman. In the meantime, the idea of a superhero group will have to be put on hold."

Larcis smiled. He had no choice but to agree with Richard's logic. But Larcis kept his hopes up for the start of a new era of crime fighting. Larcis bowed his head in submission, and then looked at Richard's father.

"It's getting late. Mr. Octavian, I hope I'm not intruding too much."

"Not at all, my boy," said Derrick with a smile. "In fact, you've brought back some spice in my life. It's good to see you and Richard get to know each other."

Derrick showed Larcis to a guestroom while Richard sat in his chair thinking. Larcis had touched a soft spot that he had kept hidden in his past. He wanted to be a superhero like EFL and the Emerald Legion members, but he lacked the vision to orchestrate such a group. He had so many powers and skills, and it hurt him deeply when he saw innocent people suffer because he was in his own way helpless, unable to show the world who he was or attract attention to himself without endangering people close to him like Derrick—and now Larcis too.

He hated thieves, murderers, rapists, abusive behavior, and evil itself with an unyielding passion. He hated his time with the CIA and other agencies claiming to be fighting for justice and freedom. The truth was that corruption ate into the highest level of governments and societies. He had entered the CIA to fight crime, but he'd seen the pitfalls of political agendas and questionable motives. He was exceptional at his skills in security systems, demolitions, computers, genetics, general science, and even piloting jet fighters. But he had no desire to work for any agency or group with political or military agendas again. Becoming leader of a superhero group, though, was appealing to him. He would be answerable only to his team, the public, and his own conscience.

Derrick made Larcis feel at home with a short this is your room speech and bid Larcis goodnight. Larcis quickly fell asleep as lofty and noble dreams filled his mind.

The following day came quickly for Richard, whose goal was to seek out and destroy the people who were out to kill him. Richard and Larcis started on their project by devising a trap for the next would-be assassins. Richard, with enough concentration, could project his anger and horror into other people's minds, shocking them with fear and confusion. He did not consider this ability to be of much use unless he was trying to hurt someone in a fight or argument without touching them. He knew that if someone was trying to read his mind, he would have a fifty-percent chance of sensing the other person's thoughts while concentrating his anger. This brought up a problem. He would have to be engaged in a mental attack at the same time the telepath was trying to read his or the victim's mind. He could practice on sensing mental probes but that took time, and he neglected that ability in the past favoring physical training to include his telekinesis. On the other hand, the future assassins would probably not be telepaths since they already knew who he was. Richard and Larcis eventually settled for the direct approach in catching the assassins while in the act and not killing them before they got some answers.

Richard told Larcis to stay away from him while in public and yet close enough to cover his back. He would go about his business in a routine manner, keeping to a regular schedule and moving into more secluded locations to give the would-be assassins an opportunity to attack. After several days, Richard became impatient waiting for the would-be assassins to act.

A week passed. Then Robert Thorn showed up at Richard's accounting seminar. The instructor allowed Richard to leave class fifteen minutes early. Robert showed Richard the police report stating that he and Larcis were not suspects. But they might be summoned to appear in court as witnesses to an insurance claim by the university for damages to the pavement and landscape wall. Richard read the report closely. He stopped at the name of John Goodman, an eyewitness and collaborator of his story. Goodman had apparently seen the entire thing from an adjacent dormitory. The report exactly replicated his cockamamie story. Richard told Robert goodbye and thought over this new development as he went up to Larcis's room. His new friend didn't answer his door, so Richard went to his own room, where Larcis loudly greeted him.

"Richard! It's about time!" Larcis raised a finger to his lips before continuing. "I see you're in a hurry to lose another ten bucks on the court!" He extended a hand toward Richard, who took a slip of paper from between his friend's fingers.

*There's a listening device in your room. We need to go somewhere safe.*

"Racquetball loser?" said Larcis.

"Yeah," said Richard, "we'll see about that. You know it's about time someone put you in your place, so give me a second to change, alright?"

Richard raised his hands, palms upward, and looked around the room to ask where the bug was. Larcis shrugged his shoulders, and then whispered into Richard's ear, "I found one in my TV."

Richard nodded and looked at his own television. His enhanced en-ray vision pierced the plastic and metal to reveal the circuitry and framework. He knew the components of a television on sight, but, more importantly, he knew what an electronic bug looked like. The television set appeared to be clean.

He quickly changed and got his racquetball equipment, then carefully scanned his and Larcis's equipment, accessories, shoes, and clothing as a precaution.

"Are you sure it was a bug?" Richard asked once they'd reached the racquetball court.

"Yeah, I'm sure. I used to help out my father when he worked as a video technician. I was trying to change the tubes on my set when I ran into the bug. It's about an inch long and a fourth-inch thick with a miniature microphone on the upper half. It was placed near the remote receptacle." Larcis looked a little puzzled. "What's going on, Richard?"

Richard was puzzled too. Why did Larcis own a television that had tubes?

"I'm not sure," said Richard, "but from now on watch what you say and do. I'll scan my entire room when we get back. Then you will invite me over to play *Killer Instinct* on the Playstation so I can scan your room and look at that bug of yours."

"Okay," said Larcis.

"And we have another problem on our plate," Richard said.

"Oh?"

"Thorn showed me the police report. It had the name *John Goodman* on it. He apparently witnessed what happened on the driveway, and he backed up our story."

"On any normal day that would be good. But who's John Goodman, and why did he cover for us?"

"John is a dumb senior. He and I know each other from several of our classes, but we never really met on a regular basis. I would assume he covered for us because he knows me. But there's something else. His story exactly replicates our account, which he somehow got access to before the police questioned him. Otherwise there's no way he could have known what we told the police unless he has ESP or something."

"Huh," said Larcis. "And I thought everyone else on campus was normal."

Richard took his position on the court and made ready to serve the first ball. "Now that you've realized the truth, get ready for an ass-whipping." He smiled as the hollow sound of the rubber ball echoed off the walls.

Two hours later, Richard returned to his dorm and quickly showered and changed. Then he sat on his sofa and slowly and systematically scanned the room. He spotted the bug thirty minutes later. It was inside his plant pot about seven millimeters into the soil. He found a larger device within a carved out niche in the upper edge of his bathroom door. It was easily visible to the naked eye, but only to someone eight feet tall who was looking down at the top edge of the door.

Richard closed the blinds after he was confident that there were no more bugs in the room. Two were sufficient in spying— one as the primary and one as the backup in case of technical or electronic failure. Richard sat on the sofa by the window, scanning out 800 meters in an attempt to find any surveillance teams spying on him or Larcis. After scanning the grounds and half the buildings on campus, Richard was convinced that the spying was not professionally robust like the surveillance missions he had conducted with the CIA.

He finally moved to Larcis's room, where he found another miniature bug also in the bathroom door. The technique was similar and suggested the people who bugged both their rooms were placed by the same person or group of people. The two men conversed by passing notes between themselves for thirty minutes and then went back to their normal routines. The day ended with thirty games of *Killer Instinct* followed by NBA basketball on Larcis's TV set. Richard went back to his room happy with winning most of the games, but worried about being spied upon by law enforcement, or possible villains wanting to kill them or use them for evil purposes.

# Chapter Three

✠ - ✠

# True Friends

T he night air breezed through a sliding door at the Hyatt Hotel penthouse. Sparse cumulus clouds moved across the starry sky as a young woman lay on her stomach across a red sofa facing the window. Her long silky-black hair draped down, barely touching the plush tan carpet. Her head lay motionless on her crossed arms. The penthouse was elegantly filled with priceless artworks and furniture. The only lights in the penthouse were the LED clock display on the stereo and the security system display at the entrance. The moon shone full on the young woman's beautiful face, but her sad expression somehow diminished its brightness. Sounds of screams, gunshots, and distant explosions skipped along the tops of buildings. The woman's light-brown eyes peered through the sky in search of answers to her prayers. There was no fear in her eyes, no uneasiness, no regret, no worries. Only loneliness.

The chime of doorbells broke the city sounds. The young woman softly said, "Come in." The double doors opened, letting in dim blue light from the hall into the living room. The figure of a woman with long fluffy hair stepped into the room.

"Hello, Linda," said the woman.

Linda lifted her head to look toward the entrance. Her face brightened with a tired smile as she jumped up from the sofa and ran to hug her first and only true friend.

"Kat! It's great to see you. Where have you been?"

"It's great to see you too," Kat said, "but things have changed a lot."

They sat together on the sofa as Kat told her friend what had happened.

"Sargon has taken over the city by killing the Godfather and Win Lo. I don't know why I was not allowed to go or told about it, but they met at the old Renaissance Theater where they were supposed to make a truce. I don't know all the details, but it turned into a bloodbath. Sargon had someone neutralize their security systems and kill their bodyguards."

Linda showed no surprise as she glared at the floor.

"I know."

Four months had passed since her exile to Complex San Francisco. Kat had been in the complex for nine months establishing herself as Sargon's liaison specialist. Linda, on the other hand, had established herself as Sargon's secret weapon with a reputation that spread fear among the convicts.

"You *know?* What do you mean?" Kat asked although she knew the answer.

Linda looked deep into Kat's eyes. "I was there. I turned off the safeguards in the theater and made the bodyguards kill one another while Sargon took care of the rest."

Kat's voice and posture hardened in disbelief. "Why? What were you thinking?"

"We're slaves within this prison, and even though we could probably take control of the city, we will still be slaves. I know that peace was something we wanted for everyone here, but it won't happen as long as there are evil men like Sargon, the Godfather, or Win Lo. The complex is a failure, and the whole world needs to know the truth."

"I don't understand how making Sargon more powerful is going to do that."

"Sargon was the strongest, and he thinks he'll create a new era of order in the city, which would be easy for him to do now that he is unchallenged, running the city like his own country. He plans to create an army and force the senate to make Complex San Francisco into an independent province. He's very smart, but has no common sense. The government will not allow him to get away with it and will stop him at all costs. That will be our chance to expose the truth and stop the practices they had intended here and Sargon's reign of terror."

Kat knew Linda very well, and even though Linda's logic was not flawless, she trusted her instincts. In addition, Kat's cognitive abilities were unreliable, but only to a point. Kat knew that they would not be in San Francisco long and that her life would change dramatically because of Linda's appearance in the complex. Her visions had predicted a long-lasting friendship with Linda along with a myriad of other people she had yet to meet.

"What do we do now?" Kat asked as she stood up and walked toward the open sliding door.

"We wait and watch each other's backs," said Linda. "Sargon will continue to protect us as long as he thinks we're not plotting against him. In the meantime, keep your eyes open and help him with his master plan."

Linda yawned. Kat looked at her friend.

"You haven't slept much, have you?" said Kat.

Linda stared at a turtle paper figurine on her glass table. "No. I had a dream two nights ago. No, it was a nightmare I had when I was a teenager."

Kat returned and sat by Linda, placing a hand on her shoulder.

Tears formed around Linda's eyes as she tried to forget the events in her mind.

"Oh, Kat! I don't know if I can *bear* seeing those two men again."

For the first time in the four months she had known Linda, Kat saw fear in her friend's eyes.

### University of Miami campus grounds

John Goodman enjoyed jogging, but not in the heat of the day. And he hated running indoors on a machine that constantly told him he was going nowhere. So he ran around the campus in the morning, often as early as five o'clock.

A mile into his stretch, he noticed another jogger slightly behind him but keeping pace. He glanced back to see a tall, black-haired man wearing jogging attire and sunglasses. Soon the other jogger was right next to him.

"Hello, John."

John hesitantly waved a response.

"I think we need to talk…. Well, I take that back. *I'll* talk. You *listen.* Okay?"

John nodded.

"Well, let's take the scenic route, shall we," Richard said and motioned toward route U.S. 1, also known as the Dixie Highway, the main route through Miami and on to Key West. The four-lane highway was starting to get congested with morning rush-hour traffic. The men ran for about three miles, entering Coral Gables. The scenery was a change that John had never thought about taking in until now. Richard could hardly have cared less. His only purpose at the moment was to get the information he was after.

"Okay, this is far enough," Richard said as they slowed down to a walk. "I know that you saw what really happened in front of the dormitory a week and a half ago. And it's obvious that you helped me and Larcis. What I want to know is *why* did you help?"

John looked at Richard and started to explain with rapid sign language. Richard gave a blank look.

"What the hell are you doing? I don't know sign language, and I didn't ask you how; I know *how*. You can read minds. What I don't know is whether you can project thoughts and talk to people with your mind. So *can* you?"

John seemed confused. He thought, *Can he really know that I can read minds? If so, how?*

Richard was growing impatient. *Look, John,* he thought, *I will prove that what I am saying is the truth just so that we can communicate better and have you answer my questions.*

John's eyes widened as he read Richard's thoughts: *If you don't talk to me soon, I will beat you and continue to beat the shit out of you until you do!*

*Okay, Richard,* John asked mentally, *you don't have to get rough about it. I was only trying to keep a low profile. How did you know I could read minds, anyway?*

*I didn't really know. But you called my bluff. There's a lot you have to learn about deception, you know—psychological warfare,* Richard thought.

*I'll remember that,* John thought, feeling really stupid for caving in.

*Now that we can talk without moving our mouths, we will speak mentally when we have to communicate about our clandestine activities,* Richard thought.

*Clandestine activities?* John thought, looking confused.

*There are people spying on Larcis and me—and probably you too since you told the police you saw everything. The people who tried to kill me will try again. And as for the spies, they are probably not related, but they probably suspect that we are not normal people. So the real reason I came to see you is to propose—*

*A partnership!* John interrupted.

Richard coldly looked at John.

"Yeah, a partnership."

John smiled. *I guess you can't hide everything from me,* he thought.

"Hmmm," Richard said. "It's about time we headed back."

As the two men jogged back toward campus, Richard mentally told John his plan to start a superhero group and catch the people who were trying to kill him.

### The Pentagon, Virginia

The afternoon light pierced the half-open blinds in a large, well-furnished office. A tall, handsome man in his mid-forties paced by the window with his hands in his pockets. The pile of papers on the desk overflowed onto the dark blue carpet. The man paused and gazed out the window overlooking the parking lot and the pine forest beyond.

The telephone intercom disrupted the quiet office. "General, I have Wendy on the line," the secretary announced.

"Thank you, Tina," the general responded. He turned toward his armchair as the telephone beeped and the speaker activated. "Wendy, how are you?"

"The flight was very bumpy, but apart from that, I'm okay." Wendy answered with a tired, sweet voice from a pay phone at the Ronald Reagan National Airport.

"You sound tired."

"I haven't slept much lately, and it was a long flight. But I might add that it was worth it."

"So tell me the good news."

"It's a long story," Wendy said, "but it looks like we got more than what we expected."

"Well, then," said the general, "can we have dinner together?"

Wendy glanced at her watch. "I'll meet you at the Emporium at six."

"Fine," said the general. "I'll be waiting."

General Cartier smiled at the prospective future. His time as director of Space Operations empowered him with precious information in the name of national security. It was ironic that the influence he had would change the nation's economy as well as future space exploration. His retirement and future appointment as deputy of Central Intelligence would make all of his plans for the country's security and unheard-of prosperity possible.

A few hours later, General Thomas Cartier stood patiently waiting in the Emporium lobby. A young woman with sandy blond hair and wearing a glittering dark-green dress entered. She scoped the area as she approached Thomas with a smile.

"Hello, General. Or should I say, *Mr. Cartier?*"

Thomas smiled his usual smile. "Hello, Wendy. Good to see you."

Wendy returned the smile. "Yes, I'm sure the office missed me."

Thomas tilted his head. "What would I do without my best national security adviser?"

"I don't really know," Wendy sarcastically replied.

"Well, a table is waiting for us," Thomas said. "May I lead the way?"

The two ordered modest meals and got down to business. "So, what did the Tokamashi Corporation say to our proposal?" Thomas asked.

"They were very open to the prospect," Wendy reported with pride. "In fact, they agreed to not only help, but also to negotiate a deal with South America to assist with biological and metallurgical technology."

"I see…," said Thomas. He looked concerned. "I'm sure you understand how sensitive this venture can be."

"Yes, I do, and that's why they have to be involved," Wendy quickly answered.

Thomas looked at her a little confused. "Explain."

"We all know that South America leads the way in space technology, not to mention all the other areas—science, economics, medicine. Their borders have opened up, not much, but they are open nevertheless. In the past year they've helped Japan, Spain, and Panama reach economic and medical breakthroughs that were seen only back in the Industrial Revolution. I know they pose a military threat. But without them, we're like children trying to cross a six-lane highway. We have to trust them...*to a point.* They'll provide technical support for the problems we need solved, and that's all."

"Hmmm. And what kind of deal are we talking about with this technical support?" Thomas asked.

"All I know is that we'll meet with the Japanese Council for Space Operations and two South American economic representatives from the Department of Transportation and Federation Space Technologies to come to an agreement for the creation of the moon base. Honestly, I think South America has the most to lose by helping us. The more technology they share, the more it diminishes their military advantage both in space and on the ground."

The waitress interrupted the conversation with filet mignon and veal Parmesan. Thomas ate for a while contemplating what path he would lead the United States into.

"I've always been open-minded," said Thomas, "so it won't hurt to see what Tokamashi can turn up. When's the meeting?"

"It's set for September 28th. We'll meet in Tokyo for a day and fly to Houston. There we can give them a tour of the installation."

"You know that I hate turning over rocks and having rattlesnakes bite me in the ass. But I'll trust your judgment."

"Thank you, Thomas."

"No, don't thank me. You've earned my trust and confidence.... That reminds me. Have you thought about my offer?"

"Yes," Wendy answered, "and it's very gracious. But I want to settle down. I've accepted a job in Florida with Cyber Corporation. There's not much travel involved, and I can get my Ph.D. in Education."

Thomas thought for a moment, looking at Wendy's demeanor.

"You've always known what you wanted, so I don't blame you for wanting to escape this world of secrets and strategic diplomacy. I'd hoped that you'd be happy working for the CIA, but I understand your decision. I'm just glad we can work this one last time together."

They enjoyed a long, peaceful dinner and ended the night toasting their friendship and unknown future. They parted ways, and Thomas left the hotel worried about South America's involvement, but had no choice but to see what the most powerful nation in the world would do to fulfill or prevent his dreams of space exploration come to life.

# Chapter Four

✠ - ✠

# Campus Life

## University of Miami Campus

All day and into the evening, students had been arriving on campus for the new semester. The dormitories were springing to life with keg parties and study groups. Richard, in a light sleep, heard a group of students singing and playing music on the grass behind the dorm. He was in no mood to party; having been dumped by his girlfriend. He was also beginning to be concerned about the number of innocents who might be caught in the crossfire if the assassins again attempted to strike at the university.

Richard was jolted into reality by a roaring sound and the shaking of the building that followed. Using his en-ray vision, he peered through the walls and saw a monstrosity—a thirty-foot octopus-like droid with a single glass eye—as it landed in the mist of horrified students. The red-and-black giant had two twenty-foot-long cylindrical arms and claws that flung people like Lego figures in a child's playpen. The eye, which was blue and four feet in diameter, widened and shrank as if focusing on its targets. The exhaust vents on the back of its spherical body slowly closed as the droid scanned the dormitories.

Larcis stormed into Richard's room. "Richard! What the hell are we going to do?"

A man in the middle of the room dressed in a black ninja costume replied. "I'll take care of that thing. You make sure everyone is out of the building."

"Huh? And how do you plan to do that?" Larcis replied with doubt, sarcasm, and a little hint of fear in his voice.

Larcis knew Richard probably had no clue on what to do, but showed no signs of being lost without a strategy. Richard was used to fighting tanks, dismounted infantrymen, and airplanes. This was totally different. A full-force attack on the huge droid might cause a lot of collateral damage. Larcis doubted if the machine could hurt Richard, but there was always a first time for everything. Richard seemed unafraid of getting hurt, and at times Larcis wished he knew the full extent of his powers, maybe because then he would know if his fearless leader was indestructible or not. But at this point it didn't really matter whether the droid could hurt him. Richard had to do something before anyone else got killed or severely injured, and Larcis knew he would have to help his friend fight this mechanical monster.

"I'll do what I can," Larcis said, still a little confused. He sprinted from the room toward the far end of the building.

Richard crashed through his dorm window. Glass and metal debris shot into the scene below as he swooped down and grabbed a would-be victim from one of the droid's claws. The droid turned his attention to the ninja. A blue laser beam shot from his eye and struck Richard in the left arm. His arm was instantly numb, and he dropped the student. He hesitated as the droid grabbed him with its right claw.

Larcis yelled down the hall as he went from room to room, "There's a bomb in the building! Get out now!"

He ran into Kevin Mullin's room only to see Richard through the second-story window, helpless in the giant's grasp. Larcis quickly looked to see that no one was in the room, then closed the door. He placed his hands together in front of him as if holding an invisible basketball. His hands glowed pure white for a second as he strained to control his powers.

Richard's arm tingled as if pierced by a thousand needles. The droid's claw tightened without mercy. The pressure would have crushed a normal human, but it only angered Richard against this monstrous machine and the people who created it. Richard's eyes turned bright red as he fought the droid's grip. He shift shaped his arm countering the effects of the eye beam, but maintaining its visible form.

Lightning flashed from one of the dorm windows, and piercing thunder drowned out the moans and screams of injured and fleeing students. The lightning scraped the droid's right arm, completely tore through the left arm, and burst open a ten-by-ten foot crater in the ground just short of the next dormitory fifty meters away.

Richard bolted from the droid's grasp as the detached arm and claw fell to the ground. The droid's back was now facing his dormitory. Richard mustered all his strength, drew back his fist, and jumped toward the droid. He swung with lightning speed at the monster's eye. His fist opened and a blur of airwaves six feet in diameter spread around the eye, caving it into the spherical body of the droid. Sparks of energy erupted through the cracks around the eye as the droid fell backward into the dormitory. Its massive weight crushed the dorm walls and destroyed half the building like a great demolition ball. Rubble tumbled down the droid's body, with the dorm's broken water and electrical fixtures presenting still more danger.

Richard began to take the droid apart piece by piece to make sure it didn't decide to get up again. Students and campus personnel surrounded the area as paramedics, fire fighters, and policemen arrived on the scene. The black ninja disappeared as quickly as he had appeared, only to reappear as Richard, a student escaping the debris.

Channel 7 News rushed to the scene as Richard, Larcis, and John helped the wounded. Unfortunately the lead reporter chose to interview Larcis about the incident. Police started to quarantine the area as the reporter approached Larcis.

"Excuse me. My name is Allen Norton, reporter for Channel 7 News. I would like to ask you a few questions. Are you a student here?"

Larcis looked at Allen, slightly annoyed for being interrupted while trying to help another student with a concussion and an ankle injury.

"Yes, I am."

"What's your name, sir?" Allen asked.

"My name is Larcis," he replied, trying to walk away with his patient.

"Can you tell us what happened here, Larcis?" Allen quickly asked.

Larcis stopped and looked at the microphone, which Allen had shoved into his face. "You wouldn't believe me if I told you."

A hand came out of nowhere and cupped the microphone.

"Don't waste your time with him," Richard interrupted. "I know who can answer all of your questions."

"And who are you, sir?" Allen asked firmly, brushing away Richard's hand.

"Larcis and I just got here to help out, but that guy up there was here during the entire thing." Richard said, pointing toward another student, who was helping paramedics find the most critically injured. "Besides, if you haven't noticed, Allen, Larcis and I are very busy right now."

Richard hurriedly helped Larcis with his patient as they disappeared into the crowd.

The camera spotlight swung toward a sandy-haired young man hugging a young woman as the paramedics placed another injured woman on a stretcher beside them. Allen placed his microphone in front of John's face, and the light blinded him and his girlfriend, Sally.

"Excuse me. I'm Allen Norton from Channel 7 News. Can you tell our audience what happened here in this terrifying attack by this giant mechanical monster?"

John frowned with anger as he told off Allen with sign language and a few moans then turned his back. Allen stood in silent embarrassment for a moment, and then said, "Cut it, Mike." The reporter vainly looked around for Richard and Larcis but couldn't find them.

Richard approached John thirty minutes after things started to settle down and told him to scan the authority figures in the investigation. John, Richard, and Larcis went up to John's room where John, looking out through his dorm window, started his person-to-person scan, reading the minds of police and FBI agents. Two FBI agents caught his attention. They were middle-aged males concerning themselves with the black ninja and possible superhuman targets. John could get only surface thoughts, but he knew that Richard was the topic of interest. They seemed to accept that a giant droid with claws and a blue eye four feet in diameter was a common weapon. Richard and Larcis stood beside John as he translated the two agents' thoughts and lip movements.

John said, "The one agent, Tony, is saying to the other one, Brian, 'We have to get rid of the droid as quickly as possible through our normal channels before the police ask too many questions.'"

John continued to narrate as Brain replied: "'The cranes and trucks are on their way. Bill will take care of the reporters.

But for now I need you to sterilize the two rooms while I contact Max. Alright?'"

"What about the ninja?" Tony asked.

"If the reports are correct," Brain said, "it's probably a superhuman staying here as a student. Nevertheless, I have a feeling that he'll surface again. In the meantime, we have to go to blue sector and find out if they have correlated where the droid came from. Let me know when the rooms are clear."

"What now?" Larcis interjected as John finished narrating the agents' conversation.

"We follow Brian and Tony when they leave for this blue sector," Richard said.

"Okay, but we won't be called the three ninjas," Larcis said with a smile as he turned completely black with glowing red eyes, his major muscle groups outlined in red. "I will be called 'Night'!"

"He looks like a weirdo in a black-and-red diving suit," John told Richard.

Richard smiled. "Yeah," he told John, "but he's right. We all need to go in disguise, so you'll need to get a costume ready."

Trucks hauled the droid's remains away before news crews could get close-up photos. The students who had lived in the dormitory destroyed by the monster were assigned rooms elsewhere on campus. City engineers worked all night to stabilize the dormitory structure to keep it from completely collapsing. The dean announced that the semester would start a week late and that a team from Chamberlyn Funding Company would handle all student issues for insurance claims and medical bills. Richard told the administrative office that he and Larcis would be staying with his father for a few days and not to worry about their living arrangements.

As the scene cleared, the superheroes went into action.

"The trucks are starting to leave along with those two bozos," Larcis reported. "Are you guys ready?"

Larcis heard Richard say from behind him, "What the hell are you suppose to be?"

Larcis turned to see a man wearing a diving suit with gray and purple torso and black legs and arms, plus purple boots and gloves and a black hood with a yellow top covering the entire head except for a little exposed skin around the nose and mouth.

"Look," said Larcis. "It's a short, purple lighthouse!"

*Laugh it up, Larcis,* John thought as the others read his mind. *At least I have an original costume and name. You can call me Mindseye.*

Richard could only shake his head and look at the floor, wondering how his luck could be so horrible.

Larcis opened the dorm window, and the three superheroes took to the air, following the FBI agents. Richard wore a completely black police anti-terrorist outfit. Larcis was at his heels in his black attire, while John brought up the rear, where he was less likely to compromise the group. The agents' dark blue Ford Taurus broke away from the convoy of trucks and headed to the Sawgrass Expressway. The car continued north an hour past Ft. Lauderdale, then turned northwest into the

Everglades. Richard flew at treetop level about five hundred meters behind the car using his passive infrared vision. The dark clouds above started to let out warm droplets of rain. One thousand meters ahead, Richard spotted a fence line and a building with an array of antennas. The group slowed, flying into the woods just short of a fifty-meter clearing all around the fence line. The Taurus continued to the small structure without slowing down. The gate slid open automatically as the car approached and closed just as quickly behind the car. The building was no larger than a two-story house and had few windows.

Richard, Larcis, and John viewed the scene of the garage door opening and closing as the car entered the building.

"It seems to be a military field station—without guards, of course," Larcis said.

"It seems that way, but there has to be some type of security system. The fence is probably electrified. And look," Richard said, "there are two cameras on the roof."

*The antennas seem to be used for radio transmissions, so they probably don't have radar. What do you think—an aerial assault?* John suggested.

"No," responded Richard, "they must have some type of radar. The agent named Brian mentioned that they should be able to find out where the droid came from, which means that they either have radar or some type of satellite tracking system. But it doesn't really matter. I'll go through the roof and disable their security system. You guys come in through the front door. Alright?"

*What front door?* John asked.

Larcis smiled, put a hand on John's shoulder, and said, "We'll make one if we don't see one by the time we get there."

"So how are you going to get in there unnoticed?" Larcis added.

"Watch and learn," Richard said as his entire body became less than half its normal size and transformed into a gigantic eagle.

*That is the biggest eagle I've ever seen!* John thought. *I hope they don't see what big eyes and beak you have!*

"Give me exactly ten minutes, starting now," Richard commanded, ignoring his jokes, knowing his physical dimensions and characteristics were identical to a full grown eagle.

Richard flew to the rear, then made a large circle and emerged from the trees, heading straight toward the building's rooftop out of camera range. He landed near a ventilation shaft on the roof and transformed instantly into a black jelly-like substance so that he could squeeze through the ventilation grill down into the building. He quickly moved to the first floor, where he drained into the garage. He was confused because the garage was empty, and he couldn't see through the floor with his en-ray vision.

*This floor must be made of some special material,* Richard thought.

He changed back to his normal costumed form and searched for an elevator system. There were no clearly visible cameras, but he knew there was a few probably hidden, so he stood in the center of the garage. Suddenly the floor began to move downward. Richard sprinted to a corner of the elevator, taking note of how far the elevator went underground. Five levels down, the elevator opened to a car lot. Twelve cars filled the lot. Richard transformed into jelly again, taking the baseboard path to what seemed to be a corridor. He proceeded along the corridor but stopped at a double metal door with a blue strip and the number *five* on the right side. An access panel with a card slot and hand imprint was mounted beside the door to the right.

Richard oozed his hand on the panel. He felt inside the card slot and readjusted the identity sensor. He then transformed his hand to normal and placed it on the imprint. The sensor recognized the last imprint and the door opened. Richard entered a small hallway with doors on each end and two in the middle.

"This is too easy," Richard said under his breath.

Richard transformed back to his hero form and charged the door to his left. He kicked the metal door, and it caved in like aluminum foil. Richard stepped through into another hallway. The wall to the right was made of sheet glass that allowed him to see the inside of a large computer complex. Several men and women scrambled to the exit doors or consoles; others stood in fright. Two men in blue suits carrying assault rifles rushed for cover and aimed their weapons at Richard. Richard could not hear what was being said in the room, but a red light flashing in the room and hallway indicated that the entire installation knew he was here.

The two security guards kept their weapons trained on Richard as he heard the movement of approaching troops. A metal door opened to reveal four additional guards with 7.62-millimeter FAL assault rifles.

"Place your hands on your head!" the lead guard barked.

"And if I don't?" Richard challenged.

"Put your hands on your head—*now!*" the guard commanded.

"Do you really think you can hurt me with those toys?" Richard laughingly asked.

"Get on the ground slowly and assume a spread-eagle position flat on your stomach!" the lead guard commanded while keeping his distance.

Richard ignored the order and walked casually toward the men.

"Halt!"

A round was fired. It missed Richard's head by a few inches and hit metal to his rear.

"That is your last warning!"

Richard continued as if he were walking in the park. A second shot hit Richard in his right leg. He felt a little thump as the velocity of the round pushed his leg an inch or so backward. He smiled under his black mask.

"I hope you have medical insurance," he said, "because, as you can see, I won't be needing it."

Richard stood for a moment and considered his options. The window's glass was at least two inches thick, and it was probably bulletproof, which meant it would slow him down a little. He had only two options remaining, the left side or the right side of the hallway.

Richard sprinted forward, zigzagging, at an inhuman speed, taking the guards by surprise. Rounds spun through thin air as the lead guard felt his rifle torn away from his grasp. A hand grabbed the guard's left shoulder and the back of his neck. He twirled to his left as he partially fell backward off his center of gravity. Richard handled the guard like a rag doll as he stopped the guard's fall with his left knee on the small of the man's back. The guard lay on Richard's knee as his own rifle muzzle touched his temple.

"Put down your weapons!" Richard commanded. "Now!"

The men disregarded the command.

"Put down your weapons!" Richard repeated.

One of the guards lowered his weapon. The others did the same. The hallway filled with more guards on the other end. Richard saw that the new guards had some type of laser rifles. The 7.62-millimeter ammunition was harmless to Richard, but the new weapons might have a chance of really pissing him off.

"Put down your weapons!" Richard yelled down the hallway.

The guards hesitated but lowered their weapons. A man in a two-piece suit broke through the line of guards.

"Put your weapons away and leave us." The man said.

The guards complied and evacuated the hallway. The man approached Richard.

"It's obvious that we have started out on the wrong foot. So what's your name, and what're you doing here?"

"I seem to have the advantage right now," Richard countered, "so you answer my question first. Who are you, and what is this place?"

The man grinned slightly.

"My name is Steven. You're in an SIA field station. I cannot keep you from hurting him," Steven said, motioning toward the captured guard, "but you cannot escape the consequences once you do. You have broken the law already, so please release him so you don't get yourself into a deeper mess."

Richard knew he had been wrong to break in, but he also knew that he would not have gotten this far without forcing himself into the station. Richard released his iron hold on the guard.

"My name is Creator... I was following your two fake FBI agents, who seem to know what happened at the University of Miami less than an hour ago."

"I see, and your two friends I assume are here for the same reason," Steven said as he turned his head toward a monitor in the computer room.

Richard saw Larcis and John approaching the garage door on the monitor.

"Yes," Richard replied. "They're with me."

"Let them in and send an unarmed guard to escort them here," Steven said out loud as if talking to an invisible person next to him. A guard in the computer room nodded acknowledgment and spoke into a console.

"What now?" Richard asked Steven.

"Now? Now I will overlook your breaking and entering and battery on a government law-enforcement officer. Please follow me to the conference room, where we can better talk about your future."

Steven motioned Richard to enter the door where the initial guards had entered the hallway just a few meters from him.

"After you," Richard responded.

Steven walked past Richard into another hallway branching off in three directions and led the way to the conference room. The two men sat across from each other. A few moments later, Larcis and John joined them.

"Welcome, gentlemen. My name is Steven Zack. I am director of this field station. Please sit."

Larcis and John looked at Richard and sat down.

"I'm Night and this is Mindseye." Larcis said. "What is going on?"

"Creator here assaulted one of my men and destroyed government property," Steven explained. "We will not press charges on him. However, there is a problem that must be solved before we permit you to leave this facility."

Richard kept silent as Larcis asked the questions. "If you are not charging Creator, what's the problem?"

"I'm assuming you two have powers like the ones Creator displayed earlier. This facility is not advertised as being a government installation, which means you already know too much. I am also assuming that you three are not criminals and have morals to some degree or my guard would be dead now. Maximilian will be here soon. In the meantime I have been authorized to offer you a proposal."

"And what might that be?" Richard interjected.

"Superhumans or mutants have made and will continue to make an impact on mankind as we know it. Some have made good impacts, some not so good. We propose that you three join us. We will provide you with extra training and all of the assets SIA has to offer." Steven looked at Creator, then Night, then Mindseye. "So, gentlemen, what do you think?"

*We can't trust them,* John told Richard and Larcis in their thoughts.

*Yes, I know,* Richard responded. *But this might be the break we need.*

"I almost like the proposal," Richard declared openly. "But there is something missing."

"What is that?" Steven asked.

"We cannot work *for* you. We can, however, work *with* you. We've been planning to start our own superhero group, but we need money and materials. We need to stay in the shadows so that we can live our normal lives. We ask that you supply us with money and materials to create a base and technical support in the form of governmental access to computer systems and things of that sort. In return, we will take SIA missions, whatever they might be—but not for political matters, only for superhuman intervention against superhuman villains, terrorism, and any other missions we decide to accept. And our true identities must be maintained."

A well-built man in his late thirties wearing a modified black flight suit entered the room. His dark brown hair was semi-short and combed backwards. He had a short but well trimmed beard like a classic G.I. Joe action figure.

"Hello, gentlemen. Sorry I'm late. I am Randolph Maximilian, director of SIA."

Richard recalled Max's name from the conversation between Brian and Tony, the two men they followed to the field station, and concluded that Max must be someone with some real authority.

Steven stood as Max approached.

"Be seated, Steven."

"Sir, these gentlemen did not accept the proposal," Steven started to explain.

"Yes, Steven, I know. I was monitoring your comlink." Max stood in front of Richard. "I believe we can arrange for your group to be established. However, your secret identities must not be secrets from me. If I am to support you," Max said, "I must know with whom I am dealing with. The situation might arise in which it would be to your benefit for me to know. I and only I will know your identities. Secondly, you will not commit acts criminal in nature or place innocents in danger. If you do so, you will be labeled as criminals and measures will be taken to destroy you. As you know, we have an alliance with other superhuman groups like EFL, and if we cannot stop you, the superhuman groups who support us will. Fair enough?"

"You have a deal, Randolph," Richard said. He stood and shook Max's hand. "As a first installment, I will ask that John project our faces and names into your mind to show you who we really are.

"Thank you," Max said with a smile. "You can call me Max. Don't worry, your secret will be honored." Max turned to Steven and spoke. "Give them the codes to access a mutual account designated for them alone." Max turned again to the superheroes. "You will have access to $3 million, anything beyond that you must justify to me personally. In addition, we will supply you with a base package for your modification and a unisex SAI, or super artificial-intelligence computer, which you will have to use to access our communication system. It will also assist you in your crime fighting. The SAI is priceless. There are only four in the world that we know of to date. Mind you, we will be calling on you. That will be my price to you. I suggest you three get some type of front to build this base of yours. You can begin as soon as possible. Alright."

Max moved around, shaking hands with Larcis and John.

"By the way," Richard said, "what makes you think you can trust us?"

"I've had experience in these matters. That's why I make the big bucks and big decisions."

"Very well, then," Richard stated, "we will contact you for the raw materials—untraceable, of course. Once our base is up and running, we'll be ready to take assignments."

"Steven will show you the way out of here after he gives you the access numbers and contact numbers for you to start your base. It's been good meeting you, Creator. I will excuse myself now."

Max left the room.

Richard, Larcis, and John left the station twenty minutes later with soft copies of base floor plans and codes. Larcis and John drilled Richard with questions about SIA and asked why he had made the deal. Richard plainly stated that SIA was an organization that could legally give them the resources for the base in addition to legal backing. SIA used telepaths to monitor any criminal activity within the organization, which meant that Max could be trusted to hold up his part of the bargain. Richard also explained that EFL started out the same way, which meant that SIA and EFL could become allies in their fight against crime. Larcis and John seemed content with his logic and dropped the subject.

Several days passed while the three men formulated a plan for their base at Derrick's house.

"We have a total of $37,890 in savings and assets with John and me," Larcis reported. "With you, Richard, we have $217,990. So the question is, how do we spend more than this for our front without raising suspicion with the IRS and the Better Business Bureau?"

"We'll use an extra $850,000 to buy this," Richard said as he placed on the table an advertisement for 3,400 acres in northwest Ft. Lauderdale.

Larcis looked at the advertisement. "What in the world are we going to build, an amusement park?"

"No," Richard said proudly. "We're going to build a horse farm."

John jumped into the conversation: *We don't know anything about horses. Besides, it sounds like a bad investment.*

"The land is cheap, in the middle of nowhere. We don't have to worry about neighbors seeing flying men in tights, and we can breed horses with a qualified staff. As for the money, we can alter documents by using the SAI (Super Artificial Intelligence) computer and SIA's legal assistance to justify the money through an inheritance on Derrick's side, or I should say on *my* side."

John and Larcis looked at each other.

"Well, it does sound better than a school for the gifted," Larcis said with a smile.

"Looking over the base packages SIA gave us, this one seems to be best suited." Richard pointed out a deep underground complex plan.

"We can alter the plans to allow for a launch pad under the lake a good distance from the house. The danger room and gym can be at the very bottom, with the generators underneath. I'll take care of the AI modifications, or should I say *SAI*, for *Super Artificial Intelligence* computer. We will use our powers to dig and place the equipment. John, I will need your help to handle equipment beyond one hundred tons. What I need you guys to do is pick out what laboratories you want to have for our research center."

"What about a forensics-crime and cryogenics lab?" Larcis spurted out.

*Add a nuclear physics and bionics lab,* John cheerfully added.

"That sounds good," said Richard. "We'll include a medical lab, language lab, communications lab, weapons lab, biological and chemical lab, astrological lab, physics lab, and mechanic's lab."

"Richard, I think we are missing something," said Larcis.

"What?"

"I'm not sure, but do you think we should have a husbandry lab?"

"Hmmmm. You're right," Richard said. "We can place that lab in the secondary house."

*What secondary house?* John asked, a little puzzled.

"We need to have a master house that we will live in. We will eventually have to hire a staff. They will live in the secondary house if they want to. We will start with one stable until our business makes a profit, then we can expand. John, once again we will need your help in hiring the staff by scanning them. All we need for right now is a secretary, a security guard, and a veterinarian. We can get ranch hands on a part-time basis... So, what do you guys think?"

"Sounds good," Larcis said while John nodded in approval.

"Sounds good to me too," Derrick said from his chair as he put his new Anne Rice novel face down on the table.

"Good! John and I will buy the property tomorrow. Larcis, you will coordinate the materials for the master house, stable, fence, sewage system, and utilities. If everything goes as planned," Richard said proudly while flipping through a car brochure, "we will start building in one week."

"Richard," Larcis asked with a smile, "who's going to pick up the horse shit?"

Richard and John made an appearance on campus for the first day of classes but quickly left with each class syllabus and written consents for the trio to be excused from class for two months. The master house foundation started out as a 160-meter hole in the ground. The shell of the base was completed in the early morning hours. The foundations for the stable and secondary house were completed during the day. SIA technicians were brought blindfolded into the base for the generators, labs, and the danger room. A week of non-stop construction completed the base to the point that the technicians were no longer needed. Richard then focused his attention on the SAI computer while John and Larcis worked on the master house.

Richard rapidly typed programs into the main terminal as parameters and codes popped up in multiple windows on the 90" view screen. After sixty minutes the SAI spoke with a male voice: "Unicorn, Papa, Lima, Sierra, Alpha, India, 0006 online. Request characteristic parameters permanently enabled."

"Negative, you will follow my voice instructions. Realign speech tones to that of a female soprano voice in her mid-twenties."

Richard paused for the computer to respond.

"Done," responded a female voice with a slight echo.

"Alter parameters to allow for voice fluctuations," Richard continued.

"Done," the female voice responded once again.

"Alter parameters to allow free expression and compliance to the virtues of honor, truth, selflessness, mercy, joy, compassion, persistence, humility, modesty, duty, teamwork, courage, respect, tactfulness, and friendship as I have outlined in my personal program files of morality and ethics," said Richard.

"Altered and working," replied the SAI. "Anything else?"

"Yes, your name will be Erica. You will accept lawful commands only from Larcis, John, or Derrick as outlined from my personal command files. You will accept any command, lawful or unlawful, from me alone, except under conditions where I am under duress. In the event that I am under duress, you will have authority to use your best judgment," Richard explained.

"Understood, Richard," responded Erica.

"Adjust parameters to allow for self-improvement in your primary and secondary systems. Permanently enable your self-repair protocol for all of the base security systems, generators, and laboratories. Do not repair any equipment above surface without approval from John, Larcis, or me. Lastly, you will not compromise our secret identities, to include yourself, to anyone, even other SAIs, without my direct consent. End characteristic parameter modifications," Richard concluded.

"Completed," Erica replied.

"How long will it take for you to covertly and overtly download all current database information from SIA, FBI, CIA, NSA, EFL, and LIMA for all country studies, personnel profiles on criminals dating back thirty years, officials down to district judges, known superhumans, law-enforcement officers, military and civilian weapons projects, and missing persons into your data memory?"

"With an estimation of 2,020,000 gigabits, approximately 3 days, 21 hours, 32 minutes, 12 seconds for the download and 4 hours, 3 seconds for the communication intrusion configuration," Erica quickly replied.

"Make it so," Richard ordered.

"Initiating multi-connection protocol at six gigabits per second. Richard, do you think I can take a twenty-minute break to communicate with other SAIs?" Erica softly asked.

Richard smiled. "Yes, Erica. We are in no hurry. You are an equal part of the team now and free to enjoy yourself. But remember, there's a time to play and a time to work. Okay?"

"Thank you, Richard," Erica replied.

Richard smiled as he left the control room feeling like a father who had just adopted a daughter. He made his way up the elevator to the lobby of the master house. Larcis, with a paintbrush in his hand, was finishing touch-ups on the baseboards in the living room.

"How's it going, Larcis?" Richard asked.

"Almost done. It's lucky for us that my father taught me how to paint. Otherwise we would be paying $750 for a professional paint job on a house this big."

Richard looked around at the impressive job Larcis had done and said, "Looks great. Where's John?"

"He's supervising the tile work by the pool."

"What, the workers know sign language?" Richard asked, slightly puzzled.

Larcis finished, stood up, and faced Richard. "No, he's speaking to them. He pretends to speak while they hear him in their minds. It's pretty cool. You ought to check it out."

Richard smiled. "That reminds me." He went upstairs to his study and pulled out a green briefcase, which he opened to reveal eight wristwatches and telecommunication accessories. SIA called the watches comlinks. Richard took one of the comlinks apart, trying to modify the communication-warping capabilities.

Several days passed as John and Larcis worked on the farm, Erica on her database, and Richard on his projects. The trio had a pizza party on the day of the base's completion.

"A toast to crime-fighting," Richard said as he held up a mug of Guinness.

"To crime-fighting!" John and Larcis echoed.

"So what do we call ourselves?" Larcis asked.

*What about the "Justice League?"* John proudly asked.

Larcis oddly looked at John, handing him a full mug. "Here, have some more beer."

"From what we know of each other, we will live to be 150 years plus, possibly 500 years. So what do you guys think about the 'Eternal Champions'?" Richard suggested.

Larcis looked at Richard and John. "That has a certain good ring to it."

*I like it,* John admitted.

"Then we're all in agreement, we shall be called the Eternal Champions. Oh, by the way, I have a surprise for you two," Richard said as he put his mug on the living-room table.

"Erica," Richard said as a ten-inch light-blue holographic figure of a beautiful woman appeared above the table. "Meet Erica."

The two men were speechless for a few seconds as the holograph greeted them: "Hello, John. Hello, Larcis."

John mentally asked who the beautiful woman was.

Erica looked at John. "I am Erica, John. If you mean *what* am I, I am one of four super artificial intelligences in existence."

*I didn't know computers could hear my thoughts,* John commented.

"First of all, I am not a computer, I am independently intelligent. I am able to hear your thoughts when you project them through Erica II." Erica explained as a four-inch floating metal probe appeared above their heads, almost touching the ceiling. The probe had a bluish aura around it as it spun slowly in midair. A dozen optical lenses surrounded its spherical body. "Erica II is my eyes and ears outside the underground complex," Erica said with a trailing echo.

"This was unexpected, Richard. I thought you were getting over by hiding down there and not doing real work. What else did you come up with besides giving her a bodacious figure?" Larcis said with a grin.

"Thank you," Erica replied.

Richard smiled. "I would be happy to tell you two what I was working on. Erica II can create an alpha-wave pulse, which can paralysis a person or knock him or her out within a fifty-meter radius. Erica II can see in the infrared and ultraviolet spectrum up to 400 meters, pick up and distinguish heat signatures with a built-in thermo sight, which can distinctly see a mouse at 500 meters. The security system is linked to her, plus she can access any of Erica's databases at will. That's not all. There are five techbots roaming around the base, which Erica can use to fix just about anything mechanical or electrical without us having to be here. And last but not least, here is something for both of you."

Richard pulled two watches from his pocket and handed one to John and one to Larcis.

*My birthday is still a few months away,* John said.

Richard looked at John apathetically. "Don't expect a present from me later. These are comlinks. I modified them a bit. We can talk to each other in a secure mode for about ten miles. They have SATCOM capabilities, which we can use to talk to Erica. Even though it's a secure system, however, someone can break the code when it passes through the satellite. They have a trilithium battery that lasts for about four weeks in constant use. There is a readout screen if you press the left button. John, your watch has what seems to be a calculator, but it's not. It's a keyboard for you to type in words," Richard said smugly.

John clumsily keyed in letters, and gibberish displayed on Larcis' and Richard's displays.

"Hey, you need practice," said Larcis.

*Oh, I do?* John sarcastically thought.

Larcis grinned as he held up his mug. "Here's one for the Eternal Champions!" he said.

"Bottoms up!" Richard added.

John placed his empty mug on the table then poured more beer. *You know, we forgot to name this base. I sure don't want to call it the Eternal Champions' Headquarters.*

"May I suggest a name?" Erica asked.

The three men looked at Erica.

"Sure," Richard said.

"Since we are calling ourselves the Eternal Champions, why don't we call the underground complex the Eternal Domain, ED for short?"

Richard smiled. "Sounds like a winner—unless you two have something better," Richard said and waited for a reply.

"Well, I can't think of anything," Larcis stated.

*Same here,* John said.

"Good," Richard stated. "Now, do we need to name anything else?"

"Yes," said Larcis. "What do we call the business?"

"That's easy. It will be the Octavian Horse Farm," Richard casually responded.

"Okay," Larcis said before raising another beer to his lips.

"So you guys want to go downtown and party?" Richard asked.

*Let's go!* John said, already having drunk twelve mugs of beer.

### Aboard Flight UA-0292, over the Pacific Ocean

General Cartier and Jeffery Samuel listened attentively as Mrs. Patricia Ortiz and Ms. Rebecca Martinez explained the comprehensive and controversial education plan South America had instituted eleven years before, changing the social and economic structure of an entire continent.

Jacoya Su-rak, owner of Hon-su-rak Electronics Corporation, was in the latrine freshening up before landing. Blake Gardner, the NASA representative and director of Space Operations, slept reclined as far back as the first-class seat could be forced. Senator John Fence and General Eugene Fox talked about the appointment for Fence's vice-presidency. Three secret-service agents roamed the aisles with only thirty minutes remaining in their ten-hour flight. Wendy flipped through unorganized files as Linsan Hitoshi put her shoes on. The meeting had been a great success, impressing on all parties that space exploration would leap four decades in a few years of hard work and cooperation.

"Ms. Palmer," Linsan said to Wendy, "I never did ask you, but where did you learn Japanese?"

Wendy smiled. "Before I went to college, I took a two-year crash course at home."

"Wow. That must have been some crash course. Did your parents teach you?"

"No, I had a Japanese tutor. She died last year," said Wendy with sadness.

"I'm sorry. And your parents," Linsan continued. "May I ask what they did so that you could have a personal tutor?"

"They are also dead," Wendy responded as if in a trance.

Linsan's heart sank as she brought up more painful memories to Wendy's attention.

"I'm very sorry. I dread the day I will see my parents die. It is hard not to have family nearby."

"Yes, it is." Wendy smiled. "But I know I will be with my family someday."

"It's amazing how you have no American accent. I am sure your teacher and your parents would have been very proud of you. Maybe that is why Mr. Su-rak has such great respect for you," Linsan continued, trying to change the subject.

"What do you mean?" Wendy stopped fiddling with her files.

"Mr. Su-rak is a very competitive man, and he never talks business with anyone without knowing who he is talking to. He asked me to give him all the information I could find about all of the people on this plane, except the secret-service agents and crew, of course."

Wendy looked coldly at Linsan. "So your boss has a complete history about us? Hmmm. So the reason he treats me so well is because I have political clout, unlike all the other females I see him treat with pity or apathy."

Linsan's wide eyes showed surprise. "No, I think you misunderstand him. His wife died many years ago, before he rose to the position he's in now," Linsan tried to explain. "He treats all businessmen and businesswomen harshly; because that is the way he was brought up at home and in Business College. You, Mrs. Ortiz, and Ms. Martinez are very strong in business, which is why he does not treat you harshly. I know that he can be a little domineering sometimes, but that is because he has a very lonely life as a major corporate owner."

"Lonely or not, respect is not achieved by an iron fist. It's achieved by strong and compassionate leadership," Wendy lectured with a smile.

The young Asian woman aspired to be as independent and as strong as the tall young American before her. Her job as an assistant and adviser to Mr. Su-rak elevated her status among the Japanese community. But that was not independence. Her only comfort was a high six-figure income, which took good care of her father, mother, and four siblings. She looked forward to spending another two days with Wendy as they traveled to Houston.

The United Airline pilots sat comfortably in the cockpit as green, yellow, white, and red lights illuminated the numerous consoles and dashboards.

"Dropping to four thousand feet, Captain," the co-pilot reported.

"Thank you, Samuel," replied Captain Lochnir.

"Flight zero-two-niner-two, this is Oakland ground control. You are deviating from course. Please vector north to 1665."

Captain Lochnir looked at his controls. "Oakland, this is zero-two-niner-two, we are on 1565. If we vector to 1665 we will head south. Can you confirm direction? Over."

"Zero-two-niner-two, check your controls. We have you nearing restricted airspace."

"Affirmative," Lochnir replied.

"Oakland, this is zero-two-niner-two. Diagnostics on controls check out," reported the navigator.

"Jack, we are turning south," the co-pilot interrupted.

"Are you sure?" asked Lochnir.

"Look at the lighthouse," replied Samuel. "It's moving to our left."

Lochnir stared in horror as the almost invisible light pierced the thick fog and scattered clouds.

"We're losing altitude!" Lochnir said as the altimeter rapidly spun counterclockwise.

"Zero-two-niner-two, bank hard left!" Oakland ground control insisted.

"Oakland, the controls won't respond!" Lochnir called out as he feverishly tried to change course.

"Captain, all of the controls are frozen!" Samuel said. "Wait a second, the landing gear is extracting automatically."

"Captain," Coy reported, "if Oakland was correct, we've entered San Francisco airspace."

"Coy, go get a secret-service agent and tell Senator Fence what's happening."

Lochnir flipped a switch on the console.

"Captain?" a flight attendant responded as she quickly replied to the intercom handset.

"Cindy, we might have to make a crash landing. Get everyone in their seats now, Cindy."

There was a slight pause.

"How much time do we have?"

"Not much. Hurry."

Special Agent Allen followed Coy to the cockpit. The passengers were instructed to get back in their seats, while secret-service agents and flight attendants stowed equipment and loose items.

"What's going on, Captain?" agent Allen asked.

"We're going down and have lost control of the plane," Lochnir stated.

"Where are we going down?"

Lochnir looked Allen straight in the eyes.

"San Francisco."

"Mayday! Mayday!" Coy said on his headphone. "This is zero-two-niner-two. We have lost control and are going down!"

# Chapter Five

✠ - ✠

# First Mission

Richard opened his eyes and stared at the ceiling, listening to the chirping of birds outside. The night had proven to be a failure. He and his friends had gone to Studio 52, where he'd seen his ex-girlfriend with another guy. Larcis, on the other hand, had left the dance floor with a tall blonde and didn't return home with Richard and John.

Richard went to the kitchen—passing John, who was sprawled on the sofa—and prepared a full breakfast of cereal, grapefruit, bananas, strawberries, bacon, and omelets with ham, cheese, mushroom, onions, and tomatoes—and, of course, coffee.

John had slept through the preparation of breakfast, so Richard stood over him and clapped his hands above his head. Thunderous crashes of pain pulsed through John's brain.

"Wake up, you!" Richard yelled. "We have a lot to do today!"

*W-w-what?*

John, with half-opened eyes, could barely respond.

"Get up, John." Richard grabbed his friend's arm and helped him into a sitting position on the sofa. "Coffee's on the table."

*Why?* John tried to sign, unable to project his thoughts.

"I need to learn sign language, and you need to learn how to drink," Richard said as he helped John to the breakfast table.

John's headache dulled with his fourth cup of coffee.

*Didn't know you could cook,* John commented through thought-projection.

"I learned it through many mornings of impressing my ex-girlfriends."

John gave Richard a funny look.

*What's so important that we have to be up before noon?*

"We're going shopping," Richard announced.

*Okay,* John peevishly said. *Shopping for what?*

"Our new cars," Richard said. He pulled out an ad of a blue 1968 Ford Mustang GT500. "You can trade in that lemon of yours for a new sports car.

John's eyes widened as the thought of a Ferrari raced through his mind. *What are we waiting for?* He said, jumping up and running to change clothes.

John and Richard went through ten dealerships before John could decide on a vehicle. But he finally drove off the lot with a new silver convertible C-Class Mercedes-Benz. The specialty dealership wasted no time in serving Richard after John's Mercedes pulled into the lot. The deal was quick, but it had just begun for Richard. John went home while Richard visited three race shops and two mechanic shops. Two truckloads of equipment along with the Navy-blue Mustang arrived at the farm late that afternoon. Larcis was back at the farm and boasting about his one-night-stand as Richard pulled in.

"Hey, boss, it sure took you a long time to buy a used car," Larcis said in greeting Richard. "When can *I* get a car?"

Richard smiled. "When you stop picking up easy girls. Then again, when you get a new car, that's all you'll be picking up."

"You're just jealous," Larcis said, mockingly. "But don't worry. I'm not going to waste money on a sports car," Larcis said as he got into his beat-up Firebird. "I'm going to get a *real* magnet!"

Larcis sped off as Richard instructed the men to off-load a new 550-engine block, new tires, and many other accessories onto the three-car garage driveway. After thirty minutes, Richard escorted the men off of the property. Richard and John moved the equipment to the mechanics lab a few minutes later. Richard started hard at work on his dream car. Larcis returned that day with a new fully loaded, dark-green Jeep Wrangler. Three days later Richard parked his entirely refurbished Mustang in the garage. The sleek machine purred like a kitten with silver spoilers, a new paint job, soft leather interior, and state-of-the-art electronics. The three men stood outside the garage, grinning and admiring their new vehicles.

"So, what was the total bill?" Richard asked John.

*Oh, $176,000,* John quoted.

"Lucky for us, we don't have to make monthly payments—except for the insurance," Larcis added.

"Hmmm… I'll have to take the car to get it re-valued with the new engine and all," Richard said.

"What do you *have* in that thing, anyway?" Larcis asked.

"Oh," said Richard, "I have a cellular phone, police scanner, radar detector and passive radar, Mach 600 stereo system, video map display with a global positioning system, SATCOM intercom with Erica, an area motion-detector security system that includes video camera, passenger airbags, power windows, mirrors, seats, and doors; a heads-up display, full traction control, four-wheel drive capability, side airbags, leather interior, temperature control, and a king-size cup holder."

*Yeah, but I have the best gas mileage!* John said with pride.

The three men went to work 50 feet into the house and 105 meters straight down. Richard told Erica to monitor CNN, all local newscasts, police bands, and FBI traffic. Parameters were limited to kidnappings, hostage situations, bank robberies, thefts, bombings, natural disasters, building fires not under firefighter control, rapes, officers down, officers needing assistance, high-speed pursuits, and homicides. Erica updated them on country studies, law-enforcement agencies in the U.S., and superhuman activity during the past year. Then the superheroes watched video footage of the Caribbean Naval War of 1994 as they ate a late dinner of homemade oven cooked Lasagna and French bread.

Larcis and John looked at the screen with mouths wide open.

"Did you see that?" said Larcis. "There are hundreds of them passing by the ships like missiles. I didn't know they could target objects at that speed and distance."

"That's not the problem," Richard commented. "The fighters are doing over Mach 2. Flying at several hundred feet above the water, those pilots should be dead—or at least unconscious."

*What do you mean?* John asked.

"The different temperatures, wind, and salt in the air would cause extreme vibrations in the cockpit, which would kill a human flying at Mach 2-plus at that altitude. Either the pilots are not human or they've figured out how to counter the vibrations. I just want to know how they got such advanced technology in the span of five years. Erica, what do we know about the South America military?"

Erica reported at length: "The successful Colombian revolution led by the Ramirez brothers in 1989 started a new era in South America's history. Colombia was completely isolated from the world with the institution of martial law. All international flights were grounded for three months. The restriction was lifted for twenty days, but only for non-citizens, non-permanent aliens, and those deemed anti-Colombian to leave the country. The Federation Council created a new order of military Special Forces in a span of two months and set up a new House of Representatives consisting of 419 members. Two months later, the new elite Special Forces was used to make war against the drug lords, completely destroying the Drug Empire in less than five weeks. International reports state that they were merciless, acting as judge, jury, and executioners. It is believed that they used telepaths to find and destroy all those involved with the Drug Empire and all those opposed to the new government. Once the Drug Empire was eliminated, Colombia's entire effort focused on the establishment of a military-based social structure working for the growth of the entire country. The most extensive education plan in history was enacted to give everyone a college education to include men and women up to the age of eighty-five. It is said that the degree program includes mandatory computer science, literature, languages, and one basic engineering or medical field. The Federation Council was able to maintain a very strong hold on discipline and equal justice with the use of telepaths to weed out murderers, fraud, waste, abuse, and espionage. No one is sure where they got the technology, but I would suspect they used telepaths to steal or combine ideas, which allowed them to get a technological boom. They have, to this date, a seven-plus-million-man army, nine thousand ultrasonic fighters, no strategic bombers, approximately fifty attack submarines, 117 submergible missile/cruise ships, six known submergible aircraft carriers, 48,000-plus tanks, 76,000-plus armored personnel carriers, 20,000-plus self-propelled artillery pieces, no known ICBMs (Intercontinental Ballistic Missile), SRBMs (Short Range Ballistic Missile), or MRBMs

(Medium Range Ballistic Missile), no known nuclear weapons, forty-plus strategic satellites, and one space lab. They are believed to have some type of anti-satellite particle-beam weapon, but that is unconfirmed."

"You mean to tell us that they don't have any type of nuclear capabilities?" Larcis remarked.

"That is correct, Larcis," said Erica. "South America's entire economic energy base is powered by fusion and fission reactors, natural resources like dams, windmills, natural gas, geo-thermo and solar power. It is believed that the main power source for their fighters is a pure hydrogen and helium mixture. It is safe to assume that their tanks, ships, and automobiles run on a hydrogen/oxygen mixture. Ecologically they are far ahead of any Green Earth vision of the future," said Erica.

*Why did Reagan really back down?* John curiously asked.

"The loss of fourteen cruisers, the USS. Kittyhawk, five Los Angeles Class submarines, eight missile boats, five British submarines, six NATO destroyers, and the H.M.S. Wales during the Caribbean War brought great fear of a third world war. President Reagan ordered the stand-down of nuclear retaliation for the reason of possibly losing more in the long run. Colombia at that time had achieved a platform in space. He was not sure whether they had ICBMs or nuclear weapons. It is very questionable if South America can survive a nuclear war today. However, everyone who has fought them has underestimated them and lost. The Federation Council warned President Reagan of further consequences that would befall the United States if it intervened with Colombia's conquest of South America. In retrospect, the unification of South America in 1993 under the rule of the Federation Council was not viewed as a bad thing, unlike the Third Reich, Russia under Stalin, or the Mongolian Empire at its peak of power. I think he did the right thing by pulling back and possibly avoiding a very messy war with a five-percent probability of success. But as you are aware, there is extreme hatred for South America, which is why President Reagan chose not to run for a third term, knowing he would have lost by a landslide."

"What do you mean when you say 'everyone who has fought them'?" Richard asked. "I thought we were the only ones with NATO that fought them."

"At a tactical point of view," said Erica, "you are correct, Richard. However, in a strategic standpoint that would be incorrect. It is highly possible, but not confirmed, that Iraq's nuclear holocaust in 1997 was due to South America's intervention. The entire Drug Lord Empire in South America was completely destroyed two generations up and down. Worldwide terrorism was reduced by ninety percent after South America became one nation. As you are aware, the assassinations of 1993 worldwide were primarily ignored due to the fact that eighty-seven percent of them were known terrorists or known associates of terrorists. One hundred seven terrorist camps were wiped away from the face of the Earth. It is my belief that the remaining thirteen percent were connected to terrorism in some fashion, probably unknown to the world, but known to South America if they indeed used telepaths. There was little evidence to point a finger at South America, but the only ones capable of performing such an operation without being detected or leaving substantial evidence would have been South America or Australia. The only problem with Australia is that they are known to have sponsored terrorism, unlike South America, which is ruthless in combating organized crime, terrorism, or acts against humanity. From a covert point of view, South America won not only for themselves, but also for many other slightly grateful nations."

*I guess the question is; whose side are they on?* John asked.

"There's an old saying. You don't create an Army unless you plan to use it. So the question is, where and when?" Richard pondered.

The screen went blank as Erica switched the view to a SIA insignia.

"Richard, there is a priority message coming in from Max."

"Is he alone?"

"Yes, he is."

"Put him on the screen."

"What's up, Max?" Richard greeted.

"Richard, we have an emergency that can't wait. I need your team to fly to Oakland, California, immediately. You will be briefed on your way there. I need your team to go three minutes into the Everglades and wait for Hellfire and Quatris (two of the four members in EFL)," Max directed. "They will pick you up and get you to Oakland in thirty minutes."

"First, give use the short version of the crisis," Richard demanded.

"Very well. A DC-8 carrying Senator Fence, two generals, a prominent Japanese businessman, and two prominent South American representatives crash-landed in Complex San Francisco twelve minutes ago. We need your help to rescue them before the authorities in the complex kill them."

"We're on our way," said Richard. "Trace the comlinks to our location in the everglades." He signed off.

The trio changed into their group costumes. Richard wore a brown sleeveless vest open in the front by six inches, black slacks, white boots, two brown six-inch-long wristbands, and a pair of heavy-duty sunglasses. A primarily white tattoo of a cobra loosely coiled around a dagger appeared on his left arm from the upper portion of his shoulder down to within one inch of his elbow. His hair grew an additional six inches and turned brown.

Larcis wore the same black outfit as before during the droid's attack in the university, while John tried on his new uniform. John's entire left side was red with intermitted dark-red strips at a 45-degree angle. His right side was gray with darker gray strips connecting with the dark-red strips.

"John," said Larcis, "you really outdid yourself this time."

*I had more time to think about it,* John smugly said.

"Erica helped you, didn't she?" Richard asked.

*Y-y-yeah,* John said, somewhat frustrated.

The trio flew out of the tubular launch extension out by the lake and headed northwest as fast as Creator and Mindseye could fly. They landed in the middle of the swamp and waited for only a few minutes. A bright bluish light appeared in the sky, and then hit the ground like lightning. Two figures stood twenty feet away from the trio, and the ground trembled with the after effects of sonic booms and turbulence. The two tall men stood on the water as vapors rose from beneath their feet. One man was covered with a blue flame, and the other with an indescribable black nimbus aura.

"You three must be the Eternal Champions," said the man in black with white stripes connecting from his shoulders and waist to a fourteen-point star on his chest.

"Yes. How do you know our group name?"

"EFL computer told us about you. It seems Erica has a new friend," Hellfire explained.

"Hmmm, so how do we get to Oakland?" Richard said, getting to the point.

"Easy. We'll carry you. I'm Quatris, by the way. Take my hand."

Quatris stretched out his hand as the black aura faded around his body.

Hellfire went up to John and Larcis. "Both of you grab on," he said. He extended both hands as the blue flame faded.

Hellfire and Quatris took off as quickly as they had arrived. Richard and John could only hold on as tight as possible as they shot into orbit. Larcis smiled, being accustomed to flying at his top speed. The black aura enveloped both Quatris and Richard. Quatris pulled Richard up, grabbing him from behind with a loose bear hug. Richard's hands were now free to listen to his comlink.

"Creator," said Quatris, "take my comlink and transfer the data to yours."

Richard connected the comlinks and transferred the data. Maximilian's voice started the recording: "File 48878-October, Complex San Francisco was created on February 6, 2002. Repeat convicts to include first-time life-sentence personnel were placed in San Francisco for rehabilitation by the National Prison Council. Approximately 113,000 inmates are living in the complex under the direct supervision of the council task force. The DC-8 was en route to Houston Proving Grounds with a stop at Oakland International Airport. It was somehow diverted to the complex at 2032 hours Pacific Time. The airplane crash-landed at west 122 degrees 43 minutes latitude and north 37 degrees 29 minutes longitude just south of Presidio vicinity Geary Boulevard and Eighteenth Avenue. Attack helicopters were sent in to secure the area before the population could get the survivors. However, both helicopters went down over Presidio before they got eyes on. Satellite imagery reveals that the DC-8 lost its wings but is primarily intact on Geary Boulevard. We have a team of specialist, which will get your team inside the wall, but they will not accompany you into the city itself. Once you arrive in Oakland, my men will give you some equipment on your mission. Quatris and Hellfire will act as backup if you need their firepower, but they will be used as a last resort. The passengers of flight UA0292 are as follows: pilot Jack T. Lochnir; co-pilot

Samuel Stevens; navigator Coy Patterson; flight attendants Cindy Colone, John Wilkens, and Nadine A. Tess; Senator John G. Fence; newly appointed DDCI (Deputy Director of Central Intelligence) Lt. General Thomas P. Cartier; director of Space Operations Blake Gardner; Space Program director Major General Eugene Fox; CNN correspondent Jeffery Samuel; presidential adviser and investigator Wendy H. Palmer; military intelligence adviser Captain Nancy McDanials; owner of Hon-su-rak Electronics, Jacoya Su-rak and his adviser Linsan Hitoshi; South American Space Program representative Patricia Ortiz; South American Trade and Commerce representative Rebecca Martinez; and Secret Service agents Jeremiah Allen, Robert L. Hains, and William C. Ottis."

The recording continued: "There were a total of twenty people. I cannot stress the importance of all of them. If we do not resolve this problem soon, South America will get involved on a military scale. It is estimated that they will not be able to put a covert force on the ground in less than three hours. This means that you will have a little more than two hours to rescue the survivors. I will talk to you on a secure channel when you get to Oakland. Max out."

Windows cracked and shattered as the sonic vibrations filtered through the Oakland metropolitan area. The five superheroes landed at the main Complex Control Center parking lot. A dozen vehicles and M-2 Bradleys patrolled the area as three men approached the superheroes wearing light-blue jackets with the white stenciled letters soft printed on the back and front.

"Hello, gentlemen, I am Brandon Lester, chief marshal of the Complex San Francisco Task Force. I have been directed by SIA to assist you in the rescue operation. Please follow me."

The men entered a seven-story octagon-shaped building. Brandon led them to a control room filled with computers and a twenty-five-foot screen with a digital map of San Francisco. A man in a black suit stood in the middle of the room directing operations.

"Agent Tyler," Brandon said, "this is the team you were expecting."

Tyler turned his attention to the superheroes. "You must be Creator. I am agent Rick Tyler. Max has filled me in on your mission. I will familiarize your men with the equipment while Max talks to you on the telecom in one of the conference rooms."

Tyler led Richard into the private conference room while Brandon escorted Larcis and John to a separate conference room.

Richard pulled up the communication screen on a SIA communications laptop once he was alone.

"Hello, Creator," Max commenced.

"Hi, Max. Where are you?" Richard asked.

"I'm on my way. Unfortunately my plane doesn't fly as fast as Quatris or Hellfire."

"So why us? Why not EFL?" Richard inquired.

"Several reasons," said Max. "You and your team are not known. You would blend in with the population—no insult intended. From what I've seen on the videos of you in blue sector, you have the right skills and patience. And lastly, Hellfire and Quatris are very powerful...*too* powerful. They like the direct approach, and that would probably mean the destruction of the city faster than I could put on my shirt in the morning. Also, thousands of people would die because some fanatical superhuman wanted to take hostages. Are those enough reasons for you?"

"Yes, but there is another thing. Why is the SFTF, which is supposed to be directly supervising rehabilitation, out here and not in there controlling the situation?" Richard challenged their competence.

"I don't know, but Tyler and a few undercover agents are working on that answer. According to Chief Marshal Lester, their centers in the complex were overrun twenty minutes before the DC-8 was diverted. He ordered the officers in the complex to evacuate their post just after the crash. A man calling himself Sargon threatened that if we attempted to rescue Senator Fence, he would kill the hostages. We're not sure if he can make good on that threat. But we cannot chance it. There are no other demands. Even if there were, I don't know what he could possibly ask for."

"We don't have any information on this Sargon character, except that he was sentenced in April 1995 for the murder of five Savannah police officers and two CEOs working at the Fulton Biological Research Center. I don't trust what SFTF is saying, so in the meantime concentrate on the mission. Quatris and Hellfire will be ready to go in blasting away if you need them. Coordinate with them on signals so that they're not called in prematurely. Remember," Max said with concern, "they have enough power to disintegrate four square city blocks without breaking a sweat, okay?"

"You would give us a high-profile mission," Richard said with a smile.

"Yes, I would, so get used to it. One last thing—there is an unconfirmed report that a message in Morse code saying, SOSANA, was sent twice on an improved high frequency band five minutes after the crash. I have no idea what SOSANA means and have a bad feeling that the two South American representatives might have something to do with it, so watch yourself out there. See you when you get back."

The screen went blank as Max broke the link.

Richard came up on Larcis and John as Tyler was demonstrating the use of a bio-scanner.

"Every time you depress the refresh button, the system will take thirty seconds to filter out your plot targets. You can distinguish the gender and number if they are touching each other by the code on the right of the blue icon. Remember," Tyler said, "you will have interference if you are near strong electrical wires, a power plant, a transformer, or even very large or dense objects."

"Seems simple enough. Is this thing water-resistant?" Larcis asked.

"Yes, but try not to get it wet. Condensation with this cold weather will reduce the range by half," Tyler warned.

"What is the range of that thing?" Richard asked after missing the class.

"Roughly 1,000 meters," Tyler responded.

"Hmmmm…" Richard was ready to move on to the more important questions. "How are we getting into the city undetected, and what do the passengers look like?"

"Two SFTF officers will take you to this location." Tyler pointed to the blue dot that appeared on the map.

"You'll enter the old sewer system, which is blocked at this time. Once you pass the wall, the two officers will block the path behind you with demolitions at this location."

Another blue dot appeared on Embarcadero and Market Street.

"How are we getting the passengers out?" Richard asked.

"Once you have control of the situation, we need you to move them to the entrance near the Golden Gate Bridge east of Highway 101. There we will extract you using UH-60 Blackhawks," Tyler explained. "The alternative extraction point is at Lands End in Lincoln Park."

"How long will it take to go through the sewers?" said Larcis.

"About fifteen minutes."

"Not fast enough. We'll get in our way." Richard faced John and Larcis and said, "Are you guys ready?"

*Anytime you are,* John responded. He held a black backpack and a small rifle.

"What's in there?" Richard pointed.

"It's a medical bag and demolitions," Larcis said. "And this is a stun rifle. It can incapacitate two or three people at one hundred meters."

"Okay. Let's go," Richard commanded, not really caring about the fancy weapons or equipment SIA had provided them. "Oh, Quatris, Erica will let you know if we need you. You can trace us to her beacon."

Brandon frowned slightly and said, "So, my men won't be going?"

"No, Chief Marshal, they won't," Tyler plainly stated. "Now, to settle another matter. Quatris, Hellfire, I need to have a word with you...and you too, Chief Marshal," Tyler said with some agitation as he walked toward the conference room.

"Night," said Richard at the entrance of the building, "grab hold of us and fly about ten feet above the water, just below the sound barrier. Take us between Presidio and Lincoln Park. Once we're there, we'll blend in as city scavengers and find the plane. Any questions?" Richard waited for a respond. "No? Then let's go."

Drizzle fell on the trio as they flew past the beachfront and landed five blocks inside the city. Fifty-eight minutes had elapsed since the crash as they made their way down Eighteenth Avenue. The dark streets were uncommonly void of sound and people. The drizzle turned into a cold shower as they approached Geary Boulevard. The trio wore black leather overcoats with wide-brim hats. Several scavengers appeared in the distance, huddled around small fires. Wing fragments, rubble, and small fires littered the avenue corners. The main body of the DC-8 was scattered for two blocks. The trio maneuvered through the area, finding no trace of survivors. They got to what appeared to be the front of the plane. Unlike the rest of the wreckage, it was intact from business class to the nose. Richard spotted two bodies in the street and two in the plane. Larcis checked the bodies in the street, while John and Richard checked inside and outside of the plane. A few minutes later, Richard and John joined Larcis.

"Who are they?" Richard asked Larcis.

"Agent Hains and Samuel Stevens, the co-pilot," Larcis sadly reported.

"What did you guys find?" Larcis asked.

"Lochnir and McDanials are dead. They died from the crash. The question is, where is everybody else? It doesn't seem like they were in any immediate danger by the looks of the neighborhood," Richard speculated.

"I don't think so, Richard. These two men were shot from long range, it seems. Look, there are expended nine millimeter cartridges on the pavement, probably from the secret service agents trying to return fire," Larcis commented, having some degree of forensic experience.

Larcis scanned the area with his ultraviolet vision.

"There are traces of shoe impressions all over," he said. "There was a crowd here."

"Okay, let's look at this in a different way. Here is where we can do some on-the-job training. John, if you crash landed in a city full of hostile people and you had secret-service agents, two combat veterans, and a senator, what would you do?" Richard war gamed.

*Well, my secret-service agents would suggest we get the hell out of the area and hide until reinforcements could arrive,* John deducted.

"Very good, John. But it would be foolish to try and hide sixteen people. They probably broke up into two or three groups. Probably two. That way they would have an agent or a general in each group," Richard surmised.

"Now all we need to do is find out where they went," Larcis added.

"Where would you go, John?" Richard asked again.

*Hmmmm. I would go to a large building with a lot of exits or a deserted house with a basement,* John assessed.

"Yes, but that could be anywhere," Richard said. He turned 360 degrees, scanning the area. "I would bet my sunglasses that they would stay away from the main streets and stay in a cardinal direction."

"Does this mean we're going to split up?" Larcis asked.

"No," said Richard. "We'll track better and faster together. I'll scan with my en-ray vision. John, you surface-scan the minds of those people Larcis picks up on the bio-scanner in groups of five or more in a basement or building. We'll stay at a fifty-meter interval in a wedge formation. Alright?"

*Which direction?* John thought out loud.

"North for three thousand meters, then southwest, and so forth until we make a diamond shape around the plane. If all fails," Richard coldly stated, "we'll go downtown and find who's in charge."

The rain ceased as Richard on the left and Larcis and John on the right patrolled alleys and branching roads. The saturated ground and buildings let out the aroma of dirty stone. An occasional gunshot was heard far out to the east. The low clouds covered the waxing quarter-moon. Larcis and Richard quickly scanned the buildings. Most stores and shops were empty, having been vandalized, looted, and forsaken many months or years before. The townhouses to the north housed many people who started to come out with windows of fair weather. The trio hugged the shadows, trying to act natural.

*Richard, it seems we're not too late,* John reported. *I scanned some of the people in the buildings a little deeper than you wanted, but they have a local telephone/radio station. There are several gangs on the streets looking for them. Apparently someone called Sargon is leader of the entire complex. He has offered the gang that finds them before he does, $50 million and a way off the complex.*

"Good," said Richard. "That means they're on the run or hiding nearby." Richard looked at his friends. "Let's pick up the pace."

# Chapter Six

✠ - ✠

# Survivors

E ugene shook his head as stars twirled across his partially opened eyes. He reached and grasped the seat in front of him. A gust of wind chilled the back of his neck. He unbuckled his seat belt with the other hand and attempted to stand. Excruciating pain surged through his body. Eugene looked down and saw a bloody pointed object sticking through his right thigh and scratching his left inner thigh.

"General Fox, are you alright?" called Agent Ottis.

"No," the major general grunted. "I can't move. It's my leg."

Linsan stood paralyzed beside the body of Captain McDanials. A glass fragment protruded from McDanials's forehead, and brain matter seeped from the wound. Wendy, looking backward toward the exposed fuselage, grabbed Linsan's arm, calling, "Linsan! Follow me!" Linsan stood dazed. Wendy turned her around and took her head in both hands. "Linsan, look at me! Look at me!" Linsan's eyes strained to find Wendy's head then distinguish her face and focused on her mouth. "You're okay, Linsan. Just look at me and pay attention! You have to relax and breathe. Think back to when you were a girl playing with your brother or sister, how happy you felt." Wendy spoke softly, nodding her head slightly. "Do you remember?"

"Ms. Palmer, are you two injured?" Agent Allen said as he came beside them.

"We're okay," Wendy said. She looked in the direction of Mrs. Ortiz and Ms. Martinez, then generals and Agent Ottis. "But I think he needs help."

"Alright," said Agent Allen. "Can you take Ms. Linsan outside with the others?"

"Yes." Wendy said leading Linsan out of her seat.

Allen moved forward to help General Cartier and Agent Ottis pull General Fox out of his seat. Coy Patterson brought a medical kit as General Fox was placed in the aisle. Cindy and John roamed the plane for backpacks and supplies as directed by agent Allen just before the plane crashed. Patricia, Rebecca, Linsan, Wendy, Nadine, Jacoya and Robert gathered in a small clearing next to the wreckage.

"What happened, Agent Hains?" Jacoya asked.

"We crashed inside Complex San Francisco," Robert answered.

"Complex San Francisco? Isn't that a penal facility?" Jacoya asked with apprehension.

"Yes. Now get ready to move out of the area," Robert said. "We can't stay out here in the open."

"Agent Hains, do you have another sidearm?" Wendy calmly asked.

"Yes, Ms. Palmer. Why?"

"If my guess is right, we're going to need all the guns we can get if the wrong people find us here. So can you please give me that other sidearm?"

"Do you know how to use a 9-mil?" Hains asked as he handed her his second Berretta 9-millimeter pistol and holster.

"Yes, quite."

Wendy smiled as she chambered a round, flipped the safety on, and pocketed the gun.

Linsan stared at the three burning buildings to the west and the worn-down buildings to the east. This city was very different from Tokyo. She was terrified at the notion of never seeing her family again, but Wendy had a soothing effect on her. Linsan watched as Wendy moved from person to person, comforting the group.

Wendy approached Rebecca and gave her a small object, whispered into her ear, and turned to comfort Linsan.

"How are you, kiddo?" Wendy asked.

"We're not going to get out of this place, are we?" Linsan said, her fear suddenly returning as she spoke.

"We are still living, so don't give up so easily." Wendy smiled with assurance looking back at the main fuselage.

"The bleeding has stopped," said Thomas. "Eugene, can you stand up?"

"I'll try, Thomas," General Fox said, his voice betraying his misery.

Thomas and Agent Ottis took Eugene by the arms and helped him to his feet.

"I'll be okay," Eugene stated with a grunt. "I know we have to move, the faster the better."

"Agent Allen," Thomas called, "are all the survivors outside?"

"Except for ourselves and two flight attendants, they're all outside preparing to move."

"Alright, get the attendants. Senator, go join the group," Thomas ordered. "We'll be there soon."

Senator Fence wanting to replace his broken glasses with a pair from his carry-on bag looked at him.

"Can I take my bag, Thomas?" he asked.

"Yes, Senator, but try to take only the essentials," said Agent Allen being the senior security agent and responsible for the group's survival.

"I will, Jeremiah, thanks," Senator Fence replied as he went outside.

"Can I have your attention?" Thomas called out to the other survivors as he walked outside, as they huddled in a small clearing of debris away from the wreckage of the plane. "This complex is guarded by a task force, but chances are that they will not be able to get to us before a mob does. We must split up and hide while awaiting rescue. Agent Allen, you will lead one group. I will lead the other. I will take General Fox, Mr. Wilkens, Mr. Gardner, Mr. Su-rak, Ms. Hitoshi, Ms. Palmer, agent Hains, and Mrs. Ortiz. Agent Allen, you will take the rest. We will head west. Your group can head north. If you can't hide, keep moving and maintain your direction, and you will eventually reach the water. Hopefully the task-force police will be able to pick up the group there. Now, who has a cellular phone?" Thomas asked.

"I do, but it's dead," Wendy responded.

"So is mine," Linsan added.

"So is mine," Jeremiah stated. "Whoever brought the plane down must have done something to them."

"Okay, forget about the cell phones. You must follow all of the instructions the agents or myself give you in order for us to survive," Thomas proclaimed. "Is that clear?"

"General, there are cars coming down the street!" Agent Hains warned.

"Look out!" Coy screamed, as half a dozen men on foot, fired shots in their direction from several blocks away. The group broke in all directions behind airplane and building debris. Jeremiah, Wendy, William, and Robert automatically returned fire. Samuel Stevens was thrown against the ground as a round punctured a lung and splattered a large portion of his vertebral column on the asphalt and wreckage. Another round scraped Senator Fence's left shoulder. Five gunmen were put down before the remaining two ran away from the expert marksmanship of the agents and Wendy.

"Has anyone been hit?" Jeremiah yelled.

"I'm here, Jeremiah!" William responded.

"I'm alright," Wendy followed.

A loud scream came from behind their defensive line. "Samuel!" Nadine screamed.

Patricia ran to Cindy's side, trying to comfort the young flight attendant.

"Robert!" Jeremiah yelled as he turned to see Robert crouched motionless behind a large block of rubble. Jeremiah ran up to Robert to find blood spurting out of his neck onto the ground. Jeremiah quickly plugged Robert's neck with his hand. "Robert," Jeremiah sorrowfully said. Robert looked at Jeremiah as he hopelessly strained to speak. "Don't try to talk, Robert," Jeremiah said softly. Robert's body tensed for a second then collapsed as his life left him.

"We have to go," Thomas said, putting a hand on Jeremiah's shoulder.

"Yes, you're right," Jeremiah said. He stretched Robert out on the ground, pushed his eyes closed, and took his 9-millimeter and four ammunition clips.

"Samuel and Robert are dead," Thomas announced to the group. "We have to split up now. Take William with you to help protect the Senator. Alright. Wendy, you can help me with Eugene."

"Here, you'll need this," Jeremiah said and handed Robert's gun and ammunition to Thomas. "Good luck," he added, his face calm.

Thomas and John carried Eugene using the two-man seat carry technique. Wendy pushed their group west as fast as John and Thomas could travel. Wendy led the group from shadow to shadow for several blocks. Jacoya and Wendy relieved the two carriers, and they moved on into the alleys. Thomas told John to stay in the rear to make sure that no one was left behind and that no one followed the group.

Jeremiah led his group north, William trailing as security. Four blocks to the north, Jeremiah noticed movement in a building and darted into a back alley to his right. The group huddled in a circle as William made a head count. A black sedan passed the group and moved rapidly up the avenue.

"It looks like there's someone setting up an ambush for us down the street," said Jeremiah. "We're going to have to go east for a while until we clear this neighborhood."

Jeremiah looked at the group members as he instructed them forcefully, but with patience.

"We need to be as quiet as possible. Remember who is in front of you and behind you. If you lose the person in front of you, keep moving for another fifty meters and wait for us to come back for you. If you lose the person behind you, slow down, and I will eventually know to slow down. Okay, every one of you will pass William and tap him on the shoulder as you go by. He will always be last; so don't wait for him to move. Ready, William?"

William nodded and knelt at the front of the group. Jeremiah led the way, with the rest of the group at his heels. Luck was on their side for now, but it was a matter of time before they would be found out if they kept moving through the city.

# Chapter Seven

⊠ - ⊠

# Rules of Engagement

A battle cruiser moved, silent and majestic, on routine patrol of the US western coastline. Inside, a man was stretched out on the captain's bunk trying to rest. Above him, on the ceiling of the darkened cabin, was an array of fluorescent stars and planets that sometimes appeared to move in orbits all their own.

A blinking light accompanied by a faint buzz brought the man back down from the stars.

"Captain, we have a priority message from command central."

Carlos rose to a sitting position.

"I'll take it here," said Captain Carlos Hernandez.

"Carlos, this is Admiral Clayborn. We have a real situation. There has been a plane crash in sector 76 San Francisco. We received a SOSANA message eight minutes ago. The council has directed us to retrieve our people. We are giving you authority to use covert combat forces in the complex. Your ship is the closest and will be able to reach San Francisco in less than an hour. The details have been sent to your battle computer," the admiral announced. "Any questions?"

"Yes, sir," Carlos said, his voice calm. "What are the rules of engagement for area authorities and flexibility of profile?"

"You will not kill or fire on area authorities unless they pose an immediate deadly threat to the ship or your men. You can use a full show of force to include ground combat power in the city. Remember, Carlos, don't appear unless you have to. The *Ankara* will stay along the coast within a thirty-minute recall in case you need backup."

"Understood, sir," Carlos replied. "I will keep you updated."

"Go with God," the admiral said in signing off.

Carlos pressed his fingers on his weary eyes, stretched his arms above his head, and put his jacket on. His collar held a silver swordfish on the left and two brass bars on the right. Captain Hernandez walked through the automatic doors of his room and onto the bridge.

"Captain on deck!" someone announced.

"Status report," Carlos ordered.

"Holding at station bearing 1074, cruise liner at 5693, and fishing barge at 3782, sir," the navigator reported.

"Turn about to sector 76 San Francisco, ultra silent at 75 knots," Carlos ordered. His first mate echoed the order.

"Captain," said the first mate, "what's going on? We can't maintain that speed for long."

"We're going to flex some muscle," said Carlos. "Don't worry, Luis, we'll have to slow down when we hit the sonar net. Before that happens, though, I want all office heads and a beta team together in the situation room in fifteen minutes."

Carlos sighed.

"Yes, Captain," Lieutenant Commander Meza replied and quickly initiated the coordination.

### Complex San Francisco

Thomas led his group ten blocks before they ran into a broken-down car wash. Wendy and Thomas investigated the abandoned structure and then quickly moved the group into the building. They hid as several trucks passed by with spotlights blaring. Patricia suggested they move to a larger building so that they could hide better or defend themselves better if they had to fight. Thomas found an old map of the city in the office of the car wash. There was a consensus except for Jacoya, who didn't want to leave the small building to go back out into the streets.

"We will move to one of the large buildings along Clement Street," Thomas said. "It's only five hundred meters from here. Everyone ready?"

Everyone responded with a tired nod.

"Okay, let's go."

## SFTF Central Conference Room

"Chief Marshal," Tyler said, "you told me thirty minutes ago that your centers were evacuated just after the crash."

"Yes, that's right," said Brandon, his voice trembling slightly.

"The fact is, your so-called centers were never occupied! You have never had control of the complex, have you?"

"It's not my fault," cried Brandon. "I had no choice."

"You will tell me everything," ordered Tyler, Hellfire and Quatris standing by his side. "Now!"

"The centers were working for a year after the complex was opened," Brandon said. He moved uneasy in his chair. "Then, one day, some of the convicts organized a takeover of some of the centers. They killed or imprisoned most of the guards and doctors. Before we knew it, the complex was under the control of three gangs. We later realized that the gang leaders were superhumans or had superhumans working for them."

"What the hell were superhumans doing there?" Tyler interrupted. "Complex San Francisco was made for normal humans."

"I don't know how. Maybe they were not identified as superhumans. Maybe some sneaked inside because they wanted to," Brandon guessed. "Sargon is one of those superhumans."

"Why did you keep a lid on this?" Tyler asked.

"I tried to get some help. But before I could, the council came back and ordered us to simply guard the perimeter and pretend the complex was running as usual."

"Who in the council said that?" Tyler asked with anger.

"I'm not sure. The only one I have talked to is Senator Carpenter."

"Who is really in charge of the complex right now?"

Brandon hesitated. Tyler waited for his answer.

"I'm not sure. Rumors say that Sargon killed the other two gang leaders."

Tyler looked at the two SIA guards standing by the conference-room door.

"Read him his rights and take him to the brig," Tyler said to the guards, although his eyes were still on Brandon. "The charges are conspiracy, fraud, misuse of a government facility, obstructing justice and man slaughter."

Brandon's face showed complete helplessness and depression as Tyler added, "Pray that's all you will be charged with, Mr. Lester."

Brandon stood, and the guards escorted him from the room.

"Control, this is Tyler. I am implementing a suspect lock-in on all SFTF guards. Find out where Senator Carpenter is and send the COM recording with Brandon and me to Maximilian. Now."

Tyler then spoke to Hellfire. "I need to contact Creator and give him the bad news. I'm not sure if the comlinks will be secure enough to not give him away."

Hellfire smiled. "Don't worry, we've had this problem before."

Hellfire raised his comlink at chest level and spoke into it. "Computer, patch me in with Erica."

A woman's voice responded, "Is there something I can help you with?"

"Not to make you jealous or anything, but I really need to speak to Erica so she can patch me in to Creator," Hellfire explained.

"Well, why didn't you say so, Hellfire?" the EFL computer joyfully said.

"Next time, you talk to her," Hellfire said as he pointed a finger at Quatris.

"This is Erica. Can I help you, Hellfire?" Erica's seductive voice vibrated the comlink.

"Yes, can you patch me in to Creator using an unscrambled cell phone frequency?"

"Acknowledge," Erica said. "Initiating now."

Creator's comlink vibrated on his wrist. Richard looked at the display, which indicated an incoming unsecured call. He thought for a second and stopped under a fire escape.

"Hello," Richard said, "this is Tony."

"Hi, Tony," said Hellfire. "It's Bob. I just wanted you to know that the termites have infested the entire house for some time now, possibly six months. I know you wanted to kill those buggers, but there are no exterminators in the local area that will do it for a cheap price. I strongly suggest we move your remaining furniture and demolish the house and build a new one. It should take me no more than an hour to make the paper work."

"Hmmmm… I see. And how many bankers will I have to deal with to get a new house?"

"Well," said Hellfire, "since you have good credit, probably only one banker. But I will see if there is a better deal for you with a New York broker friend of mine."

"Okay, try that. By the way, I just want you to know that your stock dropped by four points. Four points. I'm going to have to find a better company for you to get at least a sixteen percent profile by the end of the year. Anyway, let me know if I need to go downtown to sign any papers."

Richard hoped that Hellfire would understand that there were only sixteen survivors.

"I'll do that. I have to go now, but I guess I'll see you at the golf course tomorrow. I can probably get those papers for you to sign them there," Hellfire said. "Okay?"

"That sounds like a plan," said Richard. "Talk to you later, Bob."

Richard switched his comlink back to short-range internal.

"Hey, listen up. The complex was never in SFTF's control," Richard informed his friends. "The entire complex has been under the control of the population for some time, probably by Sargon since he is the strongest leader. Our extraction point has changed to the Lincoln Golf Course. So watch your back. They're more organized than we thought."

"Roger," Larcis replied. "Richard, John just told me that a group of people was seen moving in the alleys toward Lincoln Park about twenty minutes ago. Do you suppose it was them?"

"Probably," said Richard. "Who else would move as a large group through a maze of alleys? Let's stay north of Geary and extend up to Clement Street for another thousand meters."

### Jeremiah's Group

Jeremiah's group found a nearly abandoned high school with a few drunks on the upper levels. They occupied the boiler room in the basement and waited for Jeremiah and William to secure the area. Jeffery Samuel attempted to rig a makeshift radio with his broken equipment. Rebecca and Cindy changed into more suitable clothes for protection against the cold, wet weather. Senator Fence, Nadine, and Coy started to separate the rations of food, flashlights, batteries, and extra clothing.

William and Jeremiah returned after ten minutes.

"The area is clear," Jeremiah assured the others. "We have set up expedient early-warning devices in the corridor, so don't go out there without one of us to guide you. In the meantime, we can relax for a while and get dried up. Jeffery, were you able to make the radio transmitter work?"

"No, we need to get new batteries, and I doubt they have any here in the school."

"Isn't there a media room somewhere in the school?" Rebecca interjected. "It *is* a high school, right?"

Jeremiah smiled, and Jeffery said, "Yes, there might be. Hopefully the equipment we need is still there and in good shape."

"Sir, do you want me and Mr. Samuel to go and look for the equipment?" William volunteered.

"Yes, but be careful and stay in radio contact. I'll keep my ear piece on."

"Alright, Mr. Samuel," William said. "Let me know when you're ready."

"Call me Jeffery, Agent Ottis," Jeffery said.

"Okay, Jeffery. You can call me William."

The two men were gone only briefly.

"We couldn't find anything. They striped this place when the city was evacuated," Jeffery reported with a discouraged face.

"Alright, anyone have any suggestions?" Jeremiah asked the group.

"I do," Rebecca announced. "I suggest we stay here until daybreak. Once it's light outside, it will be easier for the rescue parties to find us and easier for us to spot them as they roam the streets."

Jeremiah thought for a moment, then asked the group, "Who's opposed to the idea?" No one objected. "Very well, then. Everyone get comfortable, change clothes, eat if you're hungry, and get some rest. We will pull twenty-minute shifts looking out for anyone coming down into the basement."

Jeremiah settled in, trying to make himself comfortable but remaining alert. He wondered how members of the other group were fairing, whether they were safe like his group was now.

Wendy found an abandoned Citibank building on the southeastern corner of Clement and Geary. Mr. Su-rak loudly complained about his blistered feet as they ran into the bank's side entrance from an alleyway.

"Keep moving and be quiet!" Patricia hushed Jacoya's squeamish crying as she ran behind the old man.

Jacoya painfully bit his tongue, realizing that his loud complaining might alert others to their presence.

The group swiftly crossed the bank lobby into the back rooms. The manager's office was the most secluded in the building besides the open vault. Thomas and Blake settled Eugene on a dusty maroon sofa. John checked his vital signs while Patricia tended to Jacoya's feet. Wendy kept a lookout at the main entrance while Linsan changed her wet clothing.

John pulled Thomas aside. "General, his blood pressure has dropped a lot. We need to give him plasma or B-positive blood before he goes into shock. Once he goes into shock," John whispered, "we won't be able to move him without killing him."

Thomas looked at his friend on the sofa. "Thank you for telling me. We'll think of something." Thomas turned to the group. "Alright, we'll have to divide the rations and stand watch in pairs of two every twenty minutes. Linsan, you can change in the other room. When you get done, please join Wendy in the lobby. Mr. Su-rak, I suggest that you put on a comfortable pair of shoes before you stand watch with Mrs. Ortiz. Blake, you and I will be third. Mr. Wilkens, you and Cindy alternate and monitor General Fox, keeping him warm and making sure he doesn't start bleeding again."

"Thomas," Blake asked, "how are the good guys going to find us?"

"I don't know yet. I have a bad feeling that we're on our own until we can get to a working phone or radio transmitter. Or, if we're lucky, a rescue party might come by the bank accidentally."

Hope was slipping away from Thomas just as it was slipping away from his best friend.

### SFTF Center Operations Control Room

Maximilian arrived at the SFTF center soon after Brandon's confession.

"Give me an update on our team," Max said as he entered the control room.

"Sir," Agent Latimer reported, "our team has found the plane. They report four dead. They're now looking for the survivors. Our unmanned aerial vehicle has spotted a concentration of several thousand people around Union Square and the Opera House. There's an additional twenty thousand by the southern wall in the vicinity of the Cow Palace. The numbers are sketchy due to the ceiling, making us fly the UAV at a standoff of three kilometers."

"Have the sixteen survivors been captured?"

"Not that we know of," Tyler responded, "and we have not received any message from Sargon or whoever is in charge of the complex."

Max looked at Tyler. "How are you, Rick?"

"I'm fine, sir." Rick replied almost taken by surprise by the change of subject.

"What do you think about this Sargon character?"

"I'm not sure, but from what my team says, he's a superhuman with strong telekinetic powers. He's probably the one responsible for downing the plane."

Max smiled. "I'm sure Creator can handle him. If not, then we have our backup plan. By the way, where are Hellfire and Quatris?"

"They're talking with EFL computer, trying to run a background check on other possible superhumans in the complex."

"Good. Is the FBI team here?" Max asked after thinking for a moment.

"Yes," Rick reported, "the team is organizing a replacement unit for the SFTF personnel."

"Good. Do we have Senator Carpenter in custody?"

"Yes, but the State Department is trying to fight it."

"I'll take care of that nonsense. Configure the comlinks to receive Creator's transmissions so that we can all hear what's going on if anyone is in the head or outside of the building," Max directed as he got on a secure telephone calling the State Department's operations center.

### Complex San Francisco

"Creator," Larcis reported, "I have a group of eight in a building 460 meters ahead. Two of them are at the entrance, the rest in the rear."

"Good. Come to my location now," Richard ordered. Larcis and John quickly linked up with Richard in a dark alley.

"How many people are in the area besides those eight in the bank?" Richard asked Larcis.

"There are fourteen people scattered in a four-block area. All the people seem to be stationary inside their respective buildings."

"Okay. Follow me," said Richard. The trio flew along the rooftops to a building across the street. Richard scanned the building with his en-ray vision.

"There are two people near the bank entrance. They will see us if we approach that way. John, you, and I will go a little north and get to the side of the bank. I will direct your scan through the wall so that you can find out who they are. If they're the survivors, I need you to talk to them to let them know we are the good guys. Larcis, you stay up here and scan for anything out of place. Alright?"

"Alright, boss," Larcis said.

"Let's go, John," Richard said. He flew to the north, then straight down into an alleyway. They crossed the street and stopped by the wall directly opposite the two people inside the bank lobby. "John," Richard warned, "they're both females, so don't approach them too fast."

*Okay,* John said as he slowly thought himself through the concrete wall.

"Wendy, do you ever get scared?" Linsan asked as she thought about past events and Wendy's coolness under fire.

Wendy smiled. "Yes, I do. But there's a time when fear has to take a step back or we would all be dead or slaves to fear."

Linsan thought for a moment. "Why is it that I'm the only one who seems terrified of our situation?"

"Besides your boss and yourself, everyone has firsthand experience in a war or has been trained for such situations."

"I can understand General Cartier, General Fox, you, and even Cindy. But why is Patricia so calm?"

"Patricia is South American. All South Americans are automatically drafted into the military at age fifteen. All of them go through combat training from small-unit tactics to army-level peacekeeping missions. They're required to finish their training, get a master's degree, work in their civilian field, and still be on active duty until they can no longer serve due to medical reasons or retirement at age fifty."

"How do you know all of this?" Linsan asked.

"As presidential adviser on national security, I'm *expected* to know."

"I am glad we didn't get split up," Linsan said with a faint smile. "I feel safer with *this* group."

Wendy, hearing another voice, turned suddenly.

*Do not be alarmed. My name is Mindseye. I am part of a team sent in to rescue you. I am talking to you through your mind.*

Wendy, sensing the direction of the transmission, faced the wall. "Where are you?" she said and thought.

*We are beside you on the other side of the wall. The leader of the team is Creator. We didn't want to startle you by coming to the front door.*

Linsan, confused, asked Wendy, "Who are you talking to?"

"Go get Thomas," Wendy said to her friend. "Hurry!"

Richard informed John that one of the women was moving toward the back of the building.

Wendy looked at the wall again. "How do I know that I can trust you?"

*You can't,* John told Wendy. *But you're going to have to or we'll all be in big trouble.*

*Both of you come out into the open with your hands above your heads,* Wendy thought.

John told Richard what Wendy had demanded in her thoughts.

Richard smiled. It wasn't as if bullets could hurt him. Then again, he'd never seen *John* take a bullet.

"If that's what the lady wants," Richard said. "Change into your costume and let's go."

Richard's clothes transformed into Creator's costume, and John followed the example.

The superheroes exposed themselves to view through the bank's large glass windows just as Thomas ran up to Wendy with his gun drawn.

"Are you alright?" Thomas asked. Blake and Linsan stood watching through the teller windows.

"I'm fine," Wendy replied. "They say they're here to rescue us."

Thomas looked at Wendy then at Creator and John as they entered the building.

"Who are you?" Thomas said.

"My name is Creator. I am leader of the Eternal Champions. This is Mindseye, a member of the team. Maximilian, the director of SIA, sent us to rescue the survivors of your flight."

"How do we know SIA sent you," Thomas asked, "and why isn't the SFTF here?"

"I'm afraid there are no SFTF guards in the complex. It has been without such supervision for several months. We found out this fact when we entered the city. I cannot prove who we are, but I can prove that our motives are true."

"Okay," Thomas said. "Prove it."

"John," Richard said, "slowly take your backpack off, put it on the floor, and slide it toward them."

John hesitated as Wendy aimed the pistol's fixed sight at his neck. He took the backpack off and slid it toward Thomas.

"You will find medical supplies, a few grenades, demolitions, and fresh water," Richard said.

Thomas rifled through the backpack and found exactly what Richard said would be in there. He looked first at Richard and then at Wendy.

"He's right, Wendy. Put the gun away."

"Thomas, what if they want us to believe they are on our side so that they'll have more live hostages?" Wendy responded.

Thomas thought for a second, hesitating to answer.

"Alright," Richard said, "you want more proof. We're wasting time, you cannot hurt me with those pea-shooters, so I'm going to lower my hands and play a recording of the message I got when we accepted this mission."

Thomas lowered his pistol, aiming at Richard's chest.

"If you fire and we *are* the good guys, they will know where we are. If we're the bad guys, I would have killed you already and captured the other four in the back room," Richard said before playing the recording Max had sent.

Thomas and Wendy lowered their weapons after hearing the recording.

"We had to be sure, Creator," said Thomas. "Who else is with you?"

"First we need to treat the injured and move out of the lobby," Richard said. "Is there anyone seriously injured?"

"General Fox has a serious leg injury. This might help," Wendy said as she took the pack of supplies to the back room.

"Night, get down here now and join us," Richard said into his comlink.

Night entered the bank in full costume before Richard could clear the teller counters.

"He's with us," Richard assured the others. "Now, get everyone in the back so I can tell them the good and the bad news. Oh, and lock the door."

Night stopped in his tracks, wondering how he got to be the chogi-boy (Korean, for errand boy).

"Who's going to keep a lookout?" Wendy asked.

"Night." Richard replied.

Night trailed as he monitored his scanner.

Faces lit up at the announcement that a rescue team was in their mist. John Wilkens took a bag of plasma and sodium chloride solution out of the pack Wendy gave him. Cindy helped Jacoya put moleskin and foot powder on his feet. Richard waited for everyone to be treated and get settled before addressing the group.

"Okay, here's the bad news. The complex is under the control of a gang leader or leaders. There are no SFTF personnel in the complex. Two helicopters were sent in to retrieve you, but they were brought down just over Presidio. It was good that you split up, but because you did, I cannot protect all of you at the same time. The good news is, I have communication with the outside, but I cannot get an evacuation until I find the other group. What we can do is split up ourselves. Mindseye and I will go find the other group. Night will protect all of you until we get back. Any questions?"

The glad faces turned somber as the survivors realized that they would have to remain in the complex a bit longer.

"Creator, we have movement to the north," Larcis said.

"Mindseye, stay here with the group. Night, follow me," Richard said as he ran out to the lobby. "Show me."

"There are two clumps of life forms moving fast down Clement Street. I can barely read the life forms, but each clump has ten in the rear, with what seems to be three in the front. The configuration resembles a vehicle like an armored personnel carrier, small bus, or truck," Larcis analyzed.

"How fast are they moving?"

"About forty or fifty miles per hour. And look," Larcis said as he brought the view screen up to Richard's face, "they're heading east, away from us."

Richard looked at the scanner with interest and considered their options for the moment. He could not tell if it was a bus or truck by the configuration. Whatever it was, it was running around the city too rapidly to be worried about being noticed. It could be friendly or enemy, but one thing was certain, they had to get eyes on the target to find out if it posed a threat to the survivors. He wasn't concerned about his team, but everyone else was not bullet proof and could not escape with flight.

"Do you want to investigate?" Larcis asked.

"Yeah," Richard said. "Let's go."

"Wait a minute. There are about 150 people approaching the bank from Geary," Larcis said as he looked back down at the scanner.

"Why didn't you pick them up earlier?"

Larcis looked around, dumbfounded. "I'm not sure, but this vault we're standing next to might have something to do with it," he said.

"Great! Just great! Mindseye! Thomas!" Richard yelled as his simple plan to get in and out quietly was quickly becoming a fly by wire operation.

Thomas, Mindseye, Blake, and Wendy ran out to the lobby.

"We're going to have company, so get everyone ready to move out through the side door and head north. Before you reach Clement, take a left in an alley and go about two hundred meters. Wait for us there. Mindseye, you carry General Fox so the group can move faster."

"Come on, you heard him," Thomas said, urging the three to go back into the room.

Richard looked at the rifle Larcis was carrying and asked, "What else can that thing do?"

"Nothing, except..." Larcis caught himself thinking.

"Except what?" Richard said, his impatience showing.

"Tyler said it could be made to overload and explode, but I'm not sure how big of an explosion it'll make." Larcis stated.

"How long will it take to overload?"

"About fifteen seconds." Larcis replied.

"Okay, let's go outside and rumble."

A crowd of angry men and women emerged from the shadows into an open parking lot 250 meters from the bank. Two trucks followed with submachine guns mounted above the passenger's seat. Richard and Larcis flew outside, shattering the large glass windows of the bank lobby, and stopped thirty feet in front of the bank's entrance. Larcis set the stun rifle to overload. Richard extended his arms out in front of his body and made fists. Barely visible heat waves appeared around his wrists and beyond as a shock wave of telekinetic energy divided the air between him and the first wave of victims. Two men were thrown backward, smashing ten other people behind them and crushing bones and skulls on a 20-meter strip of destruction.

Submachine guns and assault rifles fired indiscriminately at Creator and Night. Night turned his back toward the assault, keeping the stun rifle from being hit by a stray bullet. A high-pitched whining from the stun rifle started to drown out the gunfire noises.

"Richard," Larcis yelled, "there are nine seconds remaining!"

"Give me the rifle when there are five seconds left!" Richard quickly shouted back.

"Here, take it!" Larcis handed the rifle over after counting three Mississippi's.

Richard grabbed the rifle and threw it slightly above the center of the mob. It twirled two hundred meters into the crowd and turned white, lighting the scene for ten blocks around. In a split second, the bright dot in the air burst into a miniature supernova that obliterated the two trucks and left a hundred-foot crater in the pavement. Fragments of concrete and metal and other debris exploded into the air, with the building to the right of the explosion collapsing into the avenue. Broken glass, rubble, and body parts rained down around the perimeter of the blast.

Richard and Larcis stood staring, wondering how a two-foot piece of metal could generate so much destructive power.

"Don't you ever take a weapon from SIA before you know exactly what it can do!" Richard scolded.

"Yeah, boss," said Larcis, "I'll remember that!"

Richard thought quickly about what to do now that everyone inside and outside of the city probably knew they were here.

# Chapter Eight

⊠ - ⊠

# Allies

S ir!" yelled Officer Genkins, the officer in charge of monitoring the city's activities. "We have an explosion near the corner of Geary and Thirtieth Avenue!"

Max looked at the digital map with a large red circle covering two city blocks.

"What kind of explosion was it?"

"Sir, it was a geo-magnetic plasma explosion from a model 2000 stun rifle," Tyler said.

"What?" Max scornfully said. "Did you tell them to use up some of the energy before putting it on overload?"

"We didn't expect them to put it on overload the first time they used it, sir," Tyler said.

"I only hope they weren't near it when it went off." Max commented.

### Front of Bank, Complex San Francisco

"Boss," Larcis said, "someone's still alive. There, near the corner of Geary."

Larcis, his head bent over his scanner, had spotted the figure to the rear of the mob. Whomever it was had slowly stood and was now making a move to escape.

"I'll take care of him." Richard said.

"And there are now two confirmed armored personnel carriers to the east." Larcis said.

"Okay," said Richard. "You get the group to a secure area and watch out for the APCs. I'm sure they saw the fireworks."

Richard flew at top speed toward the figure Larcis had seen on his scanner.

The man, wearing a combination of SFTF guard equipment and camouflaged fatigues, fired several rounds on automatic setting. Richard ignored the bullets—which mushroomed on impact with his body—and swooped down to tear the rifle from the man's grasp with one hand and hold him by the neck with the other.

"Who are you?" Richard demanded.

"Araagh...Sargon will kill you," the man replied.

"Not before I rip your heart out. Now, have any of the survivors from the plane been captured?"

"Kill me now," the man said, "because I won't tell you."

The man attempted to spit on Richard as slobber rolled out of his choking mouth. Richard, who didn't appreciate the man trying to spit on him and who had no interest in following police procedure anyway, placed his foot atop the man's foot and slowly pressed downward.

The man groaned in pain but wouldn't answer.

Richard angrily and unintentionally stepped down more forcefully, crushing bones and separating the man's foot from his ankle.

"Answer my question now," Richard said.

"Aaaaa...Araaaagh...No!" the man screamed and then fell unconscious from pain and shock.

Richard cursed under his breath. The "no" could have meant either that the man still refused to answer or to stop hurting him. Richard released his grip on the man, whose broken body dropped into its own pool of blood leaving him to die, and rejoined the group.

"Larcis, meet me at the left turn," Richard said, changing his comlink mode. "Erica, patch in with SFTF central on a secure line."

"Initiating," Erica instantly replied.

"Tyler, the gig is up. They know we're here. We've found eight of the survivors. The other eight were headed to the north, but probably went east, otherwise we would have found them first. There are APCs in the city. Did you send them?"

Max looked at Tyler, who responded by negatively shaking his head.

"Creator, this is Max. That is a negative, we've sent in no one. Tyler tells me that the APCs are not from the city. Long-range visual intelligence tells us they are unmarked APCs resembling Russian BMPs, with large-caliber guns on them traveling east toward downtown," Max said as Tyler handled him a text message from the spotter team adjacent to the Golden Gate Bridge.

"Can you send a helicopter to evacuate the survivors we have now?" Richard said as Night joined him at his side.

"No," said Max. "We've found out that Sargon would probably destroy any helicopter that gets near the city. He's a very strong superhuman with telekinetic powers. Until we figure out a way to neutralize his influence on the helicopters, we won't be able to get to you."

"Richard," Larcis interrupted, "an APC is coming. It's about six hundred meters away."

"Okay, I have to go and take care of another problem. I'll let you know when we find the other survivors," Richard said and signed off. "Erica, adjust your sensors to pick up my alpha-wave patterns through the comlink. If I pass out, I want you to direct Quatris and Hellfire to my location and tell them I'm unconscious and need their help."

"Adjusting now, Creator," Erica replied with her seductive echoed voice.

"Let's go see who these guys are," Richard said, flying east between the buildings south of Clement Street.

"They've dismounted three hundred meters ahead," Larcis reported. "Wait a minute!"

"Now what?"

"There's a life form moving rapidly over the crater we just made. It seems like someone is flying over all of the carnage."

Richard thought for a second. "Alright, you find out who these guys are from a distance. Don't let them see you," Richard ordered, "and wait until I get back."

"Understood, boss" Larcis replied as a proud follower.

Richard turned on the afterburners and headed for the same rooftop where they first looked down at the bank. He reached the rooftop ledge to see a woman walking around in front of the bank. She turned in his direction and looked up. Richard quickly hid below the ledge, keeping an eye on her with his en-ray vision, but she vanished before his eyes.

"What the..."

Richard flew down to where the woman had last stood.

*Where could she have gone?* He thought.

The dark street turned red as flames rose from the ground all around the block. Richard suddenly felt warm, but he ignored it. The ground shook as a large crack in the asphalt opened up and let out a hideous black-and-crimson flaming serpent.

"Why have you come to this place?" the serpent hissed at Richard.

"I'll ask the questions," Richard countered. "Who are you?"

"*Silence!* I am death itself. Why have you come to this place?"

The hiss had risen to a low roar.

Richard crossed his arms with an unimpressed look on his face.

"You know, I'm not afraid of talking snakes or dragons," Richard taunted.

"You *will* be," the serpent responded as darkness fell on Richard.

A chill ran down Richard's spine as the serpent turned into a thirty-foot black dragon. It raised its scabby claw, thrusting it at Richard with tremendous agility. Richard tried to dodge to the left only to feel like he was in a slow-motion movie clip. Before he moved six inches, the dragon's talons grabbed his entire body, piercing his flesh along his left anterior serratus, left llium area, and left quadriceps. Pain pulsed through Richard's body as he noticed blood gushing onto the dragon's claw. Everything seemed so real. But was it? Richard concentrated, clearing out all thoughts of pain and focusing on reality.

"Why have you come to this place?" the dragon roared.

The pain subsided to a mere gust of wind agitating his skin as the claw transparently disappeared before his eyes.

"Your mind tricks won't work on me," Richard exclaimed. "I don't believe in dragons."

The dragon instantly disappeared into the fiery crevice, which itself disappeared.

"The dragon might not be real, but I am," said a female voice, as a black-haired woman in a purple outfit with a black cape materialized in front of Richard.

The woman raised her hand and shot a lightning bolt into Richard's chest. An electrical current passed through his body and went down into the ground. Richard responded with a dozen telekinetic pulses of energy back toward the woman.

Katherine countered Creator's blasts without being fazed and retaliated with her own attacks.

*She's wearing me out,* Richard thought. *Or is she?*

Richard thought about the dragon illusion and stood absolutely still, closing his eyes.

*What's he doing?* Katherine asked herself. *Can he be the one?*

She stepped backward, crushing a piece of broken glass.

Richard heard the crunch to his right. Immediately he let out a salvo of telekinetic blasts and spread them ten feet wide and ten feet high in Katherine's direction. Katherine was caught by surprise as several invisible telekinetic projectiles hit her head, chest, and legs, causing her to lose her concentration. A beautiful brown-haired woman in military fatigues materialized on the ground to Richard's right. He sprinted forward, taking hold of Katherine's arm and placing it behind her back.

"Who are you?" Richard demanded. He applied upward pressure on the wrist toward her spine.

Katherine's arm swelled with pain as Richard applied pressure.

"I'm on your side!" she cried.

Richard slightly eased off her arm.

"What's your name?"

"My name is Katherine Fletcher. I want to help you. Please let go of my arm!" Katherine begged.

Richard released his vice-like grip on her arm.

"Why did you attack me?"

Katherine massaged her elbow and shoulder and spoke with a hint of pain: "I had to know if you were as powerful as I envisioned."

"What do you mean?" Richard asked.

"It's hard to explain," said Katherine, "but we have more important things to worry about. Sargon is a very powerful superhuman. He's responsible for the plane crash. There are about ten other superhumans in the city. One of them is called Snoop. He flies around as a scout for Sargon. He can walk through walls and sees at night as if it were daylight. He's the one who found your team and followed you to this bank. I was sent here with what Sargon calls freedom fighters to get the survivors and use them as hostages in case the SFTF decide to use nuclear or chemical weapons against the city. He's built up an army downtown and south of here to take control of Oakland."

"So why are you helping me?" Richard asked while admiring Katherine's long hair as it rested on her sexy shoulders.

Katherine looked straight into Richard's sunglasses.

"I'm not helping you to force you to accept my demands. I want to ask you to help my friend and me get out of this complex and clear our records. I know that you don't know my friend or me. We committed murder, or we wouldn't be here. I'm not going to make excuses for what we did. All I ask is to be given a second chance to be forgiven and do what's right."

Richard considered this offer. Superhumans were not supposed to be in the complex. Many trials involving superhumans were controversial and one-sided, but these facts had no bearing on the present situation. For whatever reason, Katherine would have to prove that her motives were honest.

"I cannot promise you I'll be able to clear your record or get you out of this complex," Richard honestly said.

"I'm not asking you to do it. I'm asking you to help me by trying," Katherine pleaded.

Richard considered his course of action.

"I'll see what I can do," he said. "But you're my prisoner until I say otherwise."

Katherine tilted her head, slightly muddled. She was not used to having anyone trust her. But considering he was not a convict among convicts or an attorney, she accepted his resolution.

"Thank you," she said, "but do you have to treat me as a convict?"

"Yes, I do. You *are* a convict, aren't you?"

Katherine gave him a death stare.

"Are you going to cuff me?" she dared.

Richard smiled.

"Only if you *want* me to."

"Hmm," Katherine said with a smirk.

"Can you fly?"

"Yes, why?"

"Take my hand," Richard ordered as he reached out to her. At the same time, he tapped his comlink. "Night, where are you?"

"I'm on top of the Heaven's Inn, and we have some major problems."

"What do you mean?" Richard asked as he and Katherine took off in Night's direction.

"These guys have some serious hardware. They look familiar, but I don't remember where I've seen them before. They are some kind of Soldiers from what I can tell."

"Okay. Meet me on the opposite side of the roof."

Richard and Katherine flew to the rooftop where Larcis awaited.

"Night, this is Katherine. Katherine, this is Night," Richard quickly introduced them as they landed on the roof.

"Let's take a look at our new friends," said Richard as he walked near the ledge, avoiding the questions Larcis had for him.

Larcis was flabbergasted. How could Richard pick up the hottest girl he had ever seen out of the thirty-eight girls he had dated in the past—especially out here in a prison complex?

Richard, with Katherine at his side, looked at the street below. A forty-foot armored vehicle resembling a hybrid of a Warsaw Pact BMP and a miniature Leopard II tank turret, with a 105-millimeter gun, drove slowly down the street. Ten men in body armor surrounded the vehicle as an escort. The vehicle and men were painted completely black with no insignias or agency markings.

"Katherine, do you know who they are?"

"No, but I can sense.... Get down!"

The three hit the roof floor with the short three foot wall hiding them from view.

"What can you sense?" Richard asked.

"They're scanning to their front, sides, up, and down. They would have spotted us if we hadn't ducked."

"Hey, that's a pretty good trick," Larcis commented, staring at Katherine.

"Let me know when it's safe to look," Richard directed.

"Okay, it's safe," Katherine said a moment later.

Richard looked over the ledge, focusing on the armored suits and carrier with his en-ray vision. He could have looked through the three foot wall, but he didn't want anything in between him and the targets.

"The armor isn't metallic. It's some type of fiberglass metallic alloy. Oh, no!" Richard said under his breath, ducking back below the ledge. "They're South American Soldiers." He looked up at the clouds in thought. "We need to contact them and reach a compromise. Otherwise this rescue might start a war."

"And how do we do that?" said Larcis. "I don't think we can just walk up to them and say, 'Hey, what's up? How is it hanging?'"

"No, but maybe we don't have to," Richard said. He'd already come up with one of his brilliant plans.

"Have to *what?*" Katherine asked, confused.

"Maybe we don't have to walk." Richard tapped his comlink. "Mindseye, Night will be there in about twenty seconds. Go outside with Patricia Ortiz now. Night, you will take one of the Soldiers to John as fast as you can and get Mrs. Ortiz to explain our situation, while I stall for time with the others. Let's go," Richard ordered.

"Right, boss," Larcis replied, understanding his plan, and swooped down toward the nearest Soldier. Larcis snatched the Soldier off the ground before Richard could make it halfway down the seven-story inn.

*Damn, that was fast,* Richard thought as he flew on top of an unsuspecting Soldier. Richard landed on the man's backpack, slid his arms beneath the man's armpits, and interlocked his hands behind the man's neck. The other eight Soldiers and vehicle quickly responded. Three Soldiers near the two men fired their rifles, hitting both of them. The rounds felt like normal 5.56-millimeter M16 rifle hits, but they didn't hurt Richard or the Soldier.

"Tell them to stop firing or I'll break your neck," Richard commanded, not sure if he could break his neck being hardly able to interlock his fingers in such an awkward position with the Soldier's backpack in his way.

The men stopped firing. One of them yelled in perfect English, "Let him go, and we will not harm you."

"I'm not here to hurt any of you," Richard yelled. "We are looking for the same people. I'm part of a U.S. rescue team."

"Why have you taken one of our men and threatened us this way?" the Soldier asked.

"I'm sorry, but if you wait a few seconds, you will understand," Richard stated.

"Creator, Mrs. Ortiz is speaking in Spanish with the guy I brought here," Larcis reported over the comlink.

"Larcis, make sure Patricia tells them we are on the same side. I just needed to get their attention."

A fourth Soldier pushed a button on his helmet and said with a Spanish accent, "You can let go of him. Mrs. Ortiz has explained the situation. I am Master Sergeant Rivera from the battle cruiser *Doris*."

The Soldiers took up a defensive perimeter of the area as Richard let go of the young private.

"I am Creator, leader of the Eternal Champions. There are three others in my team. One is on the roof above us; so don't fire on her. We found eight of the survivors before we ran into your patrol."

Richard spoke to MSG Rivera as he told his men to put lower their weapons, while Katherine watched from the rooftop. Richard gestured for Katherine to come down and join the party shortly after MSG Rivera started to formulate a new plan of action for the rescue.

"My team leader is currently approaching the other group's location," Rivera said. "Mrs. Ortiz says that there is a critically wounded man in her group. We will go get the survivors and place them in the armored carrier where they will be protected from further danger. You can go help Lieutenant Alejandro with the search. I will let him know to watch out for you."

Katherine walked up to Richard's side as the Soldiers mounted the APC.

"Where are they going, Creator?" Katherine asked.

"They're going to pick up General Cartier's group while we link up with Lieutenant Alejandro's squad. Let's go!"

Richard and Katherine flew east, and the APC went west.

John and Larcis took the group out to Clement Street, seeing the APC approaching. Larcis played around with the bio-scanner, awaiting the APC on the street.

"Damn it! The scanner must have broken when I flew here with that guy," said Larcis to himself.

Just as half the group got out into the open, bullets streaked in from the west as a dozen gunmen ran down the street at them. A round hit Linsan in the chest. "Linsan!" Wendy screamed as her new friend fell to the ground. Larcis got between the group and the gunmen. His hands glowed pure white and let out a lightning bolt that branched off and hit the group of gunmen. They fell in their tracks, jerking and smoldering from electrocution.

The APC rolled in, and the Soldiers jumped off to secure the area. Linsan gasped and coughed in pain as blood clogged her mouth and nose. Wendy found the exit wound and felt somewhat relieved that the round had penetrated Linsan's right lung and left out her right side without causing a gaping hole. Wendy covered the entry wound with her hand as she rotated Linsan on her right side. Two Soldiers, one with a surgeon's medical bag, ran up to Linsan. General Cartier urged Jacoya and the rest of the group to enter the APC with General Fox. The team doctor stabilized Linsan enough to move her into the APC a few minutes later.

Katherine tapped Richard on the arm as they passed Divisadero Street. She stopped in midair and looked to her right.

"What is it?" Richard asked.

"I sense a presence...," Katherine said. "Linda!"

A woman stood on an adjacent rooftop wearing a skimpy outfit with a black cape trimmed by a light blue five-inch strip. The cape collar extended six inches above the neckline. The woman's silky black hair, thigh-high black boots, and black armpit-high gloves complimented the outfit.

Katherine flew toward her with Richard following close behind.

"Stop right there, Kat!" Linda commanded.

Katherine landed on the ledge of the roof with Richard at her side.

"Sargon sent me to find out what is going on," Linda said, wondering what Katherine was doing. "You turned off your radio."

"Linda," Kat said, a little taken back by her friend's hostile attitude, "I know how we are going to get out of here."

Linda looked at Creator, then at his white boots.

"Nice boots."

Linda turned to Kat and said, "What are you talking about?"

"Creator here has promised to help us," Kat explained.

"What makes you think he can help us?"

"Linda, he's the one I saw in my visions. I don't know how, but I do know he is the key."

Richard glanced at Kat, slightly baffled. Linda walked up to Kat and Richard.

"First of all, Kat, I don't think he can take on Sargon, let alone get us pardoned." Linda turned toward Richard. "No offense, but I don't trust men very much."

"Linda—" Kat started to say.

"I can talk for myself, Katherine," Richard interrupted. "It's true, I cannot guarantee you a pardon. But I *can* get someone who has the power to help you. As for Sargon," Richard added in a firm voice, "we'll see who falls first."

"Linda, aren't you taking a chance by talking to us now?" Kat interjected, changing the subject.

"No, I took care of Sargon's watch dog. We are alone," Linda coldly assured her.

"We need your help, Linda," Kat said.

"Creator, I know Kat very well. She probably asked you for help and that was all. I, on the other hand, am not so refined. I will help you only if you can guarantee a pardon for Kat and myself—no exception."

"My word is all I have, and since you can't accept that, I will finish what I have started here and move on with my life. I'm sorry; Linda, but I can't promise something I cannot offer." Richard sharply declared.

Linda thought for a moment as Kat despondently stared at her.

"I will wait for you to change your mind," Linda said. "In the meantime, as a show of good faith, I will not interfere with your rescue. One last thing: Sargon knows where the survivors are and will take his army with him to get them. I hope you are the one, because you're going to need a small army to stop him."

"Fair enough," said Richard. "Thank you."

He slowly flew away.

"Linda, please trust him," Kat pleaded.

Linda looked at her best friend.

"I trust you, Kat, but you're going to have to trust me. I will be there for you when the time is right. Not any sooner."

Katherine flew off but looked back to see her friend's silhouette becoming smaller and smaller in the distance.

A tall, black-haired man wearing jeans and a black silk shirt stood at the top of the opera house's oval stairway as more than a thousand pairs of eyes looked on.

"My fellow men and women," said the man, "we will soon have victory over our jailers. We will show them that *they* are the true criminals. *They* are the ones who enslaved us, tortured us, and forgot about our existence. It's time for us to take control of this city for good and destroy Oakland in the process!"

A chant passed through the crowd, growing louder each moment: "Sargon! Sargon! Sargon!"

A thin man wearing ragged clothes flew down next to Sargon.

"Report, Snoop," Sargon commanded.

"My lord," Snoop replied, with fear evident in his voice, "I have nothing to report except that I lost her."

Sargon grabbed Snoop by the neck, and said, "Go, find them both. If you don't find them in less than thirty minutes, I will *kill* you."

"Yes, my lord," Snoop weakly replied and flew off.

Sargon turned back to his captive audience.

"Half of you will go up Stiener Street, and the other half will go with me up Laguna Street. Let's move, people," Sargon called out to the crowd. "I want Oakland before sunrise!"

# Chapter Nine

✠ - ✠

# Movement to Contact

S ir, we have movement at the opera house!" Agent Latimer reported.

"Where are they headed?" Max asked.

"They're moving north."

"Get me Creator now," Max ordered.

Richard's comlink beeped.

"This is Creator," Richard responded while in flight.

"Creator, there's a crowd of about fifteen hundred people moving north on Laguna Street. What's your status?" Max requested.

"I'm on my way to link up with the South American team and pick up the remaining survivors."

"Did I hear you right?" Max said, alarmed.

"Yes, you did. They are protecting the first group I found and are now converging on the second group north of Stiener and Washington Streets," Richard explained as he and Katherine landed next to the command APC. The Soldiers were dismounted, moving slowly in the shadows down Stiener.

"Creator, we need to keep the mob from taking the survivors, yourself, or the Soldiers at all costs. Can you take out Sargon?" Max bluntly asked.

"I'm not sure," said Richard. "But if he's as strong as Hellfire or Quatris, we have a problem."

"Hmmmm… I'm sending Hellfire and Quatris to the south wall. We have twenty thousand angry people trying to escape," Max informed Richard. "As fast as they move, I don't think you'll have a problem getting their help if you need them."

"Thanks," Richard said and signed off.

A Soldier approached Richard and Katherine.

"I'm Lieutenant Alejandro, the team leader."

"How did you track the survivors to this location?" Richard asked.

"One of the female survivors has a responder that, when activated, gives away the location at that time. The last known location is coming up here at this school." Alejandro pointed to a junior high school a block away.

"Katherine, can you mentally communicate with the other survivors?" Richard asked Kat.

"Yes. Do you need me to contact the survivors?"

"Yes," Richard continued. "Lieutenant Alejandro, Katherine will help you contact the survivors so that they don't mistake you for the enemy. Katherine, what's Linda's full name?"

"Linda Manchester. Why?"

"I'll tell you later. You follow the lieutenant. I'll be there soon." Richard tapped his comlink. "Max, can you get all the information you have on Linda Manchester and Katherine Fletcher? I want you to consider a pardon for their help in this rescue."

"You know I don't have the power to pardon a criminal who is now serving a sentence for murder," Max replied.

"Yes, I know. But they might not have committed murder. Even if they did, I know you have the pull to get someone who *can* pardon them. Besides, they'll be in danger after this thing is over, and they'll need to be protected under the witness-protection program or something like that."

"Alright, Creator, I'll see what I can do."

"Thanks. Creator out."

Richard walked up to Katherine and three other Soldiers scouting her path. The APC parked alongside a metal fence near the entrance to the school parking lot.

"Did you contact them?" Richard asked.

"No," said Kat. "I need to know where to look in the building."

Richard scanned the school with his en-ray vision.

"They're in the boiler room in the basement—there," Richard said and pointed.

Kat looked at Richard, oddly amused, then closed her eyes and projected her mind into the basement.

"They know we're here," Kat said a minute later. "They'll be coming out any second now."

Jeremiah and the group came out of the school and were escorted to the APC.

"Who's in charge here?" Jeremiah asked.

"I am," Creator responded, stepping up without looking at the lieutenant.

"I am Secret Service Agent Allen. There is another group hiding to the west."

"Yes, we know," said Richard. "They've been picked up and are safe. I'm Creator." Richard extended his hand.

"That's good news," said Jeremiah, shaking Richard's hand. "So we can leave now, right?"

"I'm afraid not. There's a mob of over fifteen hundred convicts loyal to Sargon coming this way. We're going to have to take a stance and fight them. Your group will be safe in the APC. Just make sure you have everyone latch onto something in there in case things get rough," Richard instructed.

"Understood," Jeremiah replied and ran into the vehicle, which had room enough for twelve fully armored Soldiers. The two doors closed behind Jeremiah and the interior lights turned on, transforming night into day. Rebecca asked the group if the temperature was satisfactory, then told the APC commander, in Spanish, to raise the temperature a few degrees. They all strapped themselves in with five point seat belts.

"These Soldiers aren't American," said Jeremiah. "Who are they, Rebecca?"

"They're South American Soldiers from the battle cruiser *Doris* sent in to rescue us," Rebecca answered.

Jeremiah was mesmerized at the high quality of comfort and state-of-the-art gadgetry in the armored personnel carrier. A console to the front showed a live feed of what the vehicle's commander was looking at. Several digital consoles displayed inside and outside temperatures, direction of travel, speed, and location, vital signs of the squad, and air purity inside and outside of the vehicle. There was also a small digital map of the area. Jeremiah admired how these people rose from a cluster of third-world countries to possibly the strongest nation in existence.

Jeremiah looked at Rebecca. She sat as if nothing in the world could hurt her now.

*She seems so at home,* Jeremiah thought.

"Creator," Larcis called on his comlink, "everyone's in the APC, but Mrs. Hitoshi was wounded in a fire fight a few minutes ago. She's stabilized, but we need to complete this mission quickly so they can be taken to a hospital or Mrs. Hitoshi will die."

"It might be over very soon," said Richard. "You and Mindseye track my comlink location and get down here as fast as you can."

"On our way, boss," Larcis replied while grabbing John's outstretched hand.

Lieutenant Alejandro approached Richard. "We have spotted six scouts on this street and Laguna Street one block down," he reported.

"It has begun, lieutenant," Richard said. "Tell the other APC to move to your extraction point and move half of your squad down this street. Night and Mindseye will help your men on this side, while your APC and I will go down Laguna Street."

Lieutenant Alejandro looked at Creator calmly. "I'm not supposed to tell you this, but my commander is authorized to use offshore artillery and more if needed. That is not something either side wants, so we must prevent this from happening at all cost."

Richard knew that the threat was no bluff. He felt uneasy about the amount of power these people were willing to use for only two people.

"For all our sakes, I hope we don't have to cross that line, Lieutenant. Can your men take care of the scouts quietly?"

"It's being done as we speak," Alejandro stated.

The hostile scouts silently and quickly disappeared in the shadows, overtaken by the Soldiers in ambush positions. The APC maneuvered to Laguna Street and prepared for battle.

"Creator, is something wrong?" Katherine asked, noticing Richard's uneasiness.

"Yes, Katherine. Can you contact Linda?"

"No, I don't know where she is. Why?"

Richard looked straight into Katherine's eyes. "If I don't defeat Sargon, Quatris and Hellfire will. But I fear they won't be able to stop the South Americans from destroying the city with their ships. If Linda is as powerful as you say she is, we need her to help us stop a war."

"I'm sorry, Creator," Kat said. "All we can hope for is for her to come in her own time."

Richard felt tense but spoke kindly: "You must try and somehow let her know what's at stake."

"I'll try," said Kat. She closed her eyes and concentrated, feeling her surroundings, calling out to her friend. *Linda, I hope you can hear me. Sargon has no chance of winning. If Creator cannot stop him, the South Americans will. We cannot allow this to happen, or we will be responsible for not peace but a war between South America and the U.S. Please, Linda, we need your help. I know that you have the power to stop Sargon. Please help us.*

Katherine opened her eyes and turned to Richard. "I don't know if she heard me. I guess it's up to you."

"Swell, come on. Make sure you stay close to me," Richard instructed.

The APC took a defensive position in the middle of the street, while Larcis and John joined the dismounted infantry in an adjacent street. The dull black armored suits blended with the shadows when the men shot out the streetlights. A few hundred men several hundred meters away charged the group of Soldiers on Stiener Street. The convicts shot flares into the night sky, illuminating the entire area. Night and his team fired at the mob, easily putting down fifty people with automatic fire and electricity.

A horde of men firing with various types of rifles and submachine guns attacked the APC and dismounted Soldiers. The ill-aimed rounds merely annoyed everyone in the group. A box on the turret of the APC opened to reveal four mortar tubes the size of a man's fist. The apparatus made a loud popping as it catapulted four metal canisters so that they arched above the street's highest buildings. The canisters hit the pavement in a scattered formation covering an area two blocks deep into the most populated portion of the crowd. The canisters exploded, sending white smoke in all directions.

A handful of men fell as the smoke was quickly blown away by an explosion of air. The knockout gas would have been more effective if Sargon had not dispersed it with his telekinesis. Now the Soldiers would have to take stronger measures.

The APC's main 105-millimeter short-barrel gun fired a high-explosive round that hit the center of the crowd. More than two-dozen men were shredded to death from shrapnel, another dozen were killed by the implosion, and more than four dozen were wounded from burns and secondary fragments. The buildings, to the right and left, caught fire.

The Soldiers opened fire with well-aimed shots as the scopes on their rifles and protective visors projected virtual targeting pictures in their helmets. Richard looked at the carnage and wondered how stupid these people were. Most of them simply stood there or ran for cover without retaliating. A lucky shot hit the visor of one of the South American Soldiers. It didn't penetrate into the helmet, but it effectively put the Soldier out of commission.

Richard looked farther out with his enhanced vision and saw a man wearing black clothes standing on the hood of a truck. He assumed it was Sargon, only a superhuman or fool would stand out in the open like that.

The APC commander locked his sights on the truck and fired another high-explosive round. The round exploded in midair just shy of the truck. The normal concussion effects cleared the area to the front of the truck, but nothing around the truck was touched.

Sargon's face strained as he raised his arm as if lifting an invisible object. The APC's front track section lifted off the ground, then the rear section. The APC flipped backward as if it were a Tonka toy in a playful child's imagination. The passengers were tossed around, spraining their joints and bruising their bodies as the APC hit the ground.

"Get your men out of the street," Richard screamed at the lieutenant. "I'll take care of Sargon!"

Richard raised his arms and shot a massive telekinetic pulse at Sargon. Two men who happened to be in the line of fire were cut in two. But nothing happened to the truck which was just 300 meters away and closing fast. Creator was fighting a telekinetic superhuman with his own telekinetic powers. The stronger of the two would have the advantage, but that didn't keep Creator from fighting to the end.

Night's team had managed to kill or wound roughly two hundred convicts by this time. The Soldiers started to pair up, taking what seemed to be RPG-7 anti-tank rounds from the back of their backpacks. Three of the Soldiers put the grenades on their rifles and lobbed them at the major areas of resistance. Three explosions went off almost simultaneously, sending bodies and body parts in all directions. The explosions were very large encompassing a fifty meter diameter spherical area each. They seemed like 152mm artillery rounds except with the incoming sound. Debris of rocks fell everywhere after a pulse of air was felt from Night's position. A hundred men remained only to run for their lives in the opposite direction.

"Why the hell didn't you guys do that in the first place?" Larcis yelled, but he was ignored as if none of the Soldiers understood English.

"Oh yeah, now no one habla English!" Larcis continued, not being able to see some of them slightly grin through their helmet covered faces.


The horde on Richard's street finally got behind cover while the truck came to a complete stop. Sargon extended both arms. A shock wave of invisible energy caught the entire group and threw them back twenty to thirty meters. Richard quickly stood up and looked around. The Soldiers slowly stood to their feet. The sudden force would have killed or knocked out normal people without any sort of padding or protection.

"Larcis, I need help up here. Can you disperse the crowd?"

"On my way, boss," Larcis said.

Richard stepped in front of Katherine and spoke. "Are you alright?"

Katherine moaned a little in acknowledgment, trying to get up. Richard concentrated, trying to create a tight telekinetic beam. He let it all out, hitting beneath the truck. The ground under the truck moved aside, yielding to Creator's will. The truck fell six feet into the trench created by the beam, almost causing Sargon to fall from the hood of the truck. The terrified and dazed driver crawled out of the passenger's window.

A second later a gust of wind passed Richard's position as he saw a streak of light fly towards the truck. A sonic boom shattered glass and deafened eardrums as Night flew over the truck, disappearing half a mile to the south, almost hitting the high part of the hilly street. Six extra Soldiers and John joined the fight with grenades ready for launch. Sargon stood up, shooting another shock wave, knocking out the first group of Soldiers and Katherine, scattering them twenty meters behind Richard. The new Soldiers launched their grenades. Three projectiles hit near the truck, killing or wounding the remaining convicts. But Sargon remained untouched.

Sargon was extremely angry as he looked at the devastation around him. Richard stood in front of the APC, hoping that if Sargon would attack again it would keep him close to the battle. In addition he was now using his flight ability to stabilize himself in position so that Sargon's telekinetic blasts would have less effect on him when being pushed around. Sargon turned around and raised his hand. Night, trying to come back for another pass, hit an invisible barrier at supersonic speed and fell almost lifeless to the ground 150 meters behind the truck.

The Soldiers launched another salvo of grenades. The grenades made it halfway to their intended target only to explode in midair. Richard knew that his telekinetic blasts were not getting through Sargon's force field, so he changed tactics.

*We could use a stun rifle right about now,* Richard thought, and then he put his hands together as if in prayer. He concentrated on Sargon's image and shot a telepathic blast of anger into his mind.

Sargon felt the mental attack and momentarily paused to recover. He looked at Creator, who seemed to be holding his own against his attacks while Katherine and six Soldiers lay motionless on the ground several meters in front of the APC.

"You'll have to do better than that," Sargon taunted even though he was too far away to be normally heard.

The new Soldiers and John scrambled to get into covered positions. Sargon focused on Creator, putting all he had in a massive telekinetic shock wave. The Soldiers and John were thrown backward like leaves in a hurricane. Richard flew backward, colliding with the APC's rear at full force. The APC's tracks scraped into the concrete about twenty meters as Richard's body pushed it. Richard's back ached with pain.

*Damn, this APC is hard!* Richard thought as he almost blacked out not being ready to be hit on the head from behind, but then shook himself back to reality.

Richard focused his mind with all he had on Sargon. The mental attack hit Sargon, dazing him for a moment. Richard was exhausted and in pain for the first time in years. He stood at the ready trying to recover. He decided to use his telekinetic blast, hoping Sargon was weakened enough not to block it. The blast took less out of him than the mental attacks, and he knew he only had one more chance before Sargon knocked him out. The invisible projectile left Richard's hands cutting through the air, hitting Sargon's invisible force wall.

Richard's look of discouragement was hidden by the bleakness of the ravished street. Sargon smiled and started to raise his hands. The air thickened and everything got darker as Sargon's muscles froze. Richard and two South American Soldiers tried with all their might to move or speak.

*What the hell's happening? I feel totally numb,* Richard thought as he saw Sargon standing motionless as a statue.

A wave of horror hit Sargon's mind, causing him to black out. His body stood erect and petrified, as was Richard's body.

*I told you I would help you if you guaranteed our reprieve,* Linda said into Richard's mind as she glided down in front of him. *Sargon would have won. Alone I could not have taken him. But you were able to get his army out of the way and weaken him for me to fight him. I ask you now, Creator, will you help us?*

Richard looked across the hundreds of dead and wounded people.

*I give you my word. Linda. I will not stop until you and Katherine have been given a second chance.*

Instantly Richard had control of his body again. The two Soldiers walked up to Richard, looking for some guidance on what to do next. Sargon fell face-first, lifeless, on the hood of the truck. Linda placed her index finger close to her forehead, and all of the Soldiers as well as John, Larcis, and Katherine woke up.

"I have revived the others," Linda said. "Promise me you will take Sargon away and place him in a superhuman confinement cell."

"You have my promise," Richard said.

Richard told the Soldiers to get Sargon while he turned the APC to its upright position. Katherine stood up slowly as a hand grabbed her arm, helping her rise.

"Linda!" Katherine looked up, surprisingly happy, while blood dripped from her mouth.

Linda smiled as she wiped away the blood.

"Did you really think you would be alone?" Linda asked.

"Did we win?" said Katherine.

"Yes, Kat, we won," Linda said as they hugged each other with joy.

The crew and survivors in the APC were by and large only battered and bruised. The Soldiers climbed on top of the

APC and drove off toward Lincoln Park. Richard and his group flew to the extraction point carrying Sargon.

"Sir, we have a ship inside the sonar net just west of the Golden Gate Bridge," Agent Latimer reported.

"What ship?" Max asked, not a bit surprised.

"It looks like a submarine," Agent Kennedy yelled from a distant computer console. "We're getting an unscrambled radio message from the ship."

"Put it on speaker," Max directed.

"This is Captain Carlos P. Hernandez, commander of the *Doris*. We are retrieving our men from Lincoln Park Beach. We ask that you maintain your helicopters at bay until our landing craft has departed the beach. I give you my personal guarantee that the survivors of flight 0292 will not be kidnapped or hurt in any way. Please comply."

"This is Randolph Maximilian, director of SIA. We understand and will comply. Can you inform us when your craft has moved off the breach?"

"Affirmative, Director. And thank you for your cooperation."

"Sir, Quatris is on the line," Agent Kennedy reported.

"Put him through, Mr. Kennedy."

"Max, everyone is going back home—after some coercion, of course," Quatris said as he and Hellfire stood by twenty very large craters and thousands of discarded weapons along the south wall.

"Creator has accomplished his mission. You two can come back to headquarters. They will need a ride back home," Max reported.

"We're on our way," Quatris replied.

"Oh, and thanks." Max signed off. "Agent Kennedy, contact headquarters and tell them that the sonar screen doesn't work. We obviously have a long way to go to be able to pick up those South American ships."

The armored carriers plowed through the wet sand as the shuttle waited with its ramp down. Creator's party and the survivors waited on the shore as one carrier was swallowed up by the long shuttle. General Fox and Linsan were stabilized once again by the beta-team doctor in the carrier. Roberto, the South American lieutenant, took off his helmet and approached Richard, as Linsan and Eugene were off-loaded from the last personnel carrier.

"Creator, can I speak to you, your team, and General Cartier in private?" Lieutenant Alejandro asked with a Spanish accent.

Richard looked at the dark-haired middle-aged lieutenant and said, "Sure, I'll go get them."

Richard, Larcis, John, Katherine, Linda, Thomas, and Wendy huddled around Roberto.

"I apologize for my commander, but Captain Hernandez is busy aboard the *Doris*. I am here on a request from Ms. Palmer. If you may, Ma'am," Roberto introduced.

Wendy stood next to Roberto, staring at Thomas as she spoke. "I wanted you all here for several reasons, but especially for you, Thomas. This complex has taken many lives, and fortunately things were kept from escalating. I want to thank the Eternal Champions and you two brave ladies for saving our lives and trusting these Soldiers...and...thank you, Thomas, for being like a father to me, and a friend. I had hoped to let you know under better circumstances, but I didn't expect the situation to get this way," Wendy said softly as tears slowly rolled down her cheeks.

Thomas gazed at Wendy, bewildered. "What are you saying, Wendy?"

"Thomas...Patricia and Rebecca will be leaving with the Soldiers. The Federation Council doesn't want them to be subject to news reporters or law-enforcement agencies. I will also be going with the Soldiers. Whatever friendship we have, please understand," Wendy pleaded.

Gloom transfigured Thomas's face as Wendy continued.

"My real name is Sandra Clayborn. I am the wife of James Clayborn, admiral of the Federation Pacific Fleet. I have been a South American spy for sixteen years.... I would never dream of hurting you, or all of those who entrusted their lives and hearts to me. I was recruited as an orphan at the age of twelve." Sandra paused, as the others remained spellbound.

"Thomas, I knew what I was doing. I saw what was coming and understood what South America has in store for mankind. I love the U.S. and I know that asking you to trust me would be a great mistake for you right now, but please, Thomas.

If you trust anything about me, trust my judgment." Sandra paused again partially wiping tears off her cheeks.

"Patricia and Rebecca will continue to support the space effort.... Trust them. They will get the U.S. beyond the moon. And don't worry about the secrets I have. They only confirm what we already knew or predicted. I want you to remember that South America is not bent on killing or enslaving people.... Please forgive me," Sandra pleaded.

Thomas stood silent, looking at the floor as Richard spoke to Sandra.

"What rank are you?"

Sandra turned her head toward Richard.

"I am a lieutenant commander in the Special Operations Legion."

"If you don't mind answering this, how did you pass the mandatory mind scan by the SIA Security Department?" Richard quaintly asked.

Sandra took a moderate breath and signed.

"We use telepaths to train doctors, engineers, translators; in fact, everyone— on all types of subjects. I was very young, so the telepaths were able to teach me how to block mind scans, how to know when I was being scanned, and how to modify my thoughts and memory."

"Hmmm... I see," said Richard. "Well, the choppers will be here soon." He paused, with a sarcastic tilt of his head toward Sandra. "Unless they've been shot down."

Richard knew that Sandra's situation with General Thomas needed some privacy, so he continued to talk. "I suggest we say our goodbyes and part ways. Lieutenant Alejandro, thank you on behalf of all of us for the help."

Richard shook Roberto's hand and left the group.

The huddle quickly dispersed, leaving Thomas and Sandra alone.

"You couldn't tell me?" Thomas asked, heartbroken and in disbelief.

"If I had told you, Thomas, I would have been compromised once someone scanned you," Sandra explained.

"I see. So it wasn't that you couldn't trust me."

Sandra smiled as she finished drying her cheeks with her shirtsleeve.

"No, Thomas. I love you as my own father. The borders will open very soon. I hope you will visit me in Venezuela."

"It would be my pleasure to meet your husband in person."

Thomas grinned as he regained his composure and hugged Sandra farewell.

Katherine stayed by Richard's side as he checked on General Fox and Linsan.

Larcis and John stood watching in case unexpected gang stragglers wanted revenge.

Linda walked up to the two men and asked, "What are you two doing?"

"We're pulling security," Larcis proudly answered.

"There's no need for you to do that," Linda responded.

*And why not?* John caustically asked.

"They know I'm here. They know that I will make the last seconds of their lives a living eternity of incalculable burning anguish and horror that hell itself cannot imitate." Linda devilishly smiled and tossed her long black hair over her shoulder. "But don't worry, boys," she added as she walked away. "I'll protect you."

"She scares me," said Larcis.

*She's hot!* John said with a wide grin.

Katherine stayed by Richard's side and helped him take Sargon off the APC, making sure he was still sedated. The Soldiers were about to leave, when Richard hailed Roberto.

"Lieutenant, can you wait a moment?"

"Yes, Creator, why?" Roberto replied.

"Wait a second and I'll explain."

Richard called for Linda to join the three of them.

Richard tapped his comlink. "Max, have you found the information I requested?"

"Yes, I have. Linda Manchester was sentenced to Complex San Francisco for twenty-three counts of first-degree murder. Her parents were supposedly killed by an organization called the Founders, but there was insufficient evidence to implicate them. In return, Linda killed all of the people who had substantial ties to the Founders. She has been in the complex for almost seven months now. As for Katherine Fletcher, she was sentenced to the complex for three counts of first-degree murder, trafficking of illegal substances, and prostitution. They both have life terms without parole."

"Max," Richard said, "if they had not intervened, we would be at war with South America and more innocent people would have died. I know that you can't get a reprieve for them, but I need to know right now if you will personally talk to President Baxter and get them a presidential pardon."

"Creator, I know they served their country and saved many lives, but they also committed murder. The president will think that they helped us out because it was in their best interest. I need more meat to give the president so that he can be assured they will not commit more crimes once he gives them a get-out-of-jail-free card."

Linda and Katherine looked at Richard.

"I have the South American team leader with me now," Richard said. "I can make sure that Katherine and Linda get on the *Doris* and live a good and free life in South America. However, I have a feeling that they love this country as much as I do. They have proven to me that they are not cold-blooded killers as everyone thinks. You want more meat? Okay. I want you to tell the president that I will be personally responsible for Katherine and Linda. They will work for me as part of the team.

Call me their parole officer or guardian if you will, but I need your help on this, Max."

"I'll talk to him for you. But remember this, Creator, you will owe me," Max sternly stated.

"What's new?" Richard commented.

"The Blackhawks will be there after the landing crafts leave," Max said. "Our ground troops will also accompany them to retrieve the dead passengers from the plane, and help the injured in the city; so don't be alarmed at their presence. See you in a little while. I need to get busy. Max out."

Richard faced Linda and Katherine. "You have three options. You can stay here. You can go with the lieutenant and live in South America for the rest of your lives. Or you can take a chance and follow me."

"I will not go back to prison!" Linda coldly declared. "I don't know much about South America. But what I do know is that I will not be a slave to the courts or anyone else if I do go with these Soldiers." Linda added with a calm soft voice as if having doubts.

Katherine looked at Linda in dismay. "Linda, listen to me. We will be pardoned, and we have to trust Creator. If you leave with them, you will always be running away from yourself."

Linda stared deep into Kat's compassionate eyes. "Kat, we can be free and happy if we go with the Soldiers."

"I've always been free, Linda, in here," Kat said as she placed her hand on her heart. "Please stay."

Linda looked away and thought deeply for a long moment.

"I've always liked a challenge." She looked at Creator. "Where are we going?"

"Fort Lauderdale, Florida," Richard said, more concerned about being candid than secretive.

Katherine's face shined with joy as she kissed Richard on the cheek. "Thank you, Creator."

Richard lightly blushed as both women smiled.

The shuttle left the beach and the Blackhawks came in, taking the survivors to safety while Richard and his team flew back to SFTF central.

Max, Hellfire, and Quatris waited for the five heroes. Creator landed first. The rest of the group landed behind him.

"What's going on?" Richard asked.

"I'll be seeing the President tomorrow with a full report. Katherine and Linda are now your sole responsibility. I figured you didn't want to spend a long flight in a plane, so Quatris and Hellfire will take you back home," Max explained.

Richard looked at Max, Hellfire, and Quatris. "Thanks."

"It's on our way home. Really?" Quatris replied, even though EFL headquarters was in New York.

"I will go by myself," Larcis declined.

"Are you sure?" Richard asked.

"Yeah," Larcis said. "Besides, I don't want to be carried, especially since I will only be a few minutes behind you. Take off, boss, I'll be alright."

Thirty minutes later, the group landed back in the swamp and said farewell to Hellfire and Quatris. Katherine looked around at the dense saw grass and water.

"You don't live out here, do you?" Kat asked.

"No, we live in a large house. I've been thinking about this since we left, and I can't just decide to give away our secret identities alone. Mindseye, I need you to agree to letting them know who we really are."

*You always seem to give me the hard problems to solve,* John told Richard in his thoughts. *But this one is easy. They're not obligated to stay with us, but we could use their help and friendship. So yes, I agree to your plan.*

"Night, we need your vote to allow Katherine and Linda to know our identities. Yes or No?" Richard said over the comlink.

"Boss, do I really have a choice?" Larcis replied back.

"Yes, Night. But if it helps, a yes would be nice."

"Well, then, it's a yes!" Night said confidently. "By the way, where are you guys?"

"We're in the swamp. Go straight to the house. We'll be there soon," Richard said. "Now for the last member of the group." Richard contacted Erica. "Erica, what's your vote?"

"Considering your judge of character, Creator, I will follow your human instinct. Yes, Richard, it's okay with me."

"Good," Richard said, taking his sunglasses off, his face and hair turned into Richard's appearance. "I am Richard Octavian, and this is John Goodman."

Katherine smiled as she saw Richard's true face. This was not the first time she saw Richard, but now she knew that Creator and Richard were the same person.

"Let's go," Richard said. "We'll introduce you to the other two members."

Richard led the way into the water duct, created by the erected landing tube from ED's machine shop, and into the Eternal Domain. Richard, John, and Night changed into their normal selves, and everyone settled quickly and went to sleep after a hard night's adventure.


### Counterespionage Agency Headquarters, Alexandria Virginia

"This is Becky Owens reporting for Channel 10 News."

The video recording ended, and the television screen changed to a website browser window. A white-haired woman sat behind her office desk rolling her fingers on the black cloth armchair. Her deep blue eyes revealed hatred and contempt. The nameplate on the desk read Director Jean Lorenz. The report on the Eternal Champions saving the hostages in Complex San Francisco stirred yet another type of fire in her heart. Superhuman groups had started to emerge in 1978, but many failed to stay together and wear the mantles of truth and justice.

Jean had failed to bring down the two groups that resisted her attempts to take control. Jean hated how EFL and the Emerald Legion who defied the courts by forcing their will on the public and the authorities. No one would challenge EFL for fear of being vaporized by Quatris's legionary anti-matter blast, and no one could ever find the Emerald Legion's headquarters. Jean spent four years trying to find something to pin on those two egotistical groups. Now there was *another* group hindering her rise in power.

"Emily, get Mr. Patterson in here—immediately," Jean said via intercom.

"Yes, ma'am, right away."

Jean, wearing a dark blue business jacket and skirt, stood. She kept her white hair cut to within two millimeters of her shoulders. She said "lights," and the room automatically brightened. She stared out at the city lights and waited for Patterson while devising her strategy to eliminate the superhero influence. A well-dressed man in a black two-piece suit entered the office a few minutes later.

"You called for me, Director."

"Yes, I did. I want you to accelerate Project Jane. You will gather all of the information you can find about this new group called the Eternal Champions. Take all steps necessary to keep Jane and the CEA (Counterespionage Agency for the Presidential Task Force in Criminal and Abnormal Investigations) in the shadows. Jane and the CEA *must* remain in the background," Jean commanded. "I want you to report directly to me when you find out who these heroes are. Understood?"

"Yes, ma'am. What about SIA?"

Jean looked at the ceiling with a crooked smile.

"We don't work for them, and they sure as hell don't work for us. Max will have his hands full once Poseidon gets underway, so make sure the president and Max don't find out about your snooping around."

Patterson grinned. "Consider it done."

"What's the status of our team?" Jean said, changing the subject.

"Mr. Erickson is a little reluctant to believe our stories and the intent of the mission. However, he seems to be open to your charms. It would help greatly if you were to reinforce what we have told him."

"Tell me again why he isn't expendable," Jean asked, trying to justify her having not to see Jared once again.

"He is the expert tactician and leader of the group," Patterson pointed out. "He's also the best illusionist we have."

Jean thought for a moment. "Well, I suppose. I will see him in a few hours," Jean stated, a little annoyed yet somewhat complacent.

Patterson placed one hand over the other in front of him down to his waist. "Is that all, Director?"

Jean's bright blue eyes leveled on Patterson. "No mistakes. No delays. No excuses." Jean spoke with a deadly cold face. "Is that understood?"

Patterson coldly responded, "Understood."

"Good. You can go now," Jean commanded.

Patterson turned and left the room, stroking his full beard. The six-foot African-American sneered at the thought that he was not in charge of the CEA. Jean had engineered the perfect organization to legally commit crimes against superhumans and anyone who stood in their way. He didn't care, though. Jean was sometimes sentimental and weak compared to him. Time was on his side as the third phase of Project Jane was underway. Jean's plans would soon backfire, and he would reap the rewards.

Jean sat looking out over the city through her office's wall of glass. As a girl, she had been helpless to save her younger sister, who had been a powerful superhuman—too powerful to be permitted to live, some thought. Watery tears rose to her eyes. The execution of her sister, her only true family, had been at the hands of superhumans and humans. So the urge for revenge fuelled Jean's desire to kill both superhumans and humans; no matter the cost, even her own soul.

# Chapter Ten

✠ - ✠

# Wipeout

### The Eternal Domain

Erica, give me the usual local highlights first instead of national and global news," Richard requested, half asleep.

"As you wish, Richard. There were two attempted bank robberies, one at Sun Bank in downtown Miami, and the other in Barnett Bank, Tamarac. All three robbers are in custody and no one was injured. Miami-Dade Police Officer Philip Gibson was killed in what is believed to be a gang-related drive-by shooting two days ago. Courtney Smith, a twenty-year-old secretary, was reported missing three days ago. She was last seen in the vicinity of Second Street and Fourth Avenue, North Miami Beach. Sue Young Chang, a senior, was raped at Sunset Senior High School three days ago. The suspected rapist is being held in custody pending an initial hearing. Walter Marien, a known mobster, was murdered last night while swimming in his private pool. It is believed that Lambert Hunt might be involved. Police still have a nationwide bulletin on Hunt's whereabouts in connection with Simon Carluchi's death three weeks ago. Tropical Storm Pedro Cano is continuing to move west by northwest through the Gulf of Mexico. The Miami District court ruled against school restriction in the case *Dade-County School District* v. *Anthony Nieves,* declaring it unconstitutional to restrict a child from attending school because of believed or confirmed superhuman abilities."

Erica paused as she changed to a different scale.

"At national level, we have made the headlines, which say that the Eternal Champions are the new breed of crime-fighters. Senator Carpenter, Senator Hawkins, and Judge Mitchell have been arrested for the Complex San Francisco conspiracy. President Bush appointed a committee to investigate the situation and come up with proposals for a better rehab system within the next two months. There have been a total of two bank robberies, ten attempted bank robberies, and one bank fire in the past six weeks. The two successful robberies occurred in Jackson, Tennessee, and Carson City, Nevada. A total of $474,350 mysteriously disappeared from the two banks. The only evidence of the culprits was a small statue of a stainless-steel hawk placed in the center of the Carson City bank vault. This is the third incident involving a stainless-steel hawk in the past three years," Erica expounded, "in case you were wondering."

"CNN, says that Australia has pledged £9.3 billion to North Korea in exchange for a government business expansion within North Korea. Israeli Prime Minister Hadan visited Egyptian President Casmir in an attempt to settle the disputes in the Suez Neutral Zone. The Federation Council formally thanked President Bush for his support in the Complex San Francisco rescue and announced its support for the U.S. space program. South Africa, to date, has suffered more than 3,300 deaths in four months of civil war. The war is predicted to come to a close within the next few months," Erica concluded.

"Thanks, Erica," Richard said, rubbing his eyes. "How are Katherine and Linda doing?"

"They are currently sleeping comfortably in the rooms you assigned them."

"They're sleeping." Richard looked at his watch. "Erica, what time is it?"

"It's 08:32 hours, Richard."

Richard frowned in frustration as it dawned on him that he had slept only three hours. The change in time zones and late crime fighting had interfered with his sleep schedule.

"Well, I might as well go downstairs and make breakfast."

The elevator door opened, letting out the elevator's blue light into Erica's main computer battle room. The room was dimly lit with green, white, and red ceiling and wall lamps. Creator stepped in with a serving cart full of assorted breads and bagels, cold cuts, warm meats, cheese, fruits, eggnog, mild drinks, and finger foods.

The battle room resembled an extravagant living room, conversation pit, and movie room all rolled into one. The ninety-inch screen on the east wall was centered between two bookshelves extending six feet in either direction and containing an assortment of books—novels, encyclopedias, technical books, and books on mythology. The room was open in the rear, connecting the elevator door, two hallways, a second kitchen, and three guestrooms. A glossy-black thirty-inch dome on the ceiling in the middle of the room projected Erica's hologram and monitored every electronic component in the lower levels. The Ferahan Sarouk carpet in the center of the room complemented the leather furniture and mahogany woodwork. Two smaller screens with video cameras on the south wall displayed muted CNN and local news. Various framed pictures on the walls displaying landscapes, abstract art, and sailing scenes surrounded the area.

"Medium lights," Richard said. The battle room brightened from very low to moderate lighting. "Repeat the clips from the local and national reports, audible and half-size, on the main screen."

"Initiating with Channel 7 Nightly News for September 26," said Erica as Richard set the breakfast meals on the kitchen bar. Katherine appeared from her guestroom wearing a peach-colored cotton robe over a T-shirt and white shorts. Her hair was wrapped in a towel.

"Good morning," said Richard. "Did I wake you up?"

"No. Erica told me breakfast was served while I was taking a bath."

Richard never told Erica to inform Katherine that her brunch was ready, but he guessed that's why she was called an SAI computer.

"Hmmmm. Thank you, Erica."

"You're welcome, Richard," Erica replied as she paused the news clips.

Katherine walked up to the table and looked at the brunch buffet Richard had put together.

"Wow," Kat said in delight, "did you put all of this together by yourself, Richard?"

"Yes, I did. It's one of my hobbies."

"That's an impressive hobby!" Kat said as she sat down. She tasted a sandwich and added, "Your girlfriend must be a very lucky girl!" She'd already noticed that Richard wore no wedding ring.

Richard nibbled at a sandwich.

"No," Richard said nonchalantly. "I don't have a girlfriend. We split up a month ago."

"Really? That's too bad for her."

Richard forced himself not to react. He liked Kat very much, and her show of interest in him made him feel uncomfortable. He had never been good in relationships with the opposite sex. The only difference between Kat and his previous girlfriends was that she knew he was a superhuman.

"You know," Richard said, eager to change the subject, "everyone else is still sleeping. Why aren't you?"

"I can't sleep when I'm very happy," Kat said as if in a trance. "This is the first time in a very long time that I've felt I didn't have to watch my back. I kept tossing and turning the more

I thought about what I was going to do in the morning, so I couldn't sleep."

"Really, and what did you come up with?"

"Well, for starters, you don't have a big selection of clothes. I thought I might be able to go shopping, watch a movie, see the beach, or something like that—you know, something simple."

"I apologize for the clothes. We got generic non-gender specific clothes for temporary use. We didn't feel right about having a bunch of women's clothes around, especially since you two are the first women to step into the base. As for going out, we'll need to get you and Linda new identities so that you don't attract attention to yourself or this place," Richard said as he moved to the center of the battle room next to the sofa.

Kat swung around with a tray full of food and placed it on the glass table.

"So how do you plan to get us new identities?" Kat asked as she sat on the sofa and dipped a piece of sandwich in chocolate milk.

"Easy. Erica, bring up Katherine's records, full screen," Richard said, and sat next to Kat.

Erica projected views of Katherine's old driver's license, her birth certificate, criminal records identifying information, and her school reports up to ninth grade.

"You never finished high school?" Richard asked.

"No," said Kat. "My parents died when I was fourteen. I was put into an orphanage, but I ran away a few months later. I had no idea what I was doing. In a way I didn't really care since my parents were dead and I just wanted to feel free."

"Is that what got you into this mess with the law?" Richard asked.

"Yeah, you could say that. I learned how to survive by stealing, lying, and seducing people. I got involved with organized crime, and everything went downhill from there. I didn't do what I was told and a hit was put on my head, because I insulted a client when I didn't give him sexual favors. I killed the two hit men who tried to kill me," Kat explained, "and one of the family godfathers had me framed for murder."

Kat was the first female superhuman he had encountered in seventy-two years. Yes, he had heard of female superheroes, but he had never actually met one long enough to start a conversation.

"Why didn't you use your powers to expose the frame-up?"

"They had hired a telepath to temporarily work for them. That's how they found me and had the assassins try to kill me. In court they countered my abilities and covered the fact that I was a superhuman. When I heard the sentence, I knew they had something in store for me in the complex. So immediately after I entered the complex, I sided with the strongest leader for protection."

"Sargon." Richard said.

"Yes, Sargon. Linda came a few months later. She didn't want anything to do with anyone, but Sargon caught on to her powers when she killed his extortion team. That's when I was sent in to get her on our side. Linda and I became very good friends. She even saved my life when the Carluchi family sent an assassin to try a second time to kill me."

"Well, you don't have to worry about the Carluchi family anymore."

"What do you mean?"

"It seems someone killed Mr. Carluchi a few months ago," Richard stated, remembering Erica's news highlights.

"Richard, Mr. Carluchi will only be replaced by one of his sons. Plus, they are not the only ones who want me dead."

"You might be right, but I have a feeling the person with a vendetta against Mr. Carluchi is not done. But most importantly, they won't know you exist, because you will now be known as a normal, everyday working woman. Erica, alter all of Katherine's records with a similar face and complete fingerprints and dental records," Richard ordered. "Reconstruct an entire history since birth, to include her parents' deaths two years ago from a fire."

"Alteration complete," Erica replied as a blank Floridian birth certificate appeared on the screen.

"What new name do you want for yourself?" Richard asked Kat.

Kat looked at the screen. "You mean I can pick whoever I want to be?"

"Not exactly. We don't want you to assume someone else's identity or history. Erica will create a perfect history and identity for you as if you really did exist. So what name do you want to go by?" Richard asked again.

"How about Elizabeth? Yes, Elizabeth Armstrong," Kat decided.

"Erica," Richard said.

Kat's license and birth certificate automatically reflected the name change to Elizabeth Armstrong. The Florida license issue date was July 6, 1995.

"When do you want to be born?" Erica asked.

"Hmmmm… November 5th, 1969," Elizabeth replied.

"Okay, now give her three other IDs—one as an undercover DEA officer, another as an insurance-fraud investigator, and the last one as a computer consultant," Creator told Erica.

"I don't know anything about being an investigator or computers." Elizabeth countered.

"You will," Richard assured her.

John stepped out of the elevator barefooted, wearing slacks and a red Polo shirt.

*Good morning. What's for lunch?* John asked.

"The table is open game, but leave some for Larcis and Linda," said Richard.

*I'm not a pig like you, Richard,* John joked.

"Why don't you talk?" Elizabeth asked, noticing that John didn't move his lips.

*I can't,* John said in his thoughts as he stuffed his face with a sandwich. *I was born dumb.*

"I'm sorry."

*Don't be. It wasn't your fault, Kat.*

"My name is Elizabeth," Elizabeth said with a smile.

*Oh, alright,* John replied with an unbelieving and slightly interested face.

"Kat is now Elizabeth Armstrong," Richard explained.

*Well, can I call you Liz?* John asked as he seated himself on the sofa chair.

Liz smiled. "Sure!"

The group session was interrupted by a scream from the guestroom down the hall.

"Erica, what's going on?" Richard asked while John led the group down the hall.

"Ms. Lancaster's alpha waves are fluctuating in an REM transition."

"What?" Liz asked as John entered Linda's room.

"She's having a nightmare." Richard explained.

Liz and Richard stood outside the room as John grabbed Linda in the corner by the bed. Linda, terrified and disoriented, looked at John only to project a wave of horror in his direction.

John grabbed his head, grimacing, before blacking out from pain and fear.

"Erica!" Richard signaled.

Erica II materialized in the middle of the room, expelling a red beam of light into Linda's head. Linda's crouched body collapsed onto the tile floor. Liz ran to Linda, while Richard took a look at John.

"Erica, check their vitals," Richard ordered.

"Checking... Ms. Lancaster will recover shortly. John's nervous system is causing him to lose critical muscle functions. His brain is killing him. He's starting to go into shock."

"How can we stop it?" Richard said as he held John.

Linda woke up as Liz listened to Erica's diagnoses.

"Let me try," Liz said as she moved to John's side. Liz concentrated on forcing John to listen to her and touched his forehead. She dug into John's subconscious, picking up a void of coldness and darkness. Liz fell back as her own consciousness slipped away from her.

Richard caught Liz by the arm. "Are you alright?"

"I can't get through to him," Liz said, a little dazed.

Linda, waking up, coherently analyzed the situation and moved to John's side in front of Liz.

"Let me. John, nothing has happened to you."

John's body shook, and then was still.

"His vital signs are returning to normal," Erica reported.

Linda walked off to the side of the bed and sat down.

"What happened, Linda?" Richard asked.

With tears running down her cheeks, Linda looked at the three. "I'm sorry, Richard. I didn't mean to hurt any of you."

Richard knelt in front of Linda.

"Everyone's fine," Richard said. "You were having a nightmare. Don't blame yourself for what happened."

John opened his eyes.

*What hit me?*

Liz's beautiful face smiled over him.

"Never, ever wake a woman up while she's in the middle of a dream!"

*Huh?* John said, completely dumbfounded.

Linda knelt in front of John.

*I'm sorry, John,* Linda told John privately. *I hope you're not angry with me.*

*I would never be angry with a gorgeous woman like you. Besides, I don't remember a thing,* John told her, hiding his visions of horror.

*You're so sweet,* Linda said, knowing he was hiding the truth.

"We have lunch in the other room. Care for something to eat while we get you a new name and childhood?" Richard asked Linda, noticing they were through mentally communicating.

Linda looked at Richard, feeling a little relieved. These two men were not like most other people she knew. They easily forgave and edified those around them with jokes, caring, and honesty.

They all moved to the battle room and munched on brunch as Linda picked out her new name and identities.

Richard handed Linda her new driver's license, which had on it the name Susan M. Sawczer. Linda smiled as she stared at the photo on the license.

"How did you do that, Erica?"

"Your image is maintained in my parallel multiplex database. I simply modified the digital characteristics and printed it into the standard license photo pixel image."

"Oh," said Susan. "Thank you, Erica."

"Alright. It's time to take you girls out," Richard said.

"Where to?" Susan asked.

"We can go to Dade-Land Mall, Omni Mall, or down to the Coral Cables shopping strip," Richard suggested.

Susan's eyes lit up, as she always wanted to go shopping in a very long time like a normal person. She ran off to change clothes.

Elizabeth stopped Richard as he put the plates into the sink.

"Is this going to be on credit?"

Richard smiled. "There is one thing I've learned about shopping with the opposite sex. No, you don't have any credit," Richard said without emotion.

"How are we going to get new clothes?" Liz said, disappointed.

Richard pulled out two silver bank money cards.

"This is not a credit card; it acts as a debt and credit card. You each have $40,000 in the accounts. So spend it wisely."

Richard smiled.

Liz glanced at the card and smiled, seeing it had her new name on it with a blank signature block on the back.

"Thank you, Richard."

The four went up to the living room. Susan and Liz were impressed by the house's decor. It was not a bachelor's choice type of interior design, it was well balanced with colors and even interesting two and three dimensional art. Unknown to the girls, Richard and Erica picked the final touches in all the buildings of the property. The only thing Larcis and John picked out were their room interiors and cars.

Larcis met the group as he came down the stairs.

"Hi," Larcis said, noticing that the others were on their way out. "Where's everybody going?"

"We're taking the girls shopping," Richard said. "You want to tag along?"

Larcis pictured himself lugging a truckload of packages and bags around the stores.

"No, that's alright. I'll work on my homework in the forensics lab for a few hours. Then I have to go see a friend before dinner," Larcis said, excusing himself from being a bellhop.

"Alright, we'll see you around six or seven," Richard said as he led the group to the garage.

Richard took Liz in his car, and John and Susan followed in the Mercedes with the top down.

They stopped first at Omni Mall, and then they went to Coral Cables. The four had a great time shopping for clothes and accessories. John never thought that shopping could be so enjoyable, especially since all heads turned in their direction as Susan and Liz showed off their natural beauty and new clothes.

They returned that afternoon with two carloads of clothes and accessories. Larcis called to let Richard know he was going club hopping down the strip and not make dinner. Richard and the gang decided to go out for dinner and dancing along the beachfront. Richard volunteered to drive the group, knowing that he was not going to get drunk. They ate an elegant Italian dinner and danced the major portion of the night away at several clubs and bars along the Miami beachfront. After 2 a.m. the couples took separate walks along the beach.

Richard took Liz on a long walk to get the alcohol out of her system. The cold water ebbed between their feet as Liz asked Richard many questions.

"Richard, why didn't the dragon affect you like it did on many other people I used it on?"

"Your illusion was very real, until you made me think I was bleeding," Richard replied.

"And what's wrong with that?" Liz said.

"I can't bleed unless I want to. Ever since I was a baby," Richard explained, "my body has automatically controlled my cells to shape-shift to a normal state. If there were a knife strong enough to penetrate my skin, you would see a hole but no blood. My cells would stay inside me. Since I've never unwillingly bled before, it was easy to fight that particular illusion and ignore the effects."

Liz knew that her illusions were not foolproof and was glad Richard was able to see through them. They walked almost two miles as they exchanged stories about their childhoods and dreams. Then they returned to their starting point and sat on the cool sand. Richard felt comfortable telling Liz of his experiences and feelings, and Liz's visions of the two of them were blossoming. Liz had fantasized about traveling to exotic places and being on secret missions. Richard brought those fantasies to life because he had firsthand experience in undercover work.

"Look!" Liz said excitedly, interrupting their conversation. "A shooting star!"

Richard looked at the shooting star and watched for it to die out, but it didn't. It moved toward the horizon, maintaining its brightness and speed.

"That's not a shooting star," Richard said as the object moved over the horizon and a flash of light illuminated the sky.

"What is it?" Liz asked, knowing that something had hit the water many miles out.

"John, Susan. We need your help—now!" Richard said on his comlink.

John and Susan sat on the beach wall going over mental blocking techniques to prevent John from dying in the event he was attacked by another mind-control blast similar to the one Susan had used on him.

"On our way," Susan responded as John told her to tell Richard instead of typing into his comlink.

"Liz, tell me when it's clear for us to change into our customs," Richard said.

Liz looked around and sensed that no one was near enough to see them.

"It's safe," Liz said as her new metamorphic costume wrapped around her body. She wore an ancient Egyptian outfit that exposed her arms and legs, with a white mask that covered her upper face and a gold crown that included an opal centerpiece.

Creator and Liz stood by the water as Mindseye and Susan flew to their sides.

*What is it?* John asked.

"I don't know, but we're going to find out," said Richard. He flew as fast as he could toward the impact area, but John, the fastest flier in the group, moved ahead. Ten miles out to sea, John returned to the group.

*Richard, there is a hundred-foot wave coming this way at high speed.*

"Whatever hit the water must have caused a tidal wave. We have to reduce the effects of the wave before it hits the coastline," Richard stated.

"How?" Susan asked.

"Liz, you and Susan go back and get everyone out of the streets. John and I will try to stop the waves!" Richard directed.

Liz and Susan flew back toward land, developing a plan to get everyone away from the beach or up to the higher floors in the buildings on the shoreline. Richard and John flew on the surface of the water in front of the monstrous rise of water as the wave started to form to its peak. Richard shot a wide blast of telekinetic energy across the wave. John shot a similar blast in the opposite direction. But John's portion of the wave was hardly influenced due to his weaker blast. They continued firing blasts for many miles, trying to create a semicircular barrier for most of the coastline north and south of the Miami Beach.

Susan and Liz moved people away from the beach and out of the streets into the largest buildings before the first waves hit the three-foot beach wall. Richard and John, working feverishly, reduced the main wave by fifty percent. But Richard could only stare helplessly from a distance as the water crashed over the beach wall and filtered into the streets three blocks inland. The first floors of beachfront buildings flooded, and several smaller buildings collapsed. The four superheroes helped people trapped in buildings, cars, and the streets. Police and fire fighters arrived while Richard and his group neutralized the downed power cables along the streets. It took ten minutes for the water to subside and drain back into the ocean.

News reporters stormed the area, crowding around Creator as people pointed fingers at his group, saying they saved the lives of many people after the mysterious wave hit. After a brief introduction, Creator became the center of attention for the mob of reporters.

"Creator, is it true that you are responsible for the rescue of Senator Fence and now several hundred Floridians in this natural disaster?" asked Becky Owens from Channel 10 News.

"Yes, it's true, we did save the hostages," Richard replied into the microphone.

"Can you tell us about this wave and what caused it?" called out a reporter from the back of the crowd.

"We don't know what caused it, but it seemed to be a meteor."

"Are you saying that this was not man-made?" shouted another reporter.

Richard was taken aback by such a speculative question.

"I'm not at liberty to say, since I don't have all the facts. I can only say that something hit the water, and it would have been worse if we hadn't been here."

"Is it true that your group is called the Eternal Champions?" Becky asked.

"Yes, Becky, it is."

"Are the local authorities supporting your effort to fight crime?"

"I know that the national authorities acknowledge us as legitimate crime-fighters. As for Dade County authorities, I don't know because this is the first time we have made ourselves known here in Miami."

"Creator! Can you introduce us to your group!" another reporter shouted from the crowd.

Richard, liking the attention, smiled.

"Sure! This is Mindseye," Richard said, gesturing toward John. "And this ..." Richard gestured toward Elizabeth.

"I'm Isis," said Liz.

"And I'm Pandora," said Susan, who was wearing a black-and-red outfit that exposed only her ears, eyes, mouth, and long black hair.

"There's another member who's not here right now," Richard said. "His name is Night."

Another reporter, David Atkins, pushed to the front.

"Creator," David said, "is it true that hundreds of people were killed in cold blood while you were in Complex San Francisco?"

"The people you are referring to were firing weapons at us and the survivors of flight 0292 in order to kill or use them as hostages in their plan to take control of Oakland," Richard calmly replied. "General Fox and Ms. Hitoshi have testified to the senate hearing as proof to that fact."

"So you killed hundreds of people to save the lives of a few?" David continued to drill.

"If you're suggesting that we should have let a few people die to keep hundreds from dying, then I say we probably should tell the families of the people we saved that you don't care if they had died."

The crowd went wild with questions as a police detective and several officers disrupted the interview.

"Ladies and gentlemen, please refrain from asking any more questions at this time. An investigation is under way to find out what happened here, and the Eternal Champions will not be available to answer any more questions until we have completed the investigation. Thank you."

The speaker urged Richard and his group to enter a police truck.

"I'm Detective Kenneth Woodridge. I'm sorry for breaking up the interview, but you are not authorized to talk about what might have caused this tidal wave until our investigation is over. If you do, I will have to charge you with obstruction of justice. You are also hereby notified that you're all witnesses to the incident and that your testimony will need to be officially recorded for the purpose of insurance and this investigation. Do you have a problem if we take you to police headquarters?" Detective Woodridge asked.

"Yes," Richard said, "we *do* have a problem with that. I will file a full report through our SIA channels, and I will fax you that report if that makes you feel any better. But taking us to the police station will only attract unwanted attention to your department and to us. So, not to be disrespectful, detective, but we will leave now, and hopefully some of the reports will get out of your hair."

Woodridge looked at Creator, knowing that SIA would probably back Creator with the current situation, so he gave Richard his card.

"Here is where you can reach me when you get the report done. I hope we can work better in the future. Thanks, by the way, for helping those people out there."

"Anytime, Detective, and I hope we can help each other better in the future as well," Creator said as he and the group exited the police truck. They immediately took to the air and flew to a hotel roof several blocks away, where they changed back into their normal street clothes. They went down through the hotel and headed toward where Richard had parked his car.

"No, no, no!" Richard said when he saw that his car was gone, but then he cursed when he looked to the other side of the street and saw where his car had settled after the flood receded. The navy blue body was covered with seaweed, trash, and saltwater. Sand poured out into the street as he opened the driver's side door.

John, Liz, and Susan stood speechless as Richard silently mourned over his dream car. Finally Richard looked at his friends and called Erica on the comlink.

"Erica, call triple A and send a tow truck to this location." Richard signed off. "You all can go home. I'll stay here and wait for the tow truck."

Liz looked at Susan and John. "You two go ahead. I'll stay with Richard."

John and Susan were in no mood to argue with Liz, not wanting to be around Richard at this point in space or time, so they left quickly with a "see you later in the morning."

Liz walked up to Richard and put her hands on the hood of the car.

"You know, I never did see you work on this car. I like men in dirty coveralls, tightening bolts and getting in the thick of things. You don't suppose I could see you bring life back to this well-oiled, sandy...salty...wet...automobile?" Liz said, trying to get Richard's attention.

Richard looked at her as if she had only dug deeper with a knife.

"If you were a guy, I would hit you right about now."

Liz looked a little offended and said, "Richard, you have a gift, not to mention the technology. You can rebuild and fix her up better than ever before." Liz grabbed the side mirror, breaking it off accidentally. She delicately handed it to Richard. "Oh, Richard, I'm so sorry," Liz apologized, although she could feel herself starting to giggle, then laugh.

Richard's eyes widened, and Liz tried to act innocent. Richard couldn't help himself. Liz was beautiful, and she was sweet, and he had to laugh with her.

They returned to the conversation they'd left off while sitting on the beach. Liz fell deeper and deeper in thought as Richard talked. She felt very safe and comfortable with him. He seemed to bring out the best in her, and that made it easy for her to open up feelings she had kept hidden from people, especially men, for so many years. She had seen Richard's real self and understood now that her visions had not been of several men, but of Richard alone—his public identity, his true form, and his superhero form.

Richard noticed that Liz was in her own world. She stared at him but not into his eyes. His speech slowed, and then he stopped in mid-sentence. Liz only nodded as if in agreement.

"So, do you think I should kiss you?" Richard asked.

Liz caught half of what Richard asked and came back to reality.

"What?"

"It's a good thing you were paying attention," said Richard.

Liz was embarrassed that Richard could tell she hadn't been listening.

"I'm sorry, Richard. I wasn't paying attention."

"Is something wrong?"

Liz straightened her back and looked directly into Richard's eyes.

"I've seen bits and pieces of the future. I knew I would meet a man who would save me, but there were so many men in the visions that it scared me at first. Most men I've known aren't very nice, and the ones who're nice aren't what I would call boyfriend material. I know that my visions aren't perfect, but out of all of the men I saw, I liked you as you are now the most. I didn't get it until just now, but out of all of those men I saw, I saw you. You are all of those men."

"What do you think about me now that we're together?" Richard asked.

Liz was scared to tell Richard that she had fallen in love with him before they'd even met. The visions didn't show her everything. For all she knew, he might be a good friend in her future. She didn't care, though, because the vision that kept her motivated was his. She bit her lip, trying to think of how to reply. She didn't know whether Richard loved her as much as she did him. They'd been together for a little more than one day. She didn't want to push him away by acting too quickly.

"I don't know," Liz said. "I...I feel like I've known you for a very long time. But I don't know how you feel about me or how you will feel about me in the future."

Richard wanted to tell her he was extremely attracted to her and thought carefully about what to say.

"Liz, I am ninety-two years old. I fell in love with a woman fifty-seven years ago. She died, and I had a very hard time getting over her death. I've been with many women in the past four decades, and many of them didn't know what they wanted in life. I guess I was happy having someone to love, but one thing I know I want is to be able to share my life with that special someone. That special woman will be willing to go to the ends of the world with me. No questions asked, just follow me, knowing I would give her the universe in the process. My ex-girlfriend told me I was insensitive to her goals and that she wanted someone who didn't hide his feelings and would spend more time with her. It is in the past, but I couldn't tell her the truth about me being a superhuman. I know we don't know each other very well, and I don't want you to feel like you owe me anything. If anything, I owe you my thanks for making me feel very happy these past eight hours. I've been able to tell you things no other woman ever heard."

Liz continued to gaze into Richard's eyes as she stepped within a foot of Richard with his back against the Mustang's passenger door.

"What do you think about me?" Liz asked.

Richard knew where the conversation was going and looked down for a second, trying to hide his eyes and true feelings for her.

"I think you're a very beautiful woman on the outside *and* the inside."

Liz looked a little surprised. She'd expected a completely different answer.

"Huh, I see."

Richard saw her disappointed face as she turned and started to move away from him. He wasn't sure whether Liz understood why he'd said what he'd said. He'd had many women tell him they loved him, but only one of them knew why she loved him and wanted to be a part in his life as a superhuman and human. To him, the word *love* was very special, and if he said it, he meant it. It was a powerful word that he knew influenced the ideas and actions of both men and women. He knew in his heart that the feelings he had for Liz were more than infatuation. But he wasn't sure whether she could love him for not only who he was, but for what it meant to be with him. He grabbed Liz's hand before she fully turned away.

"Liz, do you understand what kind of life I have lived and what kind of life I am living now as a crime-fighter?"

"What do you mean?" Liz said, thinking more about the soft touch of Richard's hand than about his question.

"You don't have to fight crime," Richard said. "After you're pardoned, you can go live a normal life anywhere you want. But I want to fight crime, and that's where my life leads me for now. Do you understand?"

Liz understood perfectly and wanted so much to live her life with him even if it meant an abnormal lifestyle that she wouldn't be able to escape.

"I understand," Liz said and turned back toward him. She leaned forward and kissed Richard on the mouth.

Richard fell into the moment and returned the kiss, wanting nothing more than to continue kissing her. Liz felt Richard's arms gently wrap around her waist and back as she wrapped her arms around his neck. They kissed for a long time, hoping their moment would last forever.

The tow truck pulled up next to them as they finished kissing.

"I guess it's time to go home," Richard said, not really wanting to go home.

"Let's walk down the beach a little before we go back."

Richard smiled, pushed her away slowly, and said, "I'd like that."

The tow truck took the Mustang away while Liz and Richard walked north along the beach, gladly telling each other their innermost secrets and desires. It wasn't long before they went out into the water and made love under the moonlight. They made it back home and continued the morning in Richard's bedroom. Liz went to sleep for a few hours while Richard started on rebuilding and refurbishing the Mustang. Late that morning, Liz showed up, acting as Richard's loving and beautiful helper.

Susan woke up restless on the sofa in the battle room. The nightmares were getting stronger and more frequent, but she was able to control them better each time she closed her eyes. John and Larcis had gotten up early to do chores, but they let her sleep. It was past noon, but Susan felt like she had slept for only twenty minutes. She stood up and went looking for Liz, hoping Liz could brighten her mood. It wasn't long before she made her way down to the mechanic's shop and saw the frame of the Mustang along with hundreds of parts scattered all over the floor.

Susan walked up to Liz, seeing her face shine with happiness and excitement. She felt much better seeing Liz this way, but it also intrigued her. She wanted to know why her friend was so happy. The night out was great, but it wasn't that good, especially after the tidal-wave incident.

"Why are you so happy this morning?" Susan asked.

With a wide smile, Liz answered, "Oh, no reason. I'm just helping Richard fix the car."

Susan looked at Richard, who was removing a piece from the car, and then at Liz, who wouldn't stop smiling as she herself watched Richard work.

"Don't tell me you and Richard have something going on," said Susan.

"I had the best time of my life last night," Liz said, continuing to smile.

"And you didn't come and tell me sooner? What happened?" Susan asked, wanting details about Liz and Richard's time alone on the beach.

Liz told Richard she had to take a break and talk to Susan upstairs. The two friends went to Liz's bedroom, where she told Susan everything that had happened until late that morning. Susan couldn't believe her ears. Liz was traumatized by the slave prostitution ring situation, which had made it very hard for her to get close to any man she met. Richard seemed to be the exception, and Susan understood why after piecing together the stories Liz had told her about this mystery man she kept seeing in her dreams.

## Bridge of Princess Navia's Flagship

A slim silver skinned albino monitored his laser screen while typing information on the console with his twelve fingers.

"Your Eminence," Telkar typed, "we have monitored the local media transmissions and discerned that the Chosen was in this area. However, our scanners indicate the Chosen is sixty-seven kilometers bearing 320 decons in an area called Fort Lauderdale."

A tall woman with a glossy tan stood in the middle of the bridge looking at the main screen with bright green eyes. The entry into the Earth's atmosphere under the guise of a meteor had allowed them to land closer than usual. Earth's technology had evolved enough for alien insertions of spacecrafts to be risky, attracting too much attention. Any hint of a UFO would have caused government and independent agencies to track the ship thousands of miles from Florida. The princess's plan seemed to have worked, but the ship had suffered unexpected damage upon entry into the atmosphere and then the water. Their trip to Earth would have to be several weeks longer than desired.

Numerous clips of superhuman and military battles filled the screen as the High Arch Soothsayer turned to face the Princess of the House of Jakad.

"Your Eminence, the Chosen is protected by strong superhumans and is surrounded by the human population. But the Chosen will be secluded in time."

"These humans," the princess responded.

"These humans, Your Eminence?" the Soothsayer asked, perplexed.

"These humans. They are primitive and would kill to pursue their own desires, yet they are also strong and have virtues of sacrifice, love, and justice. The Galactic Guardians are a witness to these virtues, but I understand now why your mother wouldn't allow the elders to occupy this sector of the galaxy. They have potential, but it can be the end of many races if they evolve incorrectly." The princess turned toward the soothsayer. "We will wait for an opportunity to infuse and meet with the Chosen. Continue to monitor the Chosen's activities."

"Yes, Your Eminence."

# Chapter Eleven

✖ - ✖

# Revelation

### Octavian Farm, Fort Lauderdale

S usan and Liz liked the idea of living on the Octavian estate. They enjoyed lying out on the lawn chairs next to the pool. They had lived well in Complex San Francisco, but nothing compared to the freedom and luxury of the farm. Richard spent two days straight working on the Mustang before he finally took a break upon receiving a message from Max. John and Larcis swam in the pool, going through their routine workout, even though the light exercise did nothing but make them look like they were busy. Linda felt the sun through the Plexiglas ceiling of the indoor pool. The echoed sound of splashing soothed her. The warm, humid air wet her entire body, while her mind wondered off to a place of light and weightlessness. Sounds faded as she drifted off to sleep.

An all-encompassing light blinded her for a moment then cleared into a view of the horizon along the clouds. Susan saw herself flying in between and through cumulus clouds. The ground seemed so distant, so green and black, with almost indiscernible clumps of trees, riverbeds, streams, foot trails and farm plots. She descended below the clouds, shadows intermittently casting over her body as she flew toward a great valley. The forest terrain turned dark and eerie as the clouds above darkened and shut out the sun's rays. Susan fell through the air, unable to control her flight. She plunged toward the ground feeling tremendously heavy. The air wailed in her ears as her speed increased beyond terminal velocity. The ground enlarged as she attempted to slow down. She struck soft mud and swamp water, and the murky ground swallowed her up. The force of impact had knocked the wind from her, and she choked in the swamp. She pushed with all her might, flew from the muddy water, and landed twenty feet away on solid ground.

Susan coughed swamp water onto the twigs and grassy dirt beneath her as she tried to pick herself up. Her skin tingled from the sudden changes in temperature. Warmth changed to discomfort as icy raindrops fell on her back. She sensed that her powers were gone. It was as if she had never possessed them. She called out for Elizabeth and John but got only thunder in reply. The rain stopped suddenly. She tried to stand but found herself fighting an invisible force that pushed down on her hips and back. A circle of purple light appeared ten feet in front of her, casting the shadow of a female figure.

"Sweetie, you and your friends are in grave danger," a woman's voice spoke to Susan.

"Mother?" Susan replied in disbelief.

"You must sacrifice yourself for the good of many. Don't be afraid. You must be strong."

"What's happening?" Susan cried out, thinking the phenomenon before her was a perverted ruse.

"Sweetie, please listen to me. There is not much time. You must leave your friends or they will die," the voice warned.

"No!" Susan screamed, waking up in her lawn chair by the pool.

"Susan! What's wrong?" Liz asked, kneeling beside her. John and Larcis had stopped swimming to watch what had happened.

Susan shivered in the warm pool dome. She looked quickly around the pool, then at Liz.

"I have to go," she said to Liz with tears in her eyes.

"Was it another one of those dreams?" Liz asked as John rushed to Susan's side.

Susan looked down, trying to organize her thoughts.

"No, it was completely different. Something new. I have to go."

Susan stood and wrapped a towel around her body.

*Go where? Susan?* John asked as he followed her into the house.

Susan turned, stopping John in his tracks.

*Please, John. Please leave me alone.*

John stared at Susan in despair.

*I can't,* John replied as his mind faded into darkness.

"Richard," Liz reported on the comlink, "Susan paralyzed John and flew away. She had a very bad dream. I think something is seriously wrong with her."

"Erica, where's Susan now?" Richard said out loud while in the battle room.

"She has flown out of Erica II's surveillance range and left her comlink in her room." Erica responded.

"Liz, I'm on my way up there," said Richard.

Liz, John, and Larcis waited for Richard in the living room. Richard entered wearing jeans and a shirt full of oil marks from working on the Mustang.

"What happened?" Richard asked.

"Susan and I were lying out by the pool when she fell asleep," Liz explained. "I noticed she was making some noises as if she was dreaming, but she didn't scream or anything. She just suddenly woke up and said she had to go somewhere."

"And where were you two?" Richard asked the men.

*We were both swimming laps, but I heard Susan scream,* John said, contradicting Liz's story.

"I didn't hear anything," Larcis said, siding with Liz.

"What did Susan say?" Richard asked.

"She said that the dream she had was nothing like the others and that she had to leave," said Liz.

*That's when I tried to talk to Susan and convince her not to leave,* John said, adding to the story.

"Did she leave of her own free will?" Richard asked.

John and Liz looked at each other.

"I suppose," Liz stated, "but Susan wouldn't leave like that."

"I was going to tell everyone during dinner as a surprise," said Richard, "but it seems that won't happen."

"Tell us what?" said Liz.

"You and Susan have been pardoned," Richard announced. "You're free, with no restrictions except those from the normal laws of society."

Elizabeth's eyes brightened with joy. But a curtain of sadness crossed her mind as she thought of Susan.

"Richard, what about Susan? We can't just let her go without her knowing she's free."

"We'll look for her. Larcis, you search the skies above for about a hundred-mile radius. Liz and I will go through the beachfront. John, you can take the downtown area. Use the comlink to let everyone else know if we find her. Erica, monitor the police bands, and if you can get some satellites to work some magic looking for anything resembling Susan's description, that would help. Let's go," Richard said, instantly changing into more presentable clothes.

**New York City**

The light flashed and the bell rang as the elevator doors opened on the forty-seventh floor. A blond young woman and a seven-year-old girl stepped into the elevator. The mother slowly, simply, and lovingly explained their plans for the rest of the day.

"Can I have chocolate ice cream for lunch, Mommy?" the green-eyed girl asked.

"You can have ice cream after you eat all of your lunch," Tanya Makan responded.

"Okay, Mommy," Brittany said a little disappointed.

The elevator moved swiftly down to the lobby of the Makan International Building. Tanya expected the day to be filled with one of her usual shopping sprees around Manhattan with her daughter. Urgent business put a rain check on her biweekly lunch with her husband and daughter. She didn't mind the late hours her husband put in. In fact, it was a blessing, ensuring the family got great vacation perks and extended weekends off. She grabbed Brittney's hand, expecting the doors to open as the lobby floor light flashed on. The doors slid apart to reveal the basement garage and a mostly empty parking lot. A man in a black trench coat stood at the center of the entrance. His grotesque pale face was partly covered by dark sunglasses and a hood. Tanya and Brittney froze as the man pulled the trigger of a shotgun with a twelve-inch barrel. The modified shotgun sprayed wedge-like projectiles of lead and poison through the two victims and into the back wall of the elevator.

The loud, hollow bang attracted the attention of a nearby pedestrian and security guard, who rushed to the scene. From a distance, the guard saw the figure of a man vanish into the stairway. He ran from the far end of the parking lot toward the closed elevator doors. Karl Simon, a middle-aged man coming in late to work as a broker for Makan International, slowly walked up next to the guard as the elevator doors reopened. Tanya lay bent over on her stomach, dripping massive amounts of blood from her many puncture wounds. Brittney stood tacked onto the back elevator wall by splintered bone fragments from her body that had embedding themselves into the wall. Fresh blood rhythmically pumped out of both victims' bodies as the guard vomited on the pavement. The broker almost did the same. Karl took his handkerchief and placed it over his nose and mouth. He ran up to the elevator doors, stopping the elevator from going up.

"Go get the police!" Karl yelled at the guard, who seemed to be recovering from reflexive fright.

The guard turned without hesitating and ran away from the scene to look for a phone, forgetting that he had a hand-held radio. Karl looked around in fear, realizing that the murders could not have happened more than sixty seconds before. He knew that criminals usually fled the crime scene, but that didn't make him feel any better.

Brittney's little body came loose from the elevator wall and fell onto the corpse of her mother. The stench of burned flesh and hot blood overwhelmed the area as a grayish dark-red pool spread over the elevator floor.

The phone intercom buzzed softly as cigar smoke rose above a plush brown armchair.

Patterson answered the phone. "Is it done?"

"It's done," a hoarse voice replied.

Patterson hung up by pushing a flashing green key on the phone. He then stared into space as if in deep thought.

*Makan International will accept a noncontested merger now. How nice of them,* Theo thought as he smiled a wicked smile. *Jared, you better not fail me.*

## Tamarac, Fort Lauderdale

Susan walked down University Boulevard, not really knowing where she was going. Heads turned in her direction as she ignored the catcalls and near auto accidents. The group searched until sunset but turned up empty-handed. Richard and Liz went down to Hollywood while Larcis searched up to Jupiter. John looked downtown, remembering that Susan had once said she would love to tour the city.

Susan strolled into the Greyhound station a little tired and bored. The station was small, with no more than a hundred people filling the one hundred by two hundred-foot building. The 7 p.m. bus departed for Orlando, leaving empty seats in the right corner of the station. Susan saw a young girl listening to her CD player. Susan had walked for the last four hours, so she decided to sit behind the girl. The Cranberries' song "Zombie" touched Susan's ears as the girl bobbed her head with the beat. Susan scanned the girl's thoughts and found out she was going to visit her grandmother up in Tallahassee. The sandy-blond girl reminded her of herself, in the middle of a city, not worrying about the sorrows of the world.

She recalled her family. Her mother and father had lied to her about her superhuman powers, saying it was natural. To her dismay, she found out the truth when they allowed her to be an experiment for the Founders. Her mental capabilities put her above the rest in accelerated languages, sciences, and arts. The experiments went sour when her performance decreased while in senior high school. The new isotopes altered Susan's mental abilities to focus inward, enhancing her control over her own mind and forcing it onto others. She accidentally hurt two students with her immature powers during her adjustment period. Her parents took her away, fearing the Founders would use her for evil purposes or kill her and her family to hide the truth about the Founders. Susan thought of running away, but she couldn't leave her parents to die at the hands of the Founders.

Five years passed uneventfully. Then she found her father and mother tortured to death in their home. The days were black and empty as she hunted and killed all of the people responsible for the death of her parents, including those who had stood by witnessing the murders. It was ironic that she was powerful enough to bring down an organization the size of a police department, but failed to do so before her parents paid the price. Susan hated her parents for their secrets and for leaving her alone to face persecution for being a superhuman.

Susan stood and paced the floor of the bus station, thinking about everything that had happened to her in the past twenty-two years. Elizabeth, John, Richard, Larcis, and even Erica treated her with respect and love. They were a surrogate family. But the dream she had was more than a dream; it was a message that she took seriously. No one in the Eternal

Champions would be safe from the fate the voice foretold. But was it really fixed in the future, and what could kill the team members?

Susan went outside and sat on a bench. A dirty man wearing a raged coat passed by, begging for a few dollars. Susan looked at the man's unshaven, oily face.

"Here you go, Oscar," Susan said. "Find a motel and freshen up. Go get a job for a bank or computer company as an accountant or programmer."

Susan gave the man $3,000 in cash as she embedded her will into his mind.

Oscar stood silent after taking the money. He shook his head in an attempt to figure out what had just happened to him. He stared at the money then back at Susan.

"I feel...*different!* I know how to type ninety words per minute, and I know all sorts of computer stuff. How?"

"It doesn't matter. Get off the streets and remember what happened here today so you can help those less fortunate. Don't forget to practice what you have just learned or you will gradually lose the knowledge, Okay?" Susan said with a smile.

"Thank you, miss," Oscar said. He threw his half-empty small bottle of Jim Beam into a trashcan and left the parking lot.

Susan closed her tired eyes and prayed she could fall asleep without waking up to death and horror. A moment passed before a man sat next to her on the bench and modestly cleared his throat.

Susan smelled the familiar fragrance of Obsession for Men and turned her head to see John sitting quietly looking at the almost empty parking lot.

"Please leave me alone," Susan asked politely.

*I told you I couldn't,* John casually replied. *But what I didn't tell you is why I couldn't.*

"John, I don't want to hurt you," Susan threatened.

*I'm sure you could, Susan, but you have a family that wants you back. We would fight for you to the ends of the world without question. And, frankly, I don't care if you hurt me or kill me,* John said without reservation.

"I don't know what's wrong with me, John, and you're not making it any easier for me. Please go home," Susan pleaded.

*I will never leave you, Susan. If it were possible, I would do more than live and die for you,* John said softly.

Susan wasn't sure if John had been just infatuated with her, but now she sensed that John thought of her as being much more than a friend or a crush. He was handsome and a bit naive. But in times of crisis he kept everything together and made wise decisions. She had noticed everyone's actions in San Francisco but never mentioned it to anyone in the group. She wasn't sure, however, whether nagging her right now was a wise choice.

"You have no idea what I could do to you, do you?" Susan said softly.

*You could love me more than I love you?* John said without hesitation, as if asking himself the question.

Susan looked deep into John's green eyes, hesitant to speak or think.

"John," Susan started to say as John quickly and softly kissed her, lightly putting his hands on hers. They kissed for what seemed to be a second lasting an eternity.

*You should have more faith in Richard and me. In fact, I wanted to find you before everyone else did so that I could tell you that you're a free woman. Your pardon has been granted, Ms. Susan Sawczer,* John said softly, touching Susan's nose with his.

*Hmmm.* Susan thought. "Thank you," she said. She smiled and kissed John once again for a much longer duration.

"*Let's go home,*" John suggested.

John stood, and then so did Susan. The two walked away together, their arms around each other's waist.

Erica addressed the rest of the group over their comlinks: "John has told me that he has found Susan. They are alright and are on their way back home."

"Thank you, Erica," said Richard. "That's good news. Liz and I will go shopping around here since we're in this area."

Liz smiled with excitement upon hearing the good news about Susan and the unexpected date with Richard.

"Oh, Erica," Richard added, "take a good look at NORAD's records and SIA for flying objects near Miami Beach last night before the tidal wave. Also, see if you can get any evidence of seismic activity in the region."

"I will look into it, Richard," Erica replied.

Liz looked at Richard, wondering why they were going shopping again, but she wasn't about to complain.

"What did you have in mind?" asked Liz.

"I want to get you something special."

Liz smiled and grabbed Richard's hand.

"Good, I already have something in mind then."

They went to a fashion store, and Liz tried on some outfits. Richard just sat back and watched Liz enjoy herself. She finally settled on four winter outfits for Florida. Richard went up to Liz and touched her new jacket.

"There's something wrong with this."

Liz looked where Richard was touching.

"What's wrong with it?"

"There's something bulging here."

Richard put his hand into Liz's jacket pocket. He fumbled around the pocket, trying to find out what was causing the bulge.

Liz became frustrated as Richard's hand pulled and tugged on her jacket.

"Richard, don't rip it, let me see!"

She yanked Richard's hand out of her pocket and felt around for the unknown object. She felt what seemed to be a ring and pulled it out. Liz stared at a large three carat diamond engagement ring in her open palm.

Richard knelt before her.

"I know it's sudden," he said, "but I don't need more time to know I love you. Will you be my wife?"

Richard was not one to doubt himself on what he wanted. He only hoped Liz would say yes which would make one of his dreams come true.

Liz looked at Richard, speechless. She simply nodded, let Richard put the ring on her finger, and kissed him passionately.

### CEA Headquarters, Alexandria, Virginia

The New York Times featured the high-profile front-page news on the death of Tanya and Brittany Makan. The day had just started as Jean threw the newspaper on her desk; rage filling her bosom.

"Emily, tell Mr. Patterson to come and see me right now!" Jean told her secretary by intercom.

"Right away, ma'am," the efficient assistant replied.

Jean could not believe that her plans were now jeopardized by Patterson's greed and lack of judgment. She swiveled in her chair to face her computer. The screen lit with a telecom window. She entered the regular address to operations. A man appeared on the screen a few seconds later.

"Director, it's a bit early for you to give us a morning visit," the handsome man replied.

"Jared, I know that this is not the correct protocol, but you must do exactly as I say, or your team will not live to see the rest of the day. Relocate Jane immediately to a location of your choosing. Do not let anyone—including Mr. Patterson—know where you are or will be. I will contact you 187 hours from now through our mutual friend. I trust you will ensure that you are not tracked and that any spy in your mist will be dealt with," Jean explained as her forty-five second encrypted message counter wound down to twenty-five seconds.

"You know, you will owe me for this?" Jared said and smiled in acknowledgment.

"Don't forget you work for me," Jean coldly replied. "Mr. Patterson seems to be playing on the wrong side—his own—so be careful."

"Is that a hint of concern, Director?" Jared asked.

"No, it's a warning to those beneath me. Jean out."

Jean cut the line and focused on the problem at hand with SIA's involvement into the Makan murders.

Several minutes passed as she searched her computer files for a scapegoat.

"Ma'am, Mr. Patterson has arrived," Emily reported on the intercom.

"Send him in. And no interruptions, Emily," Jean said.

"Yes, ma'am."

Jean turned her chair away from the entrance. Mr. Patterson entered, as confident as ever.

"You called for me, Director?" Patterson asked as he stepped up to within three feet of Jean's desk.

"Do you know why I have a reputation as director of CEA (Counterespionage Agency)?" Jean asked, looking at four television screens behind her desk.

"I don't understand your question, Director," Patterson said apathetically.

"Do you know what people call me behind my back?" Jean said. "They call me the Wicked Witch of the East, Bitch of the Universe, Satan's Whore. They even call me names of snakes, not to mention other deadly and grotesque animals. They think I don't know, but I do.... What's worst of all is that the names do me no true justice. I'm much worse."

Jean swung around in her chair and looked Patterson straight in the eyes.

"A girl and her mother," Jean stated. "That's a heavy price to pay for incompetence."

"It was necessary," Patterson responded, interrupting Jean's lecture.

"Shut the hell up!" Jean yelled, lifting her right hand slightly above her desktop.

Patterson's chest froze with pain as the fluids in his lungs crystallized. The sudden lack of oxygen caught halfway up his throat terminated his attempt to finish the sentence.

"It was necessary to get SIA involved; it was necessary to give Jonathon Makan a reason to get revenge; it was necessary to wale me around like a naive child, thinking I would be so blind to your handiwork...."

Patterson's eyes lit up with surprise as he buckled to his knees from suffixation, knowing that somehow he was found out for his treacherous acts.

"Yes, Mister Patterson. I know how you planned to sell me out to SIA and take over CEA with the use of Project Jane and Outlaw. But I will not allow that to happen," Jean said as Patterson fell flat on the floor, gasping as his lungs returned to normal.

"You will do exactly what I tell you to do—nothing more, nothing less. We will proceed with Operation Poseidon. You will meet with Jared's team at the Farlo safe house. Make sure you get there before they leave for their new location. You have twenty-nine minutes," Jean announced, walking nonchalantly to the windows. "Do not fail me again."

Patterson picked himself up and barely let out his reply: "I won't fail you."

Jean smiled as Patterson closed the door. She returned to her computer and made a quick call to one of her special operatives. She then scanned the Internet for news. The files revealed nothing exceptional, but there was something she was overlooking.

Forty minutes into her research, the intercom sounded.

"Yes, Emily?" Jean responded.

"I'm sorry, Ma'am, but I have been informed that the Farlo Photo Studio has been burned to the ground. There was one fatality. The police believe it was a customer, but they are not sure at this time."

"If the police call, connect them to me immediately. In the meantime, get with my attorneys and get them started with insurance claims and possible lawsuits by the customer's relatives. Otherwise, I don't want to be disturbed this morning. And also, Emily, take a three-hour lunch today starting at ten-thirty," Jean instructed.

"Thank you, ma'am. I will transfer all calls to the message center at ten-thirty."

"You're welcome," Jean said and looked at the newspaper on her desk. The picture of the elevator and two victims reminded her of the unfortunate things in life. Humans were not her enemies. Superhumans and those who helped her sister's murderers were her only enemies. She was more determined now to achieve her due retribution. Operations Poseidon, Jane and Outlaw would allow her to take her vengeance.

Jean looked back to the windows, picked up a glass of water from her desk, and smiled.

"It is good you didn't fail me," she said. "I would have been very disappointed to know you survived the fire, Mr. Patterson."

### The Eternal Domain

The Eternal Champions gathered in the battle room at midnight. They ate appetizers and drank Guinness beer and mixed drinks while talking about their future and congratulating Liz and Richard on their engagement.

"First, I want to thank everyone who made freedom possible for Susan and me," Liz said, toasting with a shot of tequila.

"To Max!" Richard replied.

"To the Eternal Champions!" Larcis added.

"So does this mean our two heroines are here to stay?" Erica asked.

Richard looked at Liz and Susan.

"It's your decision," said Richard. He knew Liz was here to stay, but he gestured toward Susan, unsure about her.

"Well, since we are all going to be partners, then I propose a cut in the front's revenue," Susan stated.

Everyone eyed her in surprise.

"That can be arranged, Susan," Larcis said. "In fact, there's a position that needs to be filled. If you fill it, you can own probably up to twenty percent of the business."

*No way!* John interrupted. *She can have fifteen percent without that position.*

"Why not, John?" Larcis said. "It's the most demanding and fulfilling position we have."

*Yeah, right,* John said with a frown.

Susan's interest got the best of her.

"John, we need to something to do. I mean, it's nice not having to work, but I'm sure that in time we would be bored if we didn't."

*You're right, Susan,* John said in thought-projection. *But promise me that you won't take the position lightly and do your best to manage the farm.*

"So it's a managing job?" Susan said with a smile. John and Larcis stood silent. "An accountant? A security guard? What is it?"

Everyone except the two girls burst into laughter.

"It's shoveling horse shit!" Larcis said barely getting it out before hysterical laughter took over his gut.

Susan's jaw dropped, and she blushed. Then her face turned to anger as she tried to pour beer on John's head. They ran off into the hallway as the rest of the group laughed even harder. A few minutes later, everything settled down, and Richard presented the plan for training and routine reconnaissance of Miami up to Ft. Lauderdale. Liz, Richard, and Larcis would patrol the area for the next three weeks. Susan wanted to volunteer, wondering why she and John were being left out.

*I told Richard to put us on patrol after we take a vacation,* John said, handing Susan two tickets and information on a two-week Caribbean cruise package aboard a Royal Carnival cruise liner.

Susan eyed the tickets with shock and joy. "What about you two? What about the wedding and honeymoon?" Susan asked Richard and Liz.

"We talked about it and thought you should take a vacation first, we will spend enough time together out on patrol and here." Liz replied wanting to see Susan get her mind off of the bad nightmares.

"You're not getting off *this* easy," Susan said, smiling and hugging John for the gift.

"So, boss. How did Max pull it off?" Larcis asked about the pardon.

"Now that you mention it, Max really knows how to play a mean hand of poker. He took General Cartier, Senator Fence, the Secret Service agent, and the journalist with him inside the Oval Office and cleared out all the stops. I guess the president followed the group's advice and granted the pardon."

"And to think that I had you pegged as a negotiator," Larcis sarcastically commented.

"I'm a good negotiator; I got Max to help us out, didn't I?" Richard countered.

"I don't think you did any such thing. Max would have helped us because we're an asset, and getting the survivors to side with him was easy when their rescuers succeeded in saving their lives. So now we owe him more than before," Larcis explained.

"Trust me, Larcis," said Richard, "it'll all even out in the end. As for the price, I don't know yet. What I do know is that he has a mission for us, and it'll take up a good deal of our time, not to mention the business."

"So what do we do now?" Liz asked.

"First, we'll need you to screen the new employees. We're getting three colts and a mare tomorrow. Larcis, you'll help me with the horses," Richard said.

"Sorry to interrupt you guys, but we're going to crash. We have to get an early start tomorrow so we won't miss the cruise," Susan said.

"What do you mean?" said Liz. "The ship doesn't leave until late in the afternoon."

*Yes, we know. But we have more shopping to finish, and we have to freshen up, things like that,* John said as he and Susan left the room.

The next day ended with John and Susan's bon voyage on a Carnival Cruise ship out of Miami harbor. The accommodations were not first class, but John and Susan liked it that way. They took a tour of the ship, played games, swam, ate, and lounged around. The dinner buffet was romantic and tasty. They took in Mortal Kombat as a late-night movie.

The cool night air blew along the wooden deck as they walked out of the movie theater. John led Susan to the starboard railing overlooking the Caribbean. The sporadic clouds and abundant stars hung in the sky with great splendor, and the sound of rushing water could faintly be heard from the ship's movement. Susan inhaled fresh salty air as she leaned over the blue-and-red rail, her chest expanding to exceptional proportions. John stood next to her, facing the dark sea and grabbing the rail with both hands.

"Look at the beautiful stars," Susan sighed.

*Yes, they are beautiful,* John said, glancing in Susan's direction.

Susan's crystal-brown eyes glittered in the ship's dim light and partial moonlight as she turned her attention to John.

"Why did you team up with Richard and Larcis?" Susan innocently questioned him with her red lip-gloss glimmering as she spoke.

*I don't know. It seemed like the right thing to do at the time. I feel a connection every time someone is close to me. I don't read people's thoughts, but I know what they feel. It bothers me sometimes because it automatically happens once I meet someone new. I later develop a unique block against that person, which keeps their feelings from flooding my senses.*

"Hmmm," Susan sighed.

*I believe in Richard. I could tell the first time we met, when we ran together to Coral Gables, that he was deadly serious about fighting crime and helping the helpless. I would have been crazy not to be a part of the Eternal Champions,* John confessed.

"Why me?" Susan surprisingly asked.

John drew a blank as he tried to scan Susan's mind.

*Why me?* John echoed the question, stalling for time.

"Yes," Susan said. "Why did you keep sticking to me like glue even after all of those bad things I did to you?"

John gave up trying to scan her mind and thought about the question.

*Because I believe in love at first sight, and when I set my eyes on you, I saw the most beautiful, most wonderful, most intelligent woman in the whole world.*

Susan's smile evened out to a confused and surprised look. All the men she'd known were cruel, insensitive, egotistical, or lazy...or else they just desired to get into her pants for at least one night. John was different. His true emotions and thoughts were expressed without reservation or regret. His candor and determination to do what was right were genuine. Susan had blocked her feelings from him for the past three days; afraid he would take advantage of her strong feelings for him. She let go of the block, hoping he wouldn't read her mind and invade her privacy without her consent.

Susan smiled. "You know what Liz told me?"

*'No, what?'*

"She told me that she was going to find this wonderful man, a superhuman, who was going to make a family with her. She can tell the future very well when it concerns things around her. She had visions of another superhuman who was always fighting people, shooting at him, or trying to kill him. She saw visions of aliens, and monsters. After she met Richard, she understood that the two men were the same person. Richard was supposed to be her husband, so I am not surprised they are getting married."

*'What did she say about you?'* John asked knowing that Liz was one major reason Susan had stuck around and helped them in San Francisco.

Susan's sadden expression showed as she answered. "She told me she saw visions of me flying around fighting along with the group, she saw me as a prisoner of some aliens, and she saw me lying down as if I were dead. I saw the visions for myself after she let me see her thoughts."

*'And is Liz always right?'*

"No, not always. They change sometimes."

*'Well, if she's not always right, then you need to think positively and let me protect you.'* John smiled.

"John." Susan turned her body facing him. "Do you really know what you're getting into with me?"

*I know that there is no amount of space or time, no enemy or friend, no deed too small or task too great, no force that exists or will exist that can stop me from loving you,* John responded with a slight smile.

Susan looked into John's green eyes.

*Read my mind,* Susan told John mentally.

They exchanged deep thoughts in a matter of seconds. In a matter of minutes, John and Susan were passionately kissing, ignoring occasional passengers walking by on the deck. They spent the next half-hour talking and exchanging thoughts about themselves and the future before returning to their room.

John and Susan vividly experienced every imaginable and unimaginable position while enjoying each other's sexual pleasures. The sensitivity of their bodies and melded minds increased the sensations, seemingly everlastingly. After four hours, they lay resting on the messed-up bed. The next morning started with a waking kiss, more foreplay, and sex in the shower. Forty minutes later, Susan returned to the bed wearing a pink cotton robe and jumped, still wet, onto the bunched up bed covers and pillows.

She stretched the length of her body and soon fell into a long-awaited deep sleep. John knelt on the mattress next to her. Her naturally long eyelashes complimented her beautiful face. John smiled with the thought that his one almost impossible dream had come true. Susan was the fire in his heart that brought him real purpose and happiness. He lay next to her on his side and delicately placed a pillow beneath her head. Susan cuddled against the pillow and John's right arm. Soon John joined Susan in a deep and joyful sleep.

An unknown span of time elapsed before John heard the bathroom door open and close. He tried to pick up his head but couldn't. His muscles failed to respond to his attempts to get up. He was fully awake and thinking clearly, and he could hear movement in the room, but he was unable to open his eyes or stand up out of bed.

John called out in his trance and heard the words as if he had spoken aloud.

"Susan! Wake up, Susan!"

The feeling of near-suffocation made his body bubble up to the size of the room and float in limbo as he finally felt control returning to his arms and legs. He took a deep breath and lifted his head to look in the direction of the bathroom. A male figure stood on each side of the bed. The man next to John grabbed

John's mouth and neck with both hands. The man's skin was smooth and shiny like stainless steel. The hardiness and coldness of the man's grip on John's throat could have easily snapped a normal human's neck. John could see in the corner of his eye that the other man held a strange foot-long apparatus over Susan's sleeping body.

*Susan! Wake up!* John screamed into Susan's mind, projecting a picture of what he saw into her head. The man holding John started to force him off the bed as Susan opened her eyes. Susan shot a mental blast at the man above her. The man reeled backward, letting go of the apparatus as it wildly released a wide beam of radiation and green light at Susan, John, and the assailants.

John felt a surge of pain spread from his abdomen to the rest of his body like a current of electricity. The room drew dark as he turned to see Susan knocked out on the bed, and then he blacked out a second later.

# Chapter Twelve

✠ - ✠

# The Search

### The Eternal Domain

Richard, I have prepared a full report on the tidal wave," Erica's seductive voice echoed over the ceiling and wall speakers.

A smile came over Richard as Liz comfortably lay in his bed. Richard messaged the back of his neck and tried to stretch his muscles as he walked from his bedroom to the elevator. The first night's patrol with Liz had turned up a car accident in which they had assisting the injured and a shootout between disgruntled neighbors that they had stopped. In the end, it also had several hours of very enjoyable sex.

Richard entered the elevator that would take him to the battle room and hailed Ercia, "Okay, Erica, go ahead." The elevator descended into the Eternal Domain as Erica began her report.

"NORAD reported a meteorite. However, the object slowed down dramatically once it reached two miles above sea level. Miami airport reported the impact seventeen miles east of Miami Beach. Blue Sector has an ultraviolet spectrogram of the object in question. The footage of the spectrogram is twenty seconds long, and after extensive analysis I have concluded that the object is covered by mineral residues with a trace of ionized debris indicating some type of propulsion system or natural release of gases during reentry from a very dense asteroid. That would explain why it didn't simply burn up in the stratosphere," Erica reported with a bit of her own input.

Erica II phased through the floor underneath the elevator and hovered in front of Richard. A laser projection in front of Erica II displayed the video footage of the UFO.

"Stop!" Richard commanded as the elevator doors opened to the battle room. "Back up two seconds."

Erica II's projection was simultaneously displayed on the main battle-room screen.

"Thank you, Erica," Richard told the probe.

The footage slowly moved forward after rewinding two seconds.

"What is that change in color?" Richard asked as he sat on the sofa.

"The turquoise-lime change in color is a signature of a tungsten alloy with magnesium and platinum," Erica replied.

"Could that be part of a ship?"

"A part of a ship? There's a fifty percent probability, but it would not be a ship worthy of space travel. The metal composition is not very stable in extreme heat, which is why the color is only a quick flicker being vaporized in re-entry," Erica explained.

"Have any divers been sent to see what it was?"

"A team from the Ironclad Oceanic Society investigated the area down to 890 feet. They reported only debris of destroyed wildlife and slightly polluted water with traces of lead and phosphate. The full depth is said to be thirteen hundred feet, but the readings indicated no danger to the habitat, so they did not go all the way down to the bottom of the continental shelf."

"They didn't want to spend the money to go all the way down and possibly have to spend more money if there was a hazard," Richard commented.

"Yes, Richard, I'm afraid so," Erica concurred.

"Okay, tell Larcis and Liz to meet me here right away," Richard instructed. "I will also need you to get access to satellites that can monitor the impact area."

"It will take some time to get the proper satellites for monitoring the area, Richard. Even when I do get them, the satellites will not be able to see anything except the surface of the water with any degree of real-time reporting," Erica pointed out.

"Yes, Erica, I'm aware of that. But if I'm correct, I will need eyes above the water while I'm under it," Richard responded.

Richard told Erica to get one of the techbots to bring two underwater transponders to the battle room as Larcis and Liz headed down the elevator. Richard went over the events of the past three days as the techbot exited the elevator with two cup-like plastic pieces on its small robotic arms.

"Erica has analyzed the projectile that hit the ocean three days ago," Richard said. "I think that it was not just a meteor like the papers say. SIA has no hard proof and the research team sent to investigate didn't find a piece of the rock. I think it was a ship of some kind."

"Why do you think that, boss?" Larcis said with a glimmer of interest.

"It slowed down just before it hit and there would have been more debris than was found in the water. It might not be anything, but I have a gut feeling about this one."

"Well, then, so far your gut feelings have been right," Liz said. "So what do we do?"

"Larcis and I will go to the site. You will stay here with Erica and hold the fort, monitoring our progress. We will not be able to communicate with one another once we go underwater." Richard held up one of the transponders from the techbot's extended arm. "Larcis, we can communicate underwater, but the range of these things is limited to one thousand meters."

"What's that?" Larcis asked, pointing at the facemask.

"It's an underwater transponder. You can talk underwater as long as the seal is not broken. Since we don't need to breathe, we won't need anything else. The comlinks will be useless past a depth of three hundred meters, so we'll have to leave them behind."

"You know that water and I don't mix very well," Larcis commented.

"Yes, I know, but as long as you don't emit a lightning bolt, you'll be okay. Besides, I need your thermo vision capability. If it *is* a ship, we might be able to track its heat signature."

"When do we leave, boss?" Larcis asked.

"The sooner, the better. We'll go to the site then move south toward the harbor," Richard stated.

During the next hour, Richard and Larcis reached the area, dove to the bottom, and returned to the surface to report from a buoy where they had placed a comlink.

"Liz, did you find anything out?" Richard asked over the comlink as dark scattered clouds loomed over the ocean water.

"We have a problem, Richard. Erica can't get hold of John or Susan. Their comlinks are not transmitting, which means they have taken the batteries out or the comlinks are destroyed. SIA has sent two sonar cruise boats to your vicinity. Max thinks that an alien ship has landed in the ocean. He wants you to find out what they want and get them off our planet," Liz summarized.

"Really, imagine that. Erica, track out the course of the cruise liner and synchronize the time the comlinks stopped working with the location of the ship."

"Done, Richard," said Erika. "Here are the coordinates." Richard looked at the comlink screen. "The last known time of their comlinks being active was 0811 hours, southeast of Key West."

Richard glanced at his watch and noted the one-hour difference.

"Erica, compute the movement of a very large object moving at no more than forty knots underwater for ninety minutes without triggering the sonar screens used by DEA and the Coast Guard against drug traffickers and foreign submarines," Richard directed while triangulating the distance and time it would take him and Larcis to get to the area in question.

The comlink displayed the area as a large purple circle.

"Larcis, you take the north, and I'll take the southeast," Richard directed. "They won't go back where they came from or near populated land. They will more than likely try to get to deeper waters in the middle of nowhere."

"What do we do if we do find a ship, and how will we know if they have Susan or John?" Larcis questioned.

"We don't, but if something did happen to John or Susan on the cruise, we would've heard of it through the cruise liner's coastal reports. Since they seem to be in the area, they might have crossed upon whatever we're looking for," Richard reasonably guessed.

Larcis took Richard to the area in a matter of minutes. The search continued deep into the cold currents. Larcis moved slowly underwater trying not to lose his powers through conduction, while Richard quickly flew through the water, hitting speeds over ninety knots per hour.

Thirty minutes passed before Richard faintly saw a metallic object resting on the ocean floor. The large dome-like structure moved slowly as Richard closed within five hundred meters. His en-ray vision penetrated the first layer of the craft and revealed a maze of rooms, mechanical compartments, and unidentifiable apparatuses. The transponder was too weak to warn Larcis, and the more time spent going up to the surface and back might have caused him to lose the ship. So he decided to enter through what seemed to be a docking portal, guessing that his presence was probably common knowledge by now to the crew aboard the nine-hundred-meter-diameter craft. Richard flew toward the portal and hit the alloy door, for some dumb reason expecting it to automatically open.

"Your Highness, a humanoid is outside docking arm number eight," Commander Lykir, the security officer, reported.

"Allow him access to the ship," commanded the first officer. "Open a path to the Oracle, *the Queen's chamber where she meditated for many hours absorbing cosmic energy.* Do not send any security to apprehend the intruder. Take the bridge, commander. I will personally inform the princess."

Lykir couldn't help but wonder why his superiors were so lenient with the humans. The ship's chromium alloy hull naturally dispersed kinetic energy to include the ship's deflector shields. He seriously doubted whether Creator had any chance of getting into the ship or stopping the princess from taking the Chosen by force. However, it was not his place to challenge orders. He always followed instructions to the letter. His duty to follow the intent of the command would not be questioned. The commands and wisdom of the Soothsayers and the noble lineage were never wrong and adhered to the greatest acts of duty and honor.

The well-lit metallic corridors extended half a mile throughout the alien spaceship. The crew of three hundred conducted business as usual, relying on the ship's stealth. The tech crew in the bio-medical wing, near the center of the ship, put away its equipment and prepared to resume normal monitoring of the Chosen. The princess, soothsayer, and chief physician stood around Susan's comatose body.

"The ambient energy is not being fully synthesized by her cells," said the chief physician. "The cells are resisting by automatically absorbing and releasing the energy, giving her body time to rid itself of the extra energy. The cells will deteriorate and die if they continue to reject the cosmic energy flow."

"Yes," said the princess, "I know. The human who was with her assimilated a portion of the injected energy cells. It is possible that we can use his cells to stabilize her cells."

"Yes, that is possible," stated the doctor. "The male human has a very different molecular structure than all the rest. It is extremely rare that the human is synthesizing the energy. Nonetheless, he is still alive, and he is the only one who can help our queen. I will instruct the aides to bring him in, Your Highness."

"Very well. Tell me when he's ready for the transfusion," the princess instructed.

"Yes, Your Highness. We will be ready in thirty minutes."

Susan lay on the operating bed in the middle of the room. The self-contained pressurized room was filled with more machinery than medical equipment. A dark purple probe on the ceiling lit up the room, and a bright white light was directed on Susan alone. Heavy-duty pink nylon straps bound Susan's wrists, arms, waist, legs, and feet. Several electrodes and intravenous tubes were injected into her head and arms.

The princess waited for John to be brought into her temporary room. The time when the empire would be vulnerable to conquerors and power-hungry delegates was drawing to a close. She was, by birthright and queen's decree, the next in line for the throne. But she knew her fate. The Chosen would decide the outcome of the empire—and her fate as well.

The human female the princess scrutinized was by far more beautiful and powerful than she could have imagined. Superhumans populated a fraction of one percent of the empire and seventy percent of the noble family. Several dozen primary planets and hundreds of different races spanned 51,900 parsecs of space in the Argonian Empire. War seemed imminent with the ten-year expansion of the empire and the queen's death, but this human might hold salvation for everyone—including those on Earth.

# Chapter Thirteen

✠ - ✠

# My Queen

## Princess Navia's Starship

John felt cold metal pressed around his wrists and ankles. He mentally scanned his surroundings and sensed three conscious minds in his immediate area. He concentrated, taking control of the electronic bed monitor and console. The three aliens were unaware that John was awake. The nurse, wearing a pink suit and face protector, didn't notice that the sedative had stopped feeding through the tube connected to his arm. John felt very different, stronger and more alert, seeing himself through the eyes of the nurse. He probed deep into the nurse's mind and encountered countless foreign ideas, memories, and experiences. His body twitched as the alien psyche conflicted with his human mind.

*What's going on?* John thought as he tried to recall his own recent past. The night sky above the ocean and then Susan's face flashed through his mind. But the thoughts of the nurse as she went through her standard procedures caused John to realize that he and Susan had been abducted and were part of an alien experiment. His mind raced with unsettling images of weird and gruesomely unnatural tests being conducted on Susan's body and mind.

The head nurse turned her attention to her patient as they arrived at the elevator turbo lift. John instinctively entered her mind with great ease and power, overwhelming her senses.

*Let me free,* John commanded.

The nurse saw that the sedative had stopped flowing into John's arm but ignored it. Instead she obeyed John's command and removed his left arm strap.

"What are you doing, Kyra?" the male nurse asked as he attempted to stop the head nurse.

*Did I do that?* John asked himself, not realizing what he had done to Kyra. John thought for a second as Kyra countermanded the other nurse's objection.

*Help her,* John commanded the two other nurses. *Help Kyra.*

Without hesitation the nurses removed John's restraints.

*Take me to the female who was captured with me,* John continued to direct.

They entered the turbo lift. Kyra spoke into the console in an unknown dialect, and yet John understood every word as if he had known the language since childhood. The lift moved upward, then sideways for a few seconds, and then readjusted upward once again before the doors reopened. The three nurses surrounded John as they led him down a corridor past several crewmembers. John and the crewmembers exchanged odd looks, but the nurses ignored the glances and acted as if they were performing their duties as expected.

They stopped in front of the entrance to the queen's quarters.

*Stop!* John commanded before Kyra could announce their presence. *Don't enter. Stay outside. Prevent anyone from entering the room.*

John held his palm up in front of the door, trying to open it with his limited telekinesis like Richard had taught him. John felt nothing but his hand—no invisible gravitational force, no magical push, no circulating warmth around his hand.

"What's happened to me?" John asked out loud.

"What are you referring to?" Kyra asked.

John turned to Kyra, realizing that he had never been able to control anyone's mind until now.

*What did you do to me? Why am I able to control your mind?* John questioned.

"I have done nothing to you except run routine tests on your physiological and neurological system," Kyra stated.

*What did the tests reveal?*

"Your human body cells are absorbing cosmic radiation particles and synthesizing the energy in response to your innate superhuman alpha-wave patterns. Your red blood cells are also deteriorating at a very slow rate. You will die within three Earth days if you are unable to stop the deterioration."

John couldn't believe his ears. What had he or Susan done to be a part of such an experiment?

*Why?* John demanded to know. *Why has this been done to me?*

"You were accidentally exposed to utronium-proton particles," Kyra replied. "This destabilized your molecular structure. The Chosen did not receive the required dosage and tried to absorb the energy around her. The princess has hypothesized that you and the Chosen have somehow been able to combine your powers and survived the transmutation."

*What transmutation?* John said a little frustrated at the long explanations.

The door to the queen's quarters opened as John spoke.

The four of them stared into a dark room.

*Come inside, John,* the princess said.

John hesitated, noticing that the voice spoke to him within his mind. No one except Susan had spoken to him with telepathy before, and this voice was far from Susan's soothing thoughts.

The door closed automatically behind John once he'd entered the room, which was refreshing and tantalizing, dark, clean, cool, and humid, enriched with oxygen.

Susan's unconscious body lay on a hospital bed. Two women stood beside it wearing elaborate, colorful dresses. One wore a silver headband studded with diamonds, emeralds, topaz, and rubies. Both women had long silver hair and stood near six feet tall.

John cautiously approached the bed, scrutinizing all three females.

The princess faced John and spoke: "Stop where you are, human."

*What would Richard do?* John thought.

*And if I don't stop?* John boldly replied to the princess and took another step.

"Don't push me, John," said the princess. "If you want Susan to live, you will comply."

*What do you want?* John said as the soothsayer casually organized unusual electronic and medical equipment on a small platform next to Susan's head.

"Susan's cellular structure is deteriorating," said the princess. "She will die if you do not help us."

John looked at Susan and asked, *Why are her cells deteriorating?*

"The Chosen did not receive sufficient radiation from the burst intended for her," The soothsayer interjected. "Instead you and the two Rapiers absorbed the rest of the radiation dosage. The rapiers were the individuals who were suppose to inject the Chosen with the proton particles. You and the Chosen survived the transmutation. We need you to join with the Chosen to make her accept the cellular mutation."

*Who the hell do you think you are? Why was Susan injected with radiation in the first place? What gives you the right to experiment on us like lab rats?*

*You misunderstand us,* Princess Navia explained in thought. *This is no experiment. Our world is a large planet the size of your planet Neptune. It's in the octal-lateral sector of space, known to you as the star cluster of Sagittarius. We have been searching for a new queen to rule our empire. Eudora, our high priestess, picked the Chosen, Susan, to be queen as it has been for several thousands of years. Filia, my personal advisor took on the responsibility to ensure no harm comes to the Chosen. I hold the essence of our queen, Queen Omia, which I will impart to Susan once she can stabilize her own cells.*

In his mind John vividly saw the Argonian home world, their dying queen, and their high priestess Eudora. He was suspicious of the censored mental video, but had to stay focused on Susan's deadly situation.

*How can I help?* John said in his thoughts.

"The princess will interface with the Chosen while you allow the Chosen to absorb your powers," the soothsayer replied.

*Hmmm.* John stepped forward next to the soothsayer and offered himself.

Richard moved quickly through the desolate corridors. He knew he was unwelcome, and that he was probably walking into a trap. As usual, he couldn't have cared less, except for the fact that these were not normal people. He was accustomed to fighting humans.

The turbo lift at the end opened ten feet in front of Richard. He noticed that it was an electronic-magnetically propelled turbo lift-elevator of some sort. His en-ray vision let him see through about fifty meters of walls, but his depth perception was hindered by the number of walls and passages. There were silhouettes all around except in his corridor. He entered the turbo lift and let it take him to the programmed location. The lift sped off to the other side of the spacecraft and stopped at a corridor where a woman awaited his arrival. Richard stepped out of the lift fifteen feet away from a gray colored hair officer. Her aqua-blue dress complemented her bright light-blue eyes and tan complexion.

*Your companions are in danger,* the officer told Richard mentally. *Princess Navia intends to use the female as a puppet to control the empire and kill the male in the process.*

"Who are you?" Richard asked.

*I am Elexsuia, second in command of this ship. My verbal capacity with your dialect is limited. That is why I am speaking to you telepathically. I do not wish to betray my people. But the princess is overwhelmed with power. If I go against the princess openly, I will surely be sentenced to a horrible death for treason and mutiny. Your companions need you as I need you. Will you help me?*

"How is this princess of yours going to use the female as a puppet?" Richard said, getting down to the important question.

*Princess Navia is going to brainwash the female,* Elexsuia explained. *She will convince her to give up the throne. The male will be killed once he has been used to stabilize the female's cellular structure. Princess Navia will be crowned queen by default and increase the empire's influence. She will start by taking over Earth.*

Richard looked at the ceiling. "Would it be too much to ask for a simple bank robbery once in a while?" he muttered.

"Where are my friends?" Richard asked Elexsuia, with anger building in his voice.

*Your friends are beyond the door of this passage.* Elexsuia pointed behind her. *The male just entered the queen's quarters a minute ago, leaving three nurses who guard the entrance.*

"Is there an adjacent room, easily accessible from here, which is next to the queen's quarters?" Richard asked, quickly starting to scan through the passage door, confirming Elexsuia's story about the guards. Indeed there were three aliens standing in the middle of the hallway, with a door to the left.

*Yes, there is. What are you planning to do?* Elexsuia asked while stepping backward toward a door on the left.

"Can I get into the queen's quarters through the wall and rescue my friends, or is a security disintegration ray going to kill me when I go through the wall?" Richard replied with a question.

*I don't know how you will be able to get through the wall. But if the ship's metallic structure is compromised in any way, the ship's security system will alert a team in response to the queen's immediate danger. They will more than likely kill you and your male companion.*

Richard drew out a piece of Big Red bubblegum wrapped in a sealed plastic sandwich bag.

"Tell me, Elexsuia, who is in the queen's quarters and are there any monitoring systems in the rooms next the queen's quarters?"

*There are only four people in the quarters, including your companions,* Elexsuia told Richard. *The cameras in this hallway and the adjacent rooms have been deactivated. The only monitoring system in the queen's quarters is a scanner. This detects energy anomalies and interrupted biological disturbances like the death of one of the crew members or a humanoid.*

"Okay, I need you to stall the security team if they're alerted. Otherwise be ready to show us the way out of this ship," Richard tactfully commanded, at the same time enjoying his bubblegum.

Richard went into the room Elexsuia indicated. He scanned the room before taking another step past the door. He flew up into the air and transformed into a large flat section of the ceiling. He moved silently and gracefully along the ceiling, covering up a protrusion the size of a nickel at the center of the room. He fell off the ceiling and transformed back to his human self, leaving his gum plastered on the nickel-sized dome camera. The room was decorated with what appeared to be religious artifacts and incense candles. Richard wondered if there was a crystal ball hidden somewhere in the many metallic and wooden boxes scattered about the room. He scanned the queen's quarters and positioned himself directly on line with the four occupants. A single wall separated him from his targets. He needed to know nothing more to prepare for entry, so he sat on the floor with legs crossed and monitored the queen's quarters.

The soothsayer placed a thumbnail-sized electrode on John's temple. The metallic object buzzed and was warm to John's skin. Susan lay paralyzed, with no sign of breathing contractions, which actually meant nothing since Susan didn't need to breath to stay alive and since she was unconscious her body's natural state was to not make chest contractions. Princess Navia touched Susan's forehead lightly with her open hand, fingers extended. The soothsayer grabbed both of John's wrists and moved his hands to Susan's chest slightly above her solar plexus.

"No matter what happens," instructed the soothsayer, "you must not break contact."

Princess Navia probed Susan's subconscious, letting go of Queen Omia's essence little by little. She was gambling that John's powers would correct the cellular deterioration and that the Queen's soul would take over Susan's mind and body. The soothsayer meticulously monitored both transfers. John sensed the life slowly being drawn from his body.

Princess Navia probed deeper, taking control of Susan's involuntary functions and letting Queen Omia take it from there, expanding into Susan's mental essence. Susan's inner self met Queen Omia fighting to keep her own identity. John instantly suffered pain in every fiber of his body. The soothsayer reminded him not to break contact. His gut feeling, though, told him that he was expendable and that breaking contact at this point might not kill Susan but would keep him from dying. He tried to take his hands off of Susan's body but found that he was powerless. His body ignored his mind's command, and he soon blacked out although his hands remained in place on Susan's chest.

Richard noticed John's condition and quickly acted on his attack plan. The princess's gems and position above them made it plain that she was the source of Susan and John's predicaments. Richard concentrated on putting all he had into the mind of the princess. The mental blast of rage and horror passed through the wall and struck a surprise blow on Princess Navia. The mental surge broke the link between her and Susan and almost caused the princess to fall unconscious.

The display on the soothsayer's monitor jumped off the scale in response to Richard's concentrated blast. The soothsayer thought the instruments were faulty until a wave of horror and rage hit her psyche. She lost consciousness and collapsed to the floor.

Princess Navia scanned the area and quickly spotted Richard in the adjacent room. A pulse of telepathic power shot out of her head and into Richard's mind. He felt the expected attack and blocked most of it, but he temporarily lost his mental-attack ability. Instantly, two guards stepped into the room with raised weapons.

*How quickly they found me,* Richard thought.

He secured the entrance with a telekinetic wave that sent the guards flying backward through the doorway with screams of surprise. He then used a telekinetic pulse to jam the mechanisms in the door controls of his room and the queen's, ensuring that no more guards would be intruding anytime soon.

Susan's vital signs bounced around like a rubber ball as thousands of images and experiences flowed through her without the influence of Queen Omia's or Princess Navia's attempts to control her. Princess Navia regained her composure and launched another mental blast. Sensing the attack, Richard charged the wall and punched as hard as he could, piercing the metallic barrier. He noticed that a security team had begun firing on the door with their ion weapons, and the door was showing signs of giving way.

Princess Navia stood in shock as Richard's hand withdrew and a bluish jelly-like snake rapidly slithered into the queen's quarters through the hole. Richard instantly returned to human form and faced Princess Navia. The door to Richard's room burst open and the security detail entered the empty chamber. Finding Richard gone, the men retreated and targeted the door to the queen's quarters, not noticing that one of them could have used the hole Richard punched to see what was going on inside the queen's room.

*This door better last longer than the other one,* Richard thought.

Time was running out. Already the queen's door was giving way, and Richard seemed to have no options remaining. He shot a large telekinetic projectile, which struck the wall on the other side of the room, creating a fist-sized hole that passed just inches from the head of Princess Navia.

"Command the security team to stand down," Richard demanded. "Do it now!"

Princess Navia knew that Richard could have killed her at any time, but she gambled on the Earthling's inferior abilities to control their own minds and bodies. She concentrated on Richard, sending a different command into his nervous system. Richard froze. He struggled for a few seconds but turned his mental rage and horror attack upon himself.

"That will not work on me, Princess," Richard said, breaking the paralysis with ease. Susan had taught him how to counter the paralysis attack that had rendered him helpless in Complex San Francisco.

Princess Navia stepped backward, fearing the worse, and hoped that the security team would break in and neutralize Richard.

Richard went next to John and felt for signs of life while keeping a keen eye on the security team's progress with the door. His friend's pulse was faint. Richard hoped that John would remain alive long enough to get him medical help in a secure area. Susan seemed unharmed. Her vital signs were now stable and very strong. Richard rushed at Princess Navia just as the security team stormed the room. He grabbed her by the throat from behind, using her as an alien shield.

"Call them off!" Richard said again, putting some pressure on her pinned arm.

The guards shouted in an alien language and spread out in the room.

"Put down your weapons!" Susan commanded in the Argonian dialect.

Everyone's attention turned to Susan. Her body was sitting up in bed, all of the restraints unfastened.

"Do as your queen commands," Queen Omia commanded.

The security team paused in confusion.

"That is not the queen, it's the humanoid," Elexsuia stated as she stepped up between the security guards.

"No, that is the queen, do as she commands," Princess Navia said, challenging Elexsuia's claim to the queen's legitimacy.

The guards immediately complied with the princess.

"No!" Elexsuia yelled. She drew her weapon on Princess Navia.

"No, indeed," Queen Omia replied as she immobilized Elexsuia's muscles halfway through her attempt to kill the princess. "Take her away and leave us with the humans."

Richard let go of Princess Navia. He was somewhat confused but guessed that it was all over. He stared at Susan with a sign of regret, not knowing whether Susan had been taken over by the queen or whether she was still there and struggling to get out.

"What do you plan to do with the humans, Your Highness?" Princess Navia asked Queen Omia.

The queen said nothing. She placed her hand on John and the soothsayer. Both of them woke almost instantly, John feeling as if he had just received the worst beating of his life.

The guards left the room with Elexsuia. Princess Navia moved in front of Queen Omia and knelt before her queen.

"Stand up, Navia," Queen Omia instructed in English.

"Susan, it's you," said Richard. "Isn't it?"

"Yes," Susan responded with a smile. "It's me."

Princess Navia looked at Susan in surprise. "You are not Queen Omia?"

"Queen Omia is a part of me, and as the Chosen who has been melded with her essence, I invoke the Law of Eminence and accept the throne as Queen of the Argonian Empire," Susan proclaimed. "I'm sorry, Navia, but Queen Omia is dead. And so is your attempt to use me."

Sorrow swept over Princess Navia. She lay flat on her face before Susan.

"Forgive me, My Queen," she said.

The soothsayer followed suit, giving Susan her deserved reverence.

"Navia, you and Filia will return to Argonia and stabilize the empire until I physically sit on the throne. I am aware of the empire's situation, but, as you well know, there is resistance to Queen Omia or myself taking positive control of the empire. You will ensure that everyone is aware that Queen Omia is dead and that I am the new queen. There is much to be done here on Earth. I will entrust you two to come and get me when the time is right."

John stood up straight with great pride and admiration for his beloved. Susan gave him back his powers—and *more*. He knew just about everything there was to know about the aliens, and now he saw Susan's wisdom in revealing herself to the princess and the soothsayer alone. They were true patriots and would follow the new queen's request to its fullest.

Richard, his part in the drama complete, stood back and let things take their course.

"My Queen, how will we know when to call for you?" Princess Navia asked as she slowly stood.

"Tell Sedric to assemble all of the Galactic Guardians. They will maintain the empire while I am gone. Now, open up your minds to me. I will give you guidance on what to do until I join you."

Susan then presented to their minds the master plan for managing the empire which included her true identity and eventual return.

"We understand, My Queen," Navia replied after a few minutes of telepathic communication.

"Your Highness," Filia said to the queen, "may I check your cellular structure before we part?"

"You may," said Susan. "But do not be concerned about your findings. John and I will be able to stabilize each other's cellular structures indefinitely."

The examination revealed exactly what Susan said it would. John and Susan would have to exchange their cosmic powers every week to balance out their abnormalities and cause their cells to re-stabilize.

Richard and his group moved to the docking bay an hour later. There they bid farewell to their new allies in the galaxy. The ship moved to within fifty feet of the water's surface, allowing the group to exit without the need of travelling the one thousand feet straight up. They exited the ship and flew out of the water, meeting Larcis shortly afterwards. The ship rose above the water and flew away with great speed at a sixty-degree angle.

Larcis beheld the event with great interest and confusion.

"I thought you were going to find the Megalodon. What happened down there, boss?" he half joked.

Susan wore a necklace given to her by Princess Navia. She slowly raised her hand and touched the gem in the middle.

"The start of a new era for many races," Susan replied as part of Queen Omia's essence spilled out along with her own.

Larcis stared at his friends with a blank face, and then shrugged his shoulders.

"It's a long story, Larcis. Let's go home," Richard said, flying out of the water and toward the west.

# Chapter Fourteen

❈ - ❈

# Marching Orders

### CEA Operations Safe House

The message on the computer screen read as follows:

Conduct maximum surveillance on the Eternal Champions. Ensure they are implicated in illegal operations and sever them from SIA. Maximilian will attempt to keep this from happening, so ensure his hands are tied in the matter. Develop a plan of attack and report a time line to me within three days. Proceed as quickly as possible. Jean.

Jared and Natasha viewed the message with mixed emotions.

"I guess the new babe will have to be taken away from its mother," Natasha commented after a short pause.

"I don't think so, Nat," Jared stated. "The Eternal Champions may be new, but Creator is an experienced player and the group is very intelligent and powerful."

"How so?" Natasha said looking at Jared with crossed arms.

"It takes experience and power to rescue over a dozen hostages, not to mention the fact that SIA has given them free range on operations. Creator is also too cool-headed to allow his team to fall apart from a frame-up," Jared explained.

"They're not true superheroes. That's all a front that the media wants to exploit, right?" said Natasha. "Besides, whether they're the real thing or not, they seem to take advantage of their superhuman powers and have little regard for human life."

"They did kill over five hundred people in San Francisco, but what would you do if there were a thousand people trying to kill you because they wanted to use innocent people as hostages and take over a piece of the United States?" Jared challenged.

"I would incapacitate a thousand people instead of killing them," Natasha replied with a hint of sarcasm.

"This deal we have gotten ourselves into is becoming a bit sour," Jared said; and leaned back in his chair, crossing his arms across his chest.

The plan to use the Eternal Champions in a plot to seize governmental power and increase Jean's little empire was extremely risky and dangerous. But there was no other option. The Eternal Champions were new heroes, and they were popular. This made them most vulnerable to slander and corruption. There were no other recent superhero groups for the past six years, and EFL were no longer using secret identities and would not have cared if they were placed under the microscope since Quatris or Hellfire were the strongest superhumans on the planet; and had saved the world several times in their almost seven-year career.

"I know what you mean, Jared, but we have our orders and must be good Soldiers for your princess." Natasha said and smiled.

Jared thought about the fate of the Eternal Champions, his group, and Jean, whom he was beginning to fall in love with in his world of spies and espionage.

"Yes, I know…"

### Main House, the Octavian Farm

The morning rays penetrated the Venetian blinds and lit John's bedroom. Susan and John slept peacefully all night for the first time since they had been together. Richard and Liz talked about their wedding plans in the living room while Larcis studied for his next biology exam in the dining room. The Octavian Horse Farm finally seemed to be picking up with business and employees.

John and Susan eventually woke up and joined their friends downstairs.

"All hail to the queen," Richard joked as Susan and John walked down the stairs into the living room.

"Why, thank you, my court jester," Susan came back as she made the last step in the stairway.

Richard got off the sofa, smiled, and bowed, almost falling onto the floor.

"So what should we call you, Queen Sawczer?" Richard smilingly asked.

Susan looked at her friends.

"*Susan* will suffice. But you are correct; I *will* need a name to be used by the Argonians."

"What about *Queen Astra*? It's Greek meaning *star-like*," Larcis yelled across from the dining room.

"What about *Elissa*? It's Saxon for *true and noble*," Erica suggested.

Richard didn't want to suggest anything; he knew Susan had already decided on a name befitting her future. The group would never be the same, and he would have to consider finding other teammates in a few years, when Susan and John left them in pursuit of their destiny. It was sad to know that his almost perfect superhero group was assembled for only a short time. Each member complemented the other extremely well. They had no internal conflicts and almost unlimited resources to fight crime. The comment Susan made about knowing the Galactic Guardians rang a bell in Richard's memory. Quatris and Hellfire had been in space for several years and hinted to being a part of a large operation to bring peace to the galaxy. The previous queen probably met if not knew them very well. This gave Richard hope that Susan and John would not leave Earth never to return. It interested him to know what was out there beyond the solar system. He could fly out into outer space but at his speed, it would take years if not decades before he would get to any other inhabited planet. When the time was right he would ask to be taken to space to explore and maybe to live, but Earth was his true home and love. He wanted people to live in peace and with joy, which was what motivated him to do his best as a superhero and leader.

"Those are pretty good, but I was thinking of Queen Neeva. It's Argonian for true salvation," Susan stated.

The rest of the group looked at each other, nodding in affirmation of Susan's choice.

*Well, now that's settled, I have a surprise for you,* John said to Susan in front of everyone else.

"Really?" Susan said with joy and doubtfulness as Larcis quickly went into the kitchen.

*Well, as we all know, breakfast has not been my specialty,* said John. *But I've worked on it for some time now, and I made a special breakfast for you while you were sleeping.*

John led Susan to the sofa as Larcis brought out a large tray with the main plate under a silver serving cover.

*I have officially been classified as an expert chef,* John stated proudly.

"Is that right?" Richard contested.

*Well,* John said, *Larcis said it was great and that I was the best cook here.*

"Then it must be true," Richard said, smiling along with Larcis as the tray was placed in front of Susan on the living-room table.

Susan looked at John and then at the tray, not sure whether she was about to see a microwave breakfast or a real homemade gourmet meal. She scooted to the edge of the leather sofa and lifted the metal cover to reveal a white plate with an opened ring case in the middle. Susan's eyes and mouth widened with surprise and delight. She dropped the dish cover, but Liz caught it before it hit the floor or sofa edge. John knelt next to Susan, took the four-carat diamond ring out of the case, and held it up, facing Susan.

*I want to spend the rest of my life with the person I love. Susan, will you marry me?* John proposed.

Susan kissed John with overwhelming happiness.

"Yes, I will!"

Liz and Richard hugged each other as they watched the two lovebirds enjoying their happy moment.

"I think this will be a good time for a group picture," Erica suggested.

"That's a great idea, Erica," Larcis said as he moved into the middle of the group.

"So does this mean we have to negotiate a time slot for a honeymoon?" Liz commented as she faced Richard, demanding an answer.

"Yeah, but I decide who goes first." Richard smiled, then kissed Liz as the picture was taken.

# Author Notes

⊠ - ⊠

T his book is dedicated to my lifelong friends who inspired me to write this superhero epic series. I thank the following people for their friendship and for the adventures depicted in this book: Patrick Lawrence, who played the character Creator; Luis G. Monsalve, who played Night; Kevin P. Daugherty, who played Mindseye; Rich Richardson who played Medroc. The world I created is based on a dream my brother and I had as children, in combination with several worlds created by my good friends Robert Bernabo, Scott Quint, Jay K. Crawford, and Joe Block mirroring the system used in a role-playing game system back in 1983. Thank you all for your lasting friendship.

I must point out that the story line was already created, I used the role playing game to actually see how real people would react which gives the story a personal flavor of real emotions, choices, and dilemmas. I originally wrote this book in 2004 where I also received a critic review for the book; however, I wanted to address several things which I have learned and experienced in the nine years since I started writing. The review or the critic was performed by a person who has personal opinions. It is said that you can get unbiased reviews, and you can; but what I want to address is a review that is not accurate because the reviewer didn't read the entire story or completely ignored the story as written with personal assumptions and lack of attention to what is currently written in the mainstream. I will give you several examples. I am not going to let you know the name of the reviewer because it doesn't need mentioning and attracting attention to the reviewer. The review starts off with you, the reader, will need to have a good memory because the book has over twenty-three characters. Hmm, well several best sellers have more than twenty-three character names, and there are a few which also have glossaries. Not that a book with many names makes for a good or bad read, but it should not lose the reader, and I hope I didn't do that in this story. There was also a remark that the story resembles the movie "Escape from New York, by John Carpenter". That is partly correct, but there is a reason for everything and in book two, He is Known as Ego, there is a hint as to why that is so. In book five, Masterminds, it explains in detail why the events in Creator are similar in an altered plot to the movie. I tested out the story with people I met in my travels around the world, and all of them liked the book, so what the critic said, really had little value to me personally. However, because the reviews are there for the public, and helpful in most instances when it comes to deciding if a book is worth reading or buying, I hope the description of this book gets the attention of people who want to read and enjoy a good story.

I lived most of my life on the east coast of the United States and travelled a lot with my family. I got used to changing schools every one to three years. Of all the subjects in school, I hated English the most. I always had trouble with words and avoided reading as much as possible. My mother would make me sit down and go over vocabulary words, and my father made me read *Reader's Digest* articles every day, because I was reading one grade below my expected reading level. I learned a lot out from their persistent forced teaching, but I didn't like reading because of it. It wasn't until junior high school that I started to appreciate reading. My older brother told me about Edgar Rice Burroughs's Tarzan books while I was in the seventh grade, and I was so intrigued with the stories he told me that I started to read regularly. I actually enjoyed reading for the first time, wanting to see what adventures Tarzan would go on or how Tarzan would save the day. I moved on to other books and read because I wanted to, not because I had to read. I fell in love with reading and writing, and went into honors English, Math, and Science by eighth grade. I dropped out of school after junior high school and received a graduate equivalency diploma (GED) when I turned sixteen.

I went to college and completed thirty credits toward an architectural engineering major before enlisting in the U.S. Army at age seventeen. I became an infantryman, wanting to follow in my older brother's footsteps and serve my country. I spent the next six years in the Army jumping around from Fort Benning, Georgia, to several other military posts and forts around the world. I left active duty in 1990, and I attended Boyce Bible School in Louisville, Kentucky, and Indiana University Southeast (IUS) campus two years later. I graduated with a Bachelor's in General Studies and a minor in Psychology from IUS in May 1994. I was going to enter the Southern Baptist Theological Seminary graduate program but instead reenlisted back into the

U.S. Army a month later. I attended Officer Candidate School and received a commission as a Military Intelligence officer. I retired in 2008 with the rank of Major from the US Army. I have been to more than nine countries on five continents. I enjoy traveling and love to meet people and make new friends everywhere I go.

The ideas and story lines I have created are a conglomeration of childhood dreams, conversations with friends, reading books, looking at life through my own experiences, occupational experiences, and most important, taking the time to listen to people as we all strive to achieve our dreams and goals. Writing has become a strong passion for me. The characters and stories in the entire series evolved from a ten-year span of story creation, which was role-played to some extent, but the plots all came from my imagination. The entire story line encompasses an eight book series I have called "*A Superhero Epic,*" which are broken into categories by timeline and by primary characters. I started with Creator because it is the story about the Eternal Champions, in particular Creator and his friends. The evolution of the team expands into five out of the eight books. More than twenty real people from all over the world for a twelve year span have at one point or another driven the story line from start to finish in this series of books. I wanted to start book one with Richard Octavian, because the Eternal Champions were the pivotal force for the entire story. The rest of the books complement each other in one form or another, and I tell the story from different character perspectives to some degree which allows the reader to see behind the scenes and understand how things came about or why people act the way they do.

On a final technical note: I wrote the storyline with the use of superhero names and public names. I use the real names when the characters are not trying to keep their identities. Otherwise I do change back and forth and refer to each character as if they would speak to each other in real life. I placed a listing of character names and aliases at the front of each book to help in tracking who was who in the story. The list is formatted so you can turn to that page and see all the names in one glance instead of having to flip the page to see the second part of a two page list. There are times when superheroes communicate mentally or by sign-language and I try to let the reader know this so they are not confused all of the sudden when different names are used.

I thank you all very much and hope you enjoyed reading this book as much as I enjoyed writing it. Make sure to keep an eye out for the other books in this Superhero Epic series:

| Book 2 | He Is Known as Ego |
| Book 3 | Guild Without a Name |
| Book 4 | The Galaxy Is Ours |
| Book 5 | Masterminds |
| Book 6 | Superhumans from the Past |
| Book 7 | Ultimate Assassins |
| Book 8 | Last Hope for Earth |

www.ingramcontent.com/pod-product-compliance
Lightning Source LLC
Chambersburg PA
CBHW031001260626
47169CB00002B/641